X-RATED

MELODY TYDEN

Chapter One

~Laina~

Gold danced over the water's surface, the setting sun casting its rays like a blanket over the gently swelling surf. From the table at the romantic Malibu restaurant, I had a perfect view of the ocean, but at that moment, I wished I could jump right over the glass wall beside the table and disappear into the golden liquid, letting it wash away the memory of the whole evening and all the hopes I'd brought with me.

Unfortunately, that wouldn't be possible.

"Laina? Did you hear me?" Brock sounded nervous that he would have to repeat himself, but I'd heard him perfectly well.

Reluctantly, I pulled my gaze back from the water to the handsome man sitting across from me. Clean-cut and dressed in an expensive suit, with tanned skin and white teeth that showed whenever he flashed his perfect smile, he could have been the poster child for my teenage dreams. The type of man I'd always imagined myself ending up with. Some girls liked the 'bad boys' but I'd never had trouble attracting those. Instead, I yearned for someone successful and sweet, and this time, I actually thought I'd found him.

I'd let myself believe he brought me there to propose.

I couldn't have been more wrong.

"You don't think this is going to work," I repeated in a neutral monotone, the words so familiar to me, I might as well have them inscribed on my forehead. "I heard you."

He exhaled in relief that he didn't have to repeat himself after all. "It's not you. You're great. It's just…"

"My job," I supplied for him. I'd heard this entire speech before from other handsome men; I already knew how it would go. "The job that I told you about at the beginning and you swore wouldn't be a problem. Now, it's a problem."

Even his grimace looked attractive, somehow. He didn't have a bad angle. "It's not that simple, Laina. People ask me what you do, and if I lie, it seems like I'm embarrassed about it, but if I tell them the truth, they go and look up your videos and I don't want everyone I know seeing you like that."

Again, nothing he said was new. Nothing I couldn't have predicted ahead of time.

Most men loved the idea of dating a porn star… *in theory*. I preferred the term adult actress since I took the acting side of things seriously and my fans appreciated that, but to most of the world, I was a porn star. When they met me, men thought it would be all sex and glamour, forgetting that when the cameras stopped, I was a regular woman like everyone else. Except *not* like everyone else, because I got paid to have sex with other people in front of a camera. Just because I started dating someone didn't mean I stopped working.

The reality held a lot less appeal for most men than they thought it would, but Brock assured me he would be different. For almost six months, he made me believe it, until that night when he couldn't keep up the pretense any longer.

Which of us was really the actor?

I could have pointed all of that out to him, could have argued about why it shouldn't matter to him, but what would the point be? He'd made up his mind and once the desire to be together had gone, getting it back was next to impossible. It would be better to save my breath and move on. I could still get home in time to catch the latest episode of my favourite dating show on TV.

"If that's all, I'll get myself a taxi."

Brock's frown still looked photogenic. "Don't be like that. We can still have dinner and I can drive you home."

If he'd just told me what he wanted to say before he picked me up and brought me all the way to the restaurant, I wouldn't have to get a taxi. I sure as hell didn't want to eat dinner with him. "I'm not hungry."

"Laina, come on." He reached out to take my hand as I started to stand up. "I don't want things to end this way. I'd like us to be friends."

My stomach turned as I anticipated where he might be going with this, where they *always* went. "Why?"

"Why?" he repeated, like the question made no sense. "Because I like you."

"But you'd still have the same problem introducing me to people if I were your friend as you do when I'm your girlfriend."

He couldn't argue with that so he didn't even try. "Well, we can always hang out together privately."

I thought so. Leaning closer to him, I put on the sweet smile I used in my films. "Oh, so you mean you could still come over and fuck me when you want to? Maybe bring some friends sometimes?"

Excitement sparked in his eyes at what he saw as my agreement. "I mean, if you'd like to, we could..."

Before he could get the words out, I picked up the glass of freshly-poured wine in front of me and threw it directly in his face. Sputtering in shock, he finally looked less than perfect. In fact, he looked like exactly the loser he was. "Not interested. Goodbye, Brock."

A few of the women at neighbouring tables gave me smiles of solidarity, trusting that whatever my date had done merited that treatment, and luckily, a taxi had just arrived when I stepped outside. I was able to slide into the back seat while Brock was probably still dabbing the wine out of his expensive shirt.

"Where to?" the driver asked, and I gave him the address of my Malibu Hills home. Paid for entirely with the proceeds of the career that Brock found so distasteful to mention in polite company, I was as proud of my home as I was of my job. I worked damn hard to get where I was, and nobody was going to make me feel bad about it, especially not some dime-a-dozen lawyer with an Ivy League degree and more money than courage.

As we drove up the steep hill to my drive, a large moving van sat in front of the house next to mine. With our houses separated by a row of trees for privacy, I had barely known my old neighbours but I knew they'd sold a couple of months ago. Pressing my nose to the window curiously, I caught just a glimpse of a broad back and strong biceps as a man lifted a box out of the truck, obscuring his face. Was that the new owner or just one of the moving men? Either way, he seemed like a better option than spending the evening alone, even if we only had a chat.

"Actually, let me out here," I told the driver, who swerved to the side of the road, just past the driveway, coming to an abrupt stop. By the time I paid the fare and got out of the car, the man I'd seen before was coming back out the front door and his eyes widened at the sight of me standing at the end of his drive.

"Hello," I called out, giving him a friendly wave. In my white dress, high heels and jewellery, I looked ridiculously overdressed for a stroll around the neighbourhood, especially next to his t-shirt and jeans. "Are you moving in?"

He glanced at the open door of the truck in the driveway, the back of it full of boxes, before turning back to me with a sarcastic smile. "What was your first clue?"

He meant it as a joke and I took it that way, laughing in good humour. He wasn't my usual type at all; all muscle with tattoos on his arms, his hair dark and his casual clothes, but his face looked kind. I liked the way the corners of his brown eyes crinkled when he smiled.

"I live just next door," I explained, pointing down the road at my own drive, just visible beyond the bend. "I thought I'd stop and say hi to the new owner. Is that you?"

He took a few more steps towards me, his eyes narrowing as he squinted at me thoughtfully. "You've found him. You look familiar. Have we met before?"

There was only one reason why men thought I looked familiar, meaning he'd probably come across one or more of my videos. Normally, I had no problem stating that outright, enjoying the way people tripped over themselves when they realized that they'd just admitted to watching porn, but after the dinner with Brock, I didn't have the appetite for that conversation again.

"I don't think so," I told him instead, stepping forward to meet him halfway and sticking out my hand in greeting. "I'm Laina Macintyre."

His face lit up as he took my hand, making him look even more handsome than before. "No way! I knew I recognized you!"

My name shouldn't have given me away since I used a stage name, so his enthusiasm confused me. Maybe he didn't recognize me from my work after all?

"Dorian Reid," he introduced himself, tapping his chest with his spare hand while still holding onto mine with the other. "We were in high school together. I can't believe this."

"Dorian?" I hadn't thought of the name or the boy attached to it in ages, and in my memory, he bore little resemblance to the mass of man standing in front of me. Dorian Reid had been the quiet, overweight kid with braces who sat in the back of the classroom scribbling in his notebook in our small midwestern town. The other cheerleaders had been mean to him, as they were to everyone who didn't meet their standards, but we'd chatted a few times when we ended up alone somewhere. He'd been shy but sweet, as I remembered, and if I looked deep enough into his brown eyes, I could just about see the boy he used to be. "Well, this is a hell of a coincidence."

"Or fate," he teased, laughing as he released my hand. He looked almost as surprised as I felt, but pleased to see me anyway. "I'm about ready to take a break. Would you like to come in for a drink?"

I suspected he hadn't been ready to take a break at all, not with the number of boxes still to unload, but my curiosity overwhelmed any reticence I might have felt about interrupting his progress. How the hell did Dorian Reid end up in Malibu, looking like *that*?

I had to find out.

"That sounds great. Lead the way."

~Dorian~

Laina fucking Macintyre. What were the odds that my new neighbour would be Laina Macintyre? I could work out the math if I really wanted to, but it wouldn't be necessary; we could say the odds were astronomical and leave it at that.

Somehow, she looked even better than I remembered. Her naturally blonde hair had been well taken care of, cut in a way that made her look elegant and youthful all at the same time. Those blue eyes that I used to dream about were still filled with the same quiet confidence and determination I'd always found so enticing, and in her pretty white dress and heels, she looked fresh and carefree, just as she'd always seemed. I'd never known her well enough to know if that air she gave off was her truth, but maybe after all the years that had passed, I'd get a chance to remedy that.

I'd been joking when I said it must be fate that brought me there, but in some ways, it didn't seem like it could be anything else.

"I'm sorry for the mess in here, I literally got the keys this afternoon," I apologized as I led her into the living room of my new house, completely bare other than the boxes I'd moved in earlier. I really hadn't thought things through when I invited her in. "Maybe you'd be more comfortable at your house?"

Her face tightened for a moment before she shook her head. "This is fine. I don't need anything fancy."

"Right. Sure." Fuck, I was messing this up already. Why would I invite myself over to her house? Things never came out quite the way I meant them, and nothing in real life ever went as smoothly as it did in my books. "The kitchen's back here. The realtor left some champagne in the fridge."

Together, we walked through the empty living room to the equally spartan kitchen. One wall was entirely windows, opening out into the secluded backyard with its swimming pool and outdoor gym equipment. The realtor assured me that none of my neighbours could see into my yard, just as I couldn't see into theirs, so I could work out back there in peace. That had sounded like a good thing at the time, but that was before I knew Laina lived next door.

My furniture would be arriving the next day, so at that moment, I didn't have a table or chairs, but the boxes on the counters should contain some glasses, at least. I just had to figure out which box they would be in.

"Are you moving in on your own, or have you got a family?" Laina asked, leaning against the white countertop while I began opening boxes, looking for the champagne flutes. The whole room was white: the cabinets, the appliances, the floor and the countertop. Neutral, the realtor called it, so I could add in whatever accents I wanted, completely changing the feel of the room whenever I felt like it.

I could have sworn her eyes dropped to my hand for a moment, looking for a ring, but I didn't want to read too much into that. It was a perfectly normal, polite question. "Just me. My parents think it's crazy to get a house this big for one person, but I spend a lot of my time at home."

Well, that didn't make me sound like a loser or anything.

"I mean, I work from home, so it's nice to have the space. What about you? Do you live alone?"

With my back to her, I winced as I heard the words come out of my mouth. How creepy did *that* sound?

Thankfully, Laina didn't seem offended. "Yeah, I'm on my own too, and I also work from home, so I need the extra space as well. Sounds like we have a lot in common."

In an instant, my mind took me right back to high school. Standing at my locker between classes, one of the jerks on the football team had come up behind me and grabbed the romance books I'd borrowed from the town library out of my locker, holding them up for his friends to see.

"Dory's got to read about hot girls because he knows he'll never get one in real life." The other boys all laughed as my stomach sank, my eyes darting around to see the entire hallway watching us, people stepping closer to get a good look and make sure they didn't miss anything. I hated being the centre of attention, even in a good way, and the current situation definitely didn't count as good as the guy in charge turned back to me with a sneer as he gestured to the cover with a half-naked couple in a passionate embrace. "Or maybe you like this guy instead? You want a big, strong man to fall in love with you?"

There was no right way to answer that. Denying I was gay would only suggest I thought there was something wrong with it, which I didn't even if they obviously did. "Don't wreck those, they're not mine," I managed to mumble.

"What, like this?" Tossing the other books to the floor, he held up the one in his hands and ripped the cover off as I watched in disbelief. I didn't have the money to pay for a new book; if I did, I would have just bought it myself. The library was my lifeline in that stupid town, and if I got banned from using it, I honestly didn't know what I'd do. To my horror, I felt tears coming to my eyes, and things would only get worse if they saw me crying. It felt like a nightmare coming to life.

"How much of an idiot are you, Cody?" The crowd parted to reveal Laina standing there, her hands on her hips. Popular because of her beauty, she never fell prey to the trappings of popularity, not seeming to care whether people liked her or not. I admired her all the more for that. That day, her blonde hair was pulled back in a ponytail and she had her cheerleading outfit on, probably on her way to practice. "You can't just destroy someone else's property. Give him $10 to replace it."

"No way." Cody snickered in refusal, looking around for support, but all the crowd who had been on his side a moment ago were suddenly looking the other way. No one wanted to go against Laina. "It's just a stupid book."

"A book that you just ruined for no good reason. Give him the money, now."

She crossed her arms, planting her feet firmly with her hip out, making it clear she didn't intend to back down, and the other boys started to shuffle nervously.

"Just pay him, man," one of them muttered.

"Let's get going, this is stupid."

Cody huffed, trying to maintain control of the situation. "Whatever. Take your stupid book." Tossing the two pieces of the ruined copy on the ground, he threw a $10 bill after it. "Wouldn't want you to miss jacking off on the cover tonight."

The others all laughed as they walked away and the crowd dispersed, quickly losing interest. My hands shook as I bent down to pick up everything from the floor, keeping my head down, but a pair of pretty shoes soon appeared in my line of vision.

"Here, I got it." Laina picked up the $10 bill and handed it to me first before collecting all the books. "Are these any good?"

"They're... uh, yeah, they're okay." I couldn't bring myself to look her in the face so close up. She'd talked to me before and I never managed to say anything interesting. I couldn't imagine why she'd involved herself that day. "I know people think they're stupid."

I stumbled getting back to my feet, nearly falling over, and my face flushed with embarrassment as I wished the floor would just swallow me up right there. Things couldn't get much worse.

Laina stood back up too, gracefully, just as she did everything. "If they make you happy, then they're not stupid. Sometimes, the fantasy is what we need. Sounds like we have that in common."

She gave me a wink before turning around and walking off, like it hadn't been any big deal that she'd just come to my rescue or treated me like a regular person, which was far more than most of the other kids in school did.

She'd probably never thought about that day since, but fifteen years later, she'd just said almost the exact same thing to me, and it affected me nearly as much as it had then. On the surface, at least, we had a lot more in common in the present than we had back then, but I still barely knew the first thing about her.

The next box I opened had the champagne flutes in it, and I pulled them out triumphantly, making her laugh. From the fridge, I grabbed the champagne, popping the cork and pouring out two glasses, handing one to her. "Let's make a toast: to old friends and new beginnings."

Laina took the glass from me, a smile on her lips but the emotion in her blue eyes a lot more complicated. "I'll drink to that. Cheers."

After tapping her glass against mine, she drained it down in one long drink as I watched in admiration, taking only a sip of mine. She still seemed just as effortlessly cool to me as she always had, while I still felt like the awkward, unattractive kid next to her. What did she see when she looked at me? How much did we *really* have in common?

Maybe fate had brought me there to find out.

~Laina~

I still couldn't quite wrap my head around the fact that I was standing in Dorian Reid's kitchen. With each word he spoke, I became more convinced that he really was who he claimed to be, though why he would have lied to me about it, I couldn't imagine. It just seemed so completely implausible that I still needed a bit of time to wrap my head around it.

I'd left the small town we grew up in behind a long time ago and as far as I knew, no one there had any idea what had become of me. Did that explain why I'd balked at the idea of inviting him to my house, knowing that he'd see the cameras set up and no doubt have questions about why they were there? Did it have to do with Brock dumping me that evening? I usually had no problem telling people what my job was, but for some reason, I didn't want to tell Dorian about it just yet. I'd much rather talk about him.

"What do you do for work?" I cast an appreciative glance around his modern, expensive kitchen as he continued to sip on his champagne. "You must be pretty good at it."

He blushed at the compliment, looking more and more like the sweet, shy boy I remembered with each passing minute. "Well, actually... do you remember how I used to read romance novels in high school?"

Now that he mentioned it, I did. I hadn't thought about it in a long time, but when I thought back, I could remember him often having a book tucked under his arm, trying to hide the cover from the ignorant jerks who would give him a hard time about it, as if what someone else read had any effect on their lives at all. I could never fathom why people couldn't just mind their own damn business. "I always respected how you didn't stop even when you got teased about it. You just kept doing your own thing."

He started to laugh before he realized I meant it. "Wait, are you serious? *You* respected *me?*"

"Sure. Why wouldn't I?" I leaned forward on the counter again, letting him know he had my interest, and knowing that it would push my breasts up against the edge of my dress a little more. When it came to flattering angles, I knew all the tricks. He'd just told me he was single and so was I after my date that evening. What harm would a little flirting do?

"We weren't exactly on the same social level in high school," Dorian pointed out wryly, still drinking his champagne slowly, savouring it in contrast to the way I'd downed mine, hoping it would help to erase the memories of Brock's rejection.

"High school is ridiculous," was my honest reply. "And you still haven't answered my question: what do you do these days?"

"Right. Sorry." For someone so attractive, he still held onto a lot of his previous nervous habits. I found it kind of endearing. "Well, I always loved escaping into those stories, so I started writing my own. I loved being able to control everything, give my characters the perfect lines I'd never come up with in real life, and rewrite things when they didn't go as planned. Readers liked them too, I guess. They've done pretty well."

"You're a romance author?" I blurted out the question in such surprise that he winced, but I didn't mean it in a negative way. I actually thought that sounded incredible, so I quickly clarified my reaction. "That's amazing, Dorian. Have any of your books been made into movies? Maybe I've seen one."

He laughed rather nervously. "No, no movies yet. You might have heard of them but you wouldn't know they were mine. I use a pen name."

"Why?" He must be very successful if he could afford to buy the house we were in. I didn't know how much authors usually made, but I knew enough struggling screenwriters in the film industry to know that they didn't usually live in Malibu Hills.

Dorian's response felt completely open, his attention fully on me but not in a way that felt like he was hitting on me. "Well, a couple of reasons, actually. First, people have a lot of preconceptions about men writing romance, and I didn't want to get judged before they even picked up the books."

"So, you have a female pen name?" I leaned forward again, fascinated with this whole discussion. I knew all about people judging me based on preconceptions, so I could certainly relate.

"It's gender-neutral, just some initials and a surname, so people don't know one way or the other. I don't ever show my face anywhere, so no one knows who I really am except my publisher."

Almost as a reflex, I looked him up and down again. "I think you might want to reconsider that. If you're established now, you don't have to worry about people judging you, and I think it would actually work in your favour. I can see all the young women falling over themselves at book signings. You could even be on your own covers!"

He blushed again and I almost had to laugh. He was still sweet and a little shy, just as I remembered him, except that now he had money, looks, and apparently knew all about romance too. How in the world had he managed to stay single?

"Well, that leads into the second reason I keep my real name out of things. I'm really just brutally awful at talking to people. Sitting at a table where people would come up to me and expect me to be charming and witty on the spot... you've just described my worst nightmare."

He drained the last of his champagne to go with those words, but I thought he was being pretty hard on himself. "You're doing just fine talking to me right now."

Dorian grimaced. "That's different."

"Why?" I asked again. It didn't seem much different to me. In reality, he didn't know me much better than some random woman off the street.

His shrug didn't tell me much more than his answer did. "It just is. You've always been different."

I didn't know what that meant, but it didn't sound like an insult.

"Anyway, that's what I do." Dorian spread his hands as if there were nothing more to tell. "I work from home, I write, I work out. I'm a pretty quiet neighbour so you don't need to worry about loud parties or anything like that."

It hadn't crossed my mind to be concerned, mostly because the houses were far enough apart up the hill that noise rarely carried between them. It also didn't surprise me at all to hear that he worked out. He was in excellent shape, even by Malibu standards.

"What do you do?" he asked, looking eager to get the spotlight off himself. "You're obviously doing well for yourself too. I've checked now and then to see if you made it as an actress, but I never found anything."

"How did you know I wanted to be an actress?" I asked the question partly to buy myself some time before answering his first question, and partly because he'd managed to take me by surprise again. I'd never told anyone in high school about what I wanted to do.

"It was just a guess," he admitted, his cheeks colouring yet again. I'd never met a man who blushed so much, or who looked so cute doing it. "You were always incredible in the school plays and you seemed so happy on stage. When I heard you moved to LA, it made sense. I figured you came out here to be a star. I kept waiting to see your name on movie posters."

I couldn't believe he'd paid enough attention to notice all of that. He had it exactly right too; I *had* moved to California with ambitions of being an actress, and in a way, I'd achieved exactly what I set out to. I had well over a hundred films beneath my belt, but none under my real name.

After what he'd just told me, I figured he could relate to that part of it. "I use a stage name, actually. And I am an actress, a pretty successful one."

His face lit up in delight on my behalf, making his brown eyes sparkle. "Laina, that's amazing. I don't watch a lot of movies so I must have missed you. You'll have to give me a list so I can check them out, or at least your stage name."

His enthusiasm made what I had to say next even harder, but there was no point in hiding it any longer. I didn't want him to think I was ashamed of what I did when I wasn't. "Well, none of them have been shown in theatres, so you probably wouldn't have come across them. They're all available online, on adult websites."

I could practically see the pieces falling into place, though it took him a lot longer than it would have taken most men to put it together, and his expression, which had been warm and interested, slowly turned to panic. "Oh. I... well, I would still like to watch them. I mean, the beginning, at least. Not that I want to watch you do... that... but just... to see you act, before..."

He floundered for words, his cheeks and neck turning redder by the moment until I couldn't take it anymore. Any other night, I would have laughed it off and maybe even pulled one up on my phone to see his reaction, but after getting dumped an hour earlier over the same issue, I didn't have it in me to find the bright side just then.

"If you really want to find them, it's not too hard. You need to get back to your moving, though, I've taken up too much of your time already. Welcome to the neighbourhood, Dorian. I'll see you around."

Without waiting for him to show me out, I headed back through the living room, my heels clicking on the hardwood floor as I made my way to the front door, letting myself out and closing the door behind me before breaking into a jog towards my own house, as fast as I could go without falling over in my heels.

I wouldn't be seeing him again, I would put money on that. He dealt in romance and I dealt in sex, and in my experience, the two things very rarely coexisted for long.

The whole night would be best forgotten, and as I stripped out of my dress and jewellery back in my room, I made a vow to move on, leaving behind any man who considered me beneath him simply because of how I earned my living.

In fact, that might just be the hook I'd been looking for in the new film I wanted to make. I'd been looking to make a more serious film for a while, one that still involved sex, but which had a full plot too; the best of both worlds. In the morning, I'd get started on it, and with work to distract me, the Brocks and Dorians of the world wouldn't matter at all.

Chapter Two

~Dorian~

Sleep didn't come easily that night. For one thing, my bed hadn't arrived yet, so I had to try my best to build a cocoon of blankets and pillows to make myself comfortable. More than that, though, I couldn't stop kicking myself internally over the way I'd responded to Laina when she told me what she did for a living.

If it happened in one of my books, my male character would have had the perfect reply, charming and sweet. He would have said something that made her feel validated and empowered, and maybe even laugh at the same time.

It didn't even have to be anything all that witty. "Wow, that's interesting," would have worked. "I have no idea what goes into making a movie. Can you walk me through it?"

That would have demonstrated interest without judgement, giving her back the floor to take the conversation in whatever direction she felt comfortable with. Instead, I managed to somehow sound both disapproving *and* lecherous at the same time. *I wanted to watch one of them?* Why did I say that?

Groaning at the memory, I rolled over, wrapping my pillow tightly around my ears to try to drown out my self-recriminations. This had always been my problem. Whenever I got anywhere near a woman I found attractive, I lost the ability to speak like a normal human being. I panicked and I froze, and women like Laina preferred confident, articulate men. I didn't blame them for it, but it did mean that at the age of 31, my experience with the opposite sex was shockingly limited.

I wasn't a virgin, but for all intents and purposes, I might as well be. I'd certainly never had the kind of mind-blowing sex my characters did, and therein lay my other problem at the moment. Usually, I wrote closed-door romance. The build-up of sexual tension was my comfort zone, but when it came to actually describing the act itself, it always came across as stilted and rather academic since I mostly based it on descriptions I'd read rather than my own personal experience. Afraid that people would be able to tell, I simply left those scenes out instead, leaving it to my readers' imaginations.

However, my editor had been making stronger and stronger suggestions that I should reconsider that stance. Spicy romance was all the rage at the moment, and though my books did well, she felt they could do much better by simply adding a descriptive scene or two. "It's a lot of return for not a lot of effort," she told me. "We could bring in a ghostwriter if you want."

I didn't like that idea either. My characters were *mine* and I didn't want someone else writing about them in such an intimate way. The last conversation we'd had about it, I told her I would try writing some scenes to see if I could come up with one that made me happy, but it would have to wait until after my move. That only gave me a few more days until I couldn't put it off any longer.

What would Laina think of me if she knew how much I was struggling, especially since she must know more about sex than most people on the planet?

As that thought sank in, I sat bolt upright on my makeshift bed. Maybe that was it. I desperately wanted to smooth things over with her, and if

I went to her for help, that should make it clear that I respected her experience. I'd have to come up with an excuse about why I needed help in the first place, one that would make me sound like slightly less of a loser than the truth did, but I had all night to think of one. Coming up with the right thing to say when I had time to think it over, I never had a problem with.

Even if I'd wanted to go over to see her first thing in the morning, I couldn't since my furniture delivery was scheduled during the day. Between that and unpacking, it had already passed four o'clock in the afternoon by the time I made my way down the road in the direction Laina had pointed the previous evening when she told me she lived next door. The warm sun beat down on the back of my neck and on my arms, the only parts of me exposed by my t-shirt and jeans combination.

I had no idea what her working hours might be. She probably didn't film every day, but what kind of prep work would be involved? I imagined she had to work out a lot to keep in such incredible shape. Maybe we could compare workout routines or even go jogging together...

Stop getting ahead of yourself, Dorian. I shook my head at myself to refocus. She still had to accept my apology first before I could even hope for anything else.

As I rounded the bend of the road and reached Laina's drive, all other thoughts flew out of my head as my mouth dropped open. While my new house exuded modernist style, hers looked like an Italian villa transported to the California coast. A large, airy atrium acted as a central entranceway, set back between the two wings of the house, connecting them. The shades on the glass doors were drawn, but I imagined if they were open, it would be possible to see straight into the backyard, and given the corner lot she had, that yard must be impressive.

I could see why she worked from home. The location couldn't be more stunning. It must look great on film.

Walking up to the front door, I repeated the words in my head again that I had been working out all day, and tried to ignore how my hand shook as I reached out to ring the bell. A gentle chime sounded, calm and soothing, a lot like Laina herself. I would have never imagined her in a house like this, and yet, the longer I stood there, the more it felt like her.

Given the size of the house, I expected it to take a minute or two for her to get to the front door, but eventually, the door opened a crack and she poked her head out, no doubt having already seen it was me on a security camera. Her clothes were a lot more casual than they'd been the night before, her hair pulled back into a loose bun, but she looked just as stunning to me. Maybe even more so. Behind her, I could see straight through to the back of the house, just as I'd imagined, where a gorgeous swimming pool glistened in the afternoon sun.

"Hi. Do you need something?"

Her voice sounded a lot cooler than the day before, letting me know I still had some work to do to earn her trust again, so I launched into my prepared dialogue. "I do. I need to apologize for the way I reacted yesterday. You took me by surprise, but I didn't want you to think that I had any kind of problem with your job. In fact, I think it's pretty cool that you don't try to hide it, like I do with *my* job. You're one of the few people who actually knows what I do for a living. Half my family tells people I'm a lawyer."

As I hoped, that earned me a smile, if only a small one, and she opened the door a little wider. "Seriously?"

I nodded. "You know what that town's like. You think they want people to know that I spend my time writing about people falling in love?"

"You give people an escape," she corrected me, relaxing a bit as she leaned against the doorframe. "That's what I do too. It's nothing to be ashamed of."

I hadn't thought of the similarities between our careers quite that way, but I liked the comparison, and it gave me a great opening to move on to the other reason I'd come.

"Actually, there's something I hoped you could help me with. I was thinking about it after you left."

Laina's expression immediately turned wary again, her body tensing as she crossed her arms over her chest. "What kind of thing?"

Fuck. Why did I keep making things sound dirtier than they actually were? "Nothing like that. I mean, it's about that, but not in that way. I mean…"

"Dorian." She said my name firmly, a small smile starting to play on her lips. "Calm down. Just tell me what you mean."

Taking a deep breath, I tried to start over. "I write romance, right?"

"So you said." Her shoulders dropped again, just a little, her guard coming down.

"Well, the thing is, romance usually involves sex, but up until now, my books haven't."

She blinked a couple of times, processing that. "People in your books don't have sex?"

"No. I mean, they do, but I don't write about it. They fall into bed together and suddenly, it's the next morning. Like in a mainstream movie, I guess."

"Ah, the fade-to-black." She followed my train of thought perfectly. "I've never been a fan. It's such a tease."

"That's what my editor thinks too," I admitted. "The thing is, I'm afraid to write those kinds of scenes from the female perspective. No matter how much I read, I can never know exactly what it feels like for a woman, and that's what I'm interested in: what she's *feeling* in that moment, not just who's putting which body parts where."

The description made her smile more fully, and her arms dropped to her sides again. "You don't have any female friends you can ask?"

"None that are comfortable talking about that sort of thing," I told her truthfully. "I know it's a big imposition, but I was wondering if you had some time, sometime, any time, if I could pick your brain about it? You're probably as close to an expert as I'm going to find."

That hadn't been part of my script, and I winced, hoping she wouldn't take that as an insult, but to my relief, Laina laughed. "I probably am, and no, I have no problem talking about it." She threw a glance back over her shoulder, looking at something inside I couldn't see, her expression thoughtful. "Actually, this might work out well. I'm trying to work on a script for a new film, but it's harder than I thought to make the dialogue sound natural. Do you think you could give me some pointers?"

That sounded like a perfect exchange, and a reason for us to spend more time together too. "So, you scratch my back, I scratch yours?"

Her laugh was just as inviting as I remembered it being all those years ago. "Well, we'll see how we get along before we decide if there's any scratching involved." The wink she tossed me had the blood both rising to my cheeks and heading south too. "Why don't you come in and we can talk it over a bit more?"

Gratefully, I accepted her offer, and as she turned to go back inside, I wished there was a way I could go back and let the 16-year-old version of me know that it might take another lifetime, but eventually, he'd get to see the inside of Laina Macintyre's home.

~Laina~

It seemed I had jumped to conclusions about Dorian a little too quickly. When I pulled up the front door camera on my phone and saw him standing there, I really didn't know what to expect but curiosity compelled me to go and answer the door.

His apology started out well, but when he suggested I could help him with something, I assumed it must be sexual 'help' he had in mind. I'd received more propositions than most people could imagine, of all varieties, and it felt like we were heading in that direction again until he began to stumble over his words just as he had the night before, growing more flustered by the second, and I realized he didn't mean it that way at all.

He said he didn't have any women in his life to talk about sex with, and perhaps that explained his reaction the night before too. Rather than being disapproving, he just genuinely didn't know what to say.

Unless he'd become a very convincing actor in the years since I'd seen him last, he was still just the sweet, slightly awkward guy he'd always been, and when he explained he wanted some help with his book, I had a flash of inspiration.

The movie I wanted to make would be a perfect mix of romance and sex, but although I could write a porn scene in my sleep, the flirting and tension building was a lot harder. Everything I had written that day sounded forced and cheesy, and soon, the words began to swim in front of my eyes. I'd been ready to toss my laptop across the room in frustration just before Dorian arrived, and suddenly, standing on my doorstep, was a successful romance author who wanted a favour.

Maybe fate played a part in him moving in next door after all.

"This place is incredible." Dorian's appreciative comment from behind me made me smile as I led him into the living room where I'd been working. Glancing around, I tried to see it as it might appear to someone walking in for the first time.

Walls of pale gold reflected the sun's rays that came streaming in the arch-shaped windows. Paintings hung on the walls, sculptures and vases decorated the tables and corners, and rugs covered the hardwood floors. Along one wall, another row of arches framed a wall-to-wall bookshelf, filled with hundreds of books I hadn't read; I simply liked how they looked. The furniture didn't match but each piece complemented the others, and blankets and pillows were draped across the sofas and chairs. It looked homey and lived in and, to my eyes at least, absolutely perfect.

"It's based on a villa in Italy where I did one of my first overseas jobs," I told him as I took a seat back on the couch where I'd been sitting before he arrived. "We spent a week there and I loved the way each individual item in the house told a story. At the time, I had a tiny studio apartment in downtown LA with second-hand flat-pack furniture, so it felt like a whole different world. I took a ton of pictures, and my co-stars all thought I was crazy, but I knew that someday, I would have a house just like it. When I found this place, it fit my vision perfectly. I bought it on the spot."

Dorian listened to me intently even as he remained standing, still looking around the room. Wearing a t-shirt and jeans just as he had the day before, he somehow seemed even more muscular than he had in his empty kitchen the night before. My female viewers would go crazy over a body like his, and though it had never really been my type, as he turned around, giving me a view of his rather perfect ass, I had to admit I could see the appeal.

His attention kept returning to the bookshelves in particular. "This library is amazing. Are you a big reader?"

"No." I left it at that, not wanting to go into any further detail. Someone like him wouldn't understand anyway. "I'm more of a visual person, but they look good."

They looked especially good with him in front of them. Put a pair of glasses on him, make him a Clark Kent-type, and you'd have a perfect leading man. I might just have to rewrite my main character to match.

"They do look good," he agreed good-naturedly, taking one more look around before settling into one of the chairs across from me, well out of reach. Perhaps he wanted to make it clear that he really had come there to talk business and not to hit on me. "How long have you lived here?"

In some ways, it felt like only a few months since I moved in, and in other ways, I could barely remember a time when I didn't live there. "Five years. It's a lot of space, but I consider it a business investment since it gives me a lot of room for shooting."

"Is it typical to shoot movies in your own house?" He asked the question almost tentatively, as if he wasn't sure whether I'd be offended, but now that I felt a bit clearer about his motivation, I didn't immediately look for offense. Very few people ever just asked me questions about my work, like they would with any other job, so I actually rather appreciated that he did.

"For an actress, no, but I also produce most of my films. I figured out pretty quickly that the real money was in owning the rights to the film, and as a producer, it cuts down on my costs significantly if I don't have to pay for a filming location."

"Very clever." It sounded like he actually meant it, not saying it in that patronizing way that some men would have. He leaned forward in his seat, his brown eyes full of curiosity. "Do you mind if I ask how you got into the industry?"

"Are you going to write about me?" I meant it as a joke and he took it that way, a rather dazzling smile breaking out across his face.

"Actually, I already have."

"What?" I couldn't tell if he was teasing me back, but when his cheeks began to flush again, it seemed like he might actually be serious.

"Well, not *about* you, exactly, but you were the inspiration for the backstory of a character in one of my first books. I sometimes borrow different characteristics or scenarios from people I know in real life, it makes the books feel a little more real. At least, I think so."

I could understand that. People wanted to be able to identify with a character, and the more real they felt, the more likely they would be to find something in common. Point-of-view porn videos were popular for a reason, though those had never been my style.

"Tell me about her, this character based on me." Leaning back, I tucked my legs up beneath me on the sofa, settling in for a story, and Dorian laughed nervously.

"I thought you wanted to talk about how we could work together?"

"I do, and since I haven't read your books, it'd be good to get a sense of the type of stories and characters you write about. It might help me figure out how we could complement each other. You don't have to be nervous, Dorian. I'm not here to judge, I just want you to tell me a story. What do you say?"

~Dorian~

I didn't know if it only happened to me or if other authors went through the same thing too, but whenever someone asked me to give them a summary of one of my books, my mind went completely blank. Sitting at my computer, I could remember each of my characters' birth dates, favourite foods, and childhood pets, but the second someone asked me about them, I was lucky if I could remember their names.

Somewhere in the back of my head, I suspected this could just be a deflection technique on Laina's part. I'd asked her about how she got into her career, and she flipped the conversation so that we were talking about me, without her ever having given me an answer. It hadn't escaped my attention, and yet, I didn't want to refuse her request since our truce still felt quite fragile. If I opened up to her, maybe she'd open up to me in response.

With that in mind, I took a deep breath, trying to bring the character into my head so I could talk about her in a way that supported my assertion that I actually told stories for a living.

"Her name is Jesalyn. When the book begins, she's living in Chicago where she's trying to make a career for herself, but no matter what she does, things seem to go wrong. She applies for her dream job, but they don't hire her because of a bad reference. She takes another job instead, but everyone treats her like she has the plague, even though they were nice during the interview process. The bank turns down her application for a mortgage on her perfect house, and she starts to think that maybe she's cursed."

"I think we all feel that way sometimes," Laina agreed, tucking a loose strand of hair behind her ear as she leaned forward, listening carefully.

The afternoon sun coming in the windows seemed to bathe her in a glowing light, making her look even more beautiful than usual.

"During flashbacks, we see a little bit of Jes' life in high school, and that's where you come in. She trod her own path there, never slotting into any of the stereotypical cliques that existed, just like you did. Everyone thought she was cool, but no one really knew her. One day, she stood up to one of the most popular boys in the school when he bullied another kid, and unbeknownst to her, that bully never forgot about it. His father was a powerful man with lots of connections, and once they'd graduated from college, he used his father's influence to interfere in her life, causing all these negative things to happen that she attributed to bad luck."

Would that ring any bells with her? Would she recognize the incident I referenced, and that I had been the kid she stood up for?

If she figured it out, she didn't say so. Instead, she raised one perfectly manicured eyebrow at me. "Let me guess: he's an asshole but they end up falling in love anyway."

"No. Definitely not." Bully romances might be popular, but they had never been my genre, for rather obvious reasons. "She ends up meeting a quiet guy who works in the company's IT department, someone everyone thinks is a little odd but who turns out to be a bit of a dark horse, and he helps her get to the bottom of things. Together, they come up with a plan to get back at the bully, and along the way, they fall in love."

In a way, writing that book, one of the very first I published, had been my way of writing out the story of Dorian and Laina the way I'd always hoped it would go. Having given them their happy ending, I could let go of any last lingering feelings I still had for the girl who had always been out of my league.

I thought it worked, until she turned up on my driveway and all those feelings came rushing back, a mix of teenage hormones and long-forgotten hopes. Ideally, the more time we spent together, the more I could put that behind me again and simply get to know the woman in front of me, the one I found easier to talk to by the second.

"They fall in love but they never have sex." Laina's blue eyes sparkled as she teased me, looking more comfortable with me too with each passing minute, and I had to laugh.

"They *do* have sex, I just didn't write about it."

She leaned forward again, just as I had, trying to lessen the distance between us. Maybe I could have sat a *little* closer. "You said you're looking to focus on the emotion, but it doesn't necessarily need to be emotional. Women like the filthy stuff too. A lot of my viewers are women, maybe more than you'd think. They want the visual, the 'who's putting which body parts where', as you said."

I definitely knew that. I spent enough time lurking around reader chat groups to know that women could be every bit as pleasure-focused as men in the right context. "Sure, but it has to be a mix. If it comes across as a manual, it's not sexy. There needs to be a narrative within a sex scene, as I'm sure you know, and I haven't figured out how to write that narrative in a way that's both compelling and sexy. When I've tried, it just comes across as... well, bad porn."

Once again, I held my breath as the words came out of my mouth, hoping I hadn't crossed a line, but to my relief, Laina laughed. "Trust me, I've seen enough bad stuff to know exactly what you mean. It really feels like we're talking about the same thing here, Dorian. I want to make a film that's a bit more on the emotional side, like your books. I want the buildup and I want the stakes. When they have sex, I want the viewer to know that it means something, to feel like something more is going to come out of it than just an ejaculation."

Though I had nothing in my mouth, I nearly choked anyway. I'd never had such a frank conversation with a woman in person before, but Laina seemed entirely at ease with it, so I did my best to match her confidence. "How far along are you with the script?"

For the first time, she looked almost sheepish. "Actually, I've really just started. It's something that's been in my head for so long, but when

I actually sit down to try to get it all out, it seems to get stuck. Does that make any sense?"

It made perfect sense to me. "Absolutely. That's totally normal for any writer but especially a less experienced one. I've got some tricks about how to break through that block and I'd be happy to share them with you. But in terms of working together..."

The idea had been building in my head throughout our conversation, and I decided to blurt it out right there and then, before I lost my nerve.

"I'm finishing up a book at the moment and my editor has asked me to add some spicy scenes. Every time I try, I make *myself* cringe. Maybe we could talk through your dialogue and you could help me with my sex scenes?"

Laina didn't have to think it over for long. "I think that could work. We can start tomorrow if that works for you?"

I nodded immediately, not wanting her to change her mind. I still had a lot of unpacking to do, but I'd find the time.

She seemed genuinely pleased with my agreement. "In the meantime, will you tell me your pen name? Maybe I should actually read one of your books so I know this isn't all some kind of act."

Again, she was teasing, and I laughed along with her. "It's J.M. Everlee. You might want to start with my most recent ones, they're better than my earlier ones."

"Actually, I might check out the one you were telling me about. I'm sure they're all pretty good."

I'd had much more effusive praise before, but for some reason, those words from her meant just as much to me as any five-star review. "Do you have any homework for me? If you're reading my book, what should I do?"

She thought about it for a moment. "I'll send you a couple of films I've produced, ones that I'm not in. That'll give you an idea of the type of thing I do so we can both be familiar with each other's work. If you did want to watch any of my films, they're all publicly available, so that's up to you."

"I'll... I'll just watch the ones you send me." Heat rose in my cheeks again, but somehow, I'd managed to make it through an entire conversation with her without sticking my foot in my mouth too badly. I definitely counted that entire visit as a win.

Only when I made it back to my own house did I realize she'd never actually answered my question about how she got into making porn in the first place. It looked like I would have to wait a little longer to get the answer to that question, but with the prospect of seeing her again the next day, I felt certain I'd find out sooner or later.

Chapter Three

~Laina~

After sending Dorian an email with links to free versions of a couple of my production company's films, it didn't take long to find his book online, and I breathed a sigh of relief when I saw he had an audio version available. That would make things a lot easier.

I only intended to listen to a chapter or two to get a feel for his writing and what I could learn from him, and I put the book on my house-wide speaker system so I could move from room to room while listening. However, the story quickly drew me in. I made supper while Jesalyn went through her string of 'bad luck', as Dorian had described it to me. She met Erik, the mysterious IT guy, just as I finished eating, and I couldn't stop there. I kept it on while I did my evening workout, the tension building with every stolen glance between them or the way their hands brushed against each other while they pored over phone records of the guy who'd set out to ruin Jesalyn's life.

They hadn't even kissed, and I was ready to jump into the book and scream at them both to make a move already.

Eventually, I had to get some sleep, but as soon as I woke up, before I even got out of bed, I started the book again, eager to find out what happened next. Normally, I went for a swim in the morning to help wake up, but that day, I jumped on the treadmill instead so I didn't waste any listening time. I could still hear the book in the shower as I got ready, searching my body for imperfections in the full-length mirror I'd installed in the bathroom. At 31, I still looked nearly as good as I ever had, but the camera wasn't kind. I had to keep on top of things.

With no plans that day other than working with Dorian, I dressed casually in leggings and an oversized sweater, eating my egg white omelet, yogurt and melon at the breakfast table while the book raced towards its climax.

Just as Jesalyn and Erik got trapped together inside the former bully's house after they broke in to look for the evidence that would bring him down once and for all, my doorbell rang, and I groaned in frustration before remembering that it must be the book's author at the door.

"This is all your fault!" I greeted him after flinging the door open. Dressed in jeans again, he wore a polo shirt instead of a t-shirt, slightly dressier but still on the casual side. His biceps still stood out just as much, and the tattoos on his forearms seemed even more prominent than before. I hadn't had a chance to examine them closely yet; from a distance, I couldn't tell exactly what they were.

"E-excuse me?" Dorian's smile faltered at my unexpected outburst.

"I haven't been able to stop your book since I started it. I haven't gotten anything done." With that explanation, I turned around for him to follow me, not to the living room where we'd spoken the day before, but through the opposite doors of the atrium leading out to my back-yard and the pool. The light breeze and sunny blue sky that day were gorgeous, even by Malibu standards, and we might as well enjoy them.

"You didn't have to read the whole thing," Dorian protested as he stepped out onto the tiles outside the door and stopped in his tracks. "Wow. This is gorgeous."

I happened to think so too. The pool had been the clincher for me when I viewed the house during my property search. Visible from half the house, Dorian would have seen it if he went over to the window in the living room the day before, but since he hadn't, he got the full effect of it now, seeing it from its most flattering angle.

The rectangular main pool had rounded corners, atop which sat Roman-inspired statues of men and women, tastefully nude. Slightly elevated behind the pool, the circular hot tub was framed by palm trees, and beyond it, the hill fell away to give a clear view all the way to the Pacific Ocean, the deep blue water sparkling in the sunshine beneath the paler blue sky.

Even after five years, the view managed to take my breath away at times, and clearly, it did the same for Dorian. He could barely tear his eyes off it.

Closer to the house, a covered, shaded gazebo sat to one side, and on the other side, a covered awning extended from the house which could be withdrawn depending on whether I wanted the sun or not. As Dorian looked over to the gazebo, he chuckled nervously. "Ah, that's where the first movie you sent me was filmed."

I had almost forgotten which films I had sent, but he was right. My pool area featured in several of my films since I'd be crazy not to make use of such a stunning location, and I had sent him one based on the ever-popular 'pool boy' trope. Where better to film it than next to my pool?

"So, you watched them? What did you think?"

I took a seat at the outdoor dining table beneath the awning, gesturing for him to join me. He chose a seat a little closer to me than he had the day before, but still not the one right beside me.

"I hope this doesn't come across the wrong way, but they were better than I expected them to be." Dorian gave me a sheepish shrug to accompany those words, and I accepted them at face value. He didn't mean it as an insult to me but as more of a commentary on the industry in general.

"Do you watch a lot of porn?"

His surprised cough made me smile. Although he had started to open up to me, it seemed pretty clear that he had some hang-ups about talking candidly about sex. I wondered how much that had to do with why he didn't feel comfortable writing sex scenes, beyond what he'd said about needing to understand the female experience.

Dorian did his best to cover his surprise and maintain his composure. "I'm not sure what 'a lot' is, but I'm going to say no. It's not a regular thing for me."

I leaned forward onto the table, clasping my hands in front of me. "That's interesting. Why not? You said you're single so you must masturbate. You don't use porn then?"

His red cheeks were back, as was his flustered stammering, which I expected. I was being deliberately provocative, but he brought himself back under control more quickly that time. "I, uh... no. Not really. I guess my imagination is good enough on its own."

I could believe that. The mind that came up with the story which had me enthralled for hours could probably write a sex scene better than any I'd ever created. But he didn't, which confused me now that I knew how his writing could draw people in. He was such a strange mix of confident and hesitant, talented and self-effacing, gorgeous and shy. Who was Dorian Reid, really?

"When did you first begin writing? When you used to scribble in your notebooks in high school, were you writing stories then?"

Dorian's eyes widened in surprise. "You remember that?"

"Sure. Pretty much every class, you were scratching away. I used to wonder what could be so interesting. Now, I know it was you all along."

After years of marketing myself, flirting came second nature, but my words were still true. Dorian was a puzzle I'd overlooked once before, but I had no intention of letting him fly under the radar again. Sooner or later, I was going to figure him out.

~Dorian~

Although I had tried to prepare myself for any and all conversations we might have that morning, Laina still had a way of surprising me. I'd only been in her backyard for about three minutes and already we'd touched on filming people having sex by her pool, masturbation, and the fact that she had noticed me writing in high school.

She had a way of switching between topics just as I got comfortable with the one we were on, and she had a knack of always bringing the conversation back to me instead of focusing on her. I'd noticed it, but I still needed to figure out how to counteract it. I still had a lot more to figure out about her in general.

When I received her email the night before, I sat down at the island in my kitchen to open it, giving myself a pep talk first. I spoke the words out loud since no one else could hear me. "Alright, Dorian. You're a grown man, and the beautiful woman next door has just sent you some porn that she made so you can watch it and have a reasoned discussion about it tomorrow. You are *not* going to think about her while you're watching it."

No points would be awarded for guessing how long that lasted.

At first, I tried to keep an academic mindset about it. "The lighting is really good," I commented, still talking out loud since it helped me feel more in control. "Story-wise, we're setting up some conflict right off the bat, that's good."

The owner of the house in the video appeared to be a businessman, and his trophy wife pouted about him leaving her at home all day with nothing to do. She tried to tempt him into staying, wearing only her bikini and a see-through coverup on top of it.

"I have to work," he snarled at her, smacking her ass before heading to the door. "Be good."

The woman flipped him off behind his back as he disappeared, sighing in frustration before heading to the backyard to sunbathe. She removed her top, giving the camera a good view of her flawless, artificially enhanced chest before she lay down on one of the sun loungers, face down.

Soon, the pool boy showed up. Young, but not too young, handsome but not *too* handsome, he was perfectly cast. Men could watch him thinking 'he's not *that* much better looking than me', and think they had a chance of being in his shoes. Woman could watch thinking he'd suffice for a little distraction, which was clearly all the female character wanted.

Did Laina get involved in casting the films? How hands-on did she get?

As soon as my beautiful, enigmatic neighbour crossed my mind, I couldn't think of anything else. Had she written the script for this film? I'd heard a lot worse. In particular, I liked how they kept talking through the sex scene, it wasn't just moaning and grunting once they both got naked.

Had Laina been there watching, behind the camera, while the pool boy fucked the boss' wife over the gazebo bench? Did it turn her on to watch it, or was it strictly business? And why was I getting more turned on by the idea of Laina being turned on than I was about anything actually happening on the screen?

I thought I'd left my crush on her behind a long time ago, and I didn't want to be the creepy guy obsessing over a woman who barely knew he existed. That was part of the reason I wrote the book about Jesalyn and Erik, putting my unrequited teenage feelings for Laina to rest once and for all. Ever since I gave them their happy ending, I hadn't spent any more time pining after a girl I had honestly barely known.

That night, however, watching the film she'd provided for me, I felt closer to her than ever before. When she leaned closer to me in her living room, her attention fully on me, it hadn't felt out of the realm of possibility that she might actually find me attractive too.

With a groan, I gave in to the need rising in me, unzipping my jeans and pulling my half-stiff cock out. The images on the screen weren't causing my arousal; it came entirely from my mind as I closed my eyes and imagined myself in that scene but on the other side of the camera, standing next to Laina. While the scene continued in front of us, everyone focused on the two actors, I pulled her away. We didn't go far, just a few steps behind a wall where we could still hear what was going on though we couldn't see it, and lifting her skirt, I thrust into her right there against the wall, covering her mouth with my hand to stop any noise from coming out.

In my mind, the tight grip of my hand was the feel of her body, and the woman's moans I could still hear coming from my computer were Laina's, whimpered beneath my hand.

"Fuck." Gasping for breath as my orgasm hit, I lowered my forehead to the cool marble of the countertop, resting it there as pleasure and guilt washed over me at the same time. We couldn't really be held responsible for our fantasies, could we? Hopefully, she would never find out I just did that, and once my head cleared, I quickly got up to clean the mess off my new kitchen floor.

So, when she asked me that morning if I masturbated to porn, my heart seemed to stop for a second before I could remind myself that she had no way of knowing what I'd done. I told her I relied on my imagination instead, which wasn't a lie; I just didn't mention that, most recently, that imagination had been centred on her.

Clearing my throat, I did my best to direct the conversation back to her. "Do you mind if I ask you some technical questions about your movies? Well, not yours in particular, but porn in general, I guess."

Laina's eyebrows raised curiously, a half-smile forming across her lips. "Sure. Ask away."

I could feel the colour rising in my cheek at just the thought of what I wanted to ask, but I pressed on anyway. "How much editing is there? I mean, the man is always ready, the woman is always ready, half the time he just shoves it in with no preparation at all… what goes on behind the scenes?"

The bewilderment in my tone, or perhaps my choice of words, made Laina laugh, a laugh I didn't hear nearly enough back when we were teenagers. "There is a *lot* of editing. A 30-minute film like the ones I sent you will take four or five hours to shoot. If the man's getting too close to his ejaculation, we might call a break to help him hold off. Sometimes, it's too late and he loses control, and then we have to wait until he's ready to go again. If you're ever watching a movie and the guy goes from pretty hard in one scene to a lot limper in the next one, that's probably what happened."

So, they didn't just have superhuman levels of stamina. That was good to know, though I couldn't really say for sure why I cared. Maybe because I didn't want her to compare me to them? Not that she'd given me any indication we were heading in that direction at all.

"As for women, usually, the first penetration you see in the movie isn't the actual first penetration of the day. She'll have been warmed prior to that. If we're talking anal, that's a whole other situation and there's a lot of preparation that goes into that."

"It doesn't sound all that sexy," I had to point out.

"It's not, but if you're a good enough actor, you can make people believe it is." She gave me a conspiratorial smile that had my body reacting again, making me glad my lap was hidden beneath the table. "It's the same as words on a page. There's nothing inherently sexy about that, but if you draw the reader, or in my case, the viewer in, you make them forget that it's not real."

Our creative pursuits really did give us something in common, and I returned to the question I had tried to ask her the day before, trying to make some sense in my head of how the girl I'd known in another life-time now sat beside a pool behind her multi-million-dollar Italian-style villa, running her own adult film company: "How did you realize this is what you wanted to do? I want to hear the whole story, Laina. How did you end up here?"

~**Laina**~

Talking about porn in general didn't bother me at all. With over ten years' experience, I felt like I knew the industry almost as well as anyone, and I took pride in that fact. Knowing what viewers wanted and how to give it to them was powerful, lucrative knowledge to have. I knew the 'behind the scenes' stuff that Dorian asked me about and how to make a scene look seamless even when it wasn't. Other people who weren't in the industry themselves rarely asked me about it, usually being too embarrassed or disapproving of the whole venture, so I rarely got a chance to share that knowledge with anyone else. If Dorian wanted to sit and chat about it for hours, I would have been happy to.

When he asked about my personal reasons for starting out though, just as he'd done the day before, that hit a little closer to home. Though I had no regrets about how things had turned out, the story of why I got involved in it in the first place didn't exactly fill me with pride.

Hopefully, I could answer an adjacent question to the one he'd asked and satisfy him that way. Rather than speaking about porn in particular, I could talk about why I became interested in acting in the first place. "Being an actress always appealed to me because of the power that stories have. Movies can make us laugh or cry or, in the case of porn, get turned on, even though nothing is actually happening to us. Books are just the same, so you know how it is. Did you always want to be a writer?"

Dorian leaned forward, his elbows on the table and a half-smile on his face. His forearms were the closest they'd ever been to me and I had to keep from staring at the tattoos on them. What had led to such a drastic turnaround in his physical appearance? I still needed to find that out.

"You keep doing that, you know."

I'd been so distracted by his body, his statement took me by surprise. "Doing what?"

"Changing the subject whenever I ask you about yourself."

He'd noticed that, had he? Most men weren't so perceptive. "If I do, it's only because I find you so interesting."

It was a line, but men usually fell for it anyway.

Not Dorian.

"I'm asking because I'm genuinely curious, Laina. I'd like to get to know you better now that you've reappeared in my life, almost like magic. I'd like to know what drives you and what I can learn from you. If it's not a great story, that's okay. I've got some not-so-great stories too."

The supportive tone of his deep voice wrapped around me like a warm blanket, inviting me to relax and let my guard down. As much as I found his awkward, nervous side rather adorable, this more determined Dorian was pretty attractive too.

By referring to 'not-so-great stories', I had a feeling I could guess what he thought. He must suspect I'd been manipulated into it somehow, lured in and exploited in the way that the news stories liked to sensationalize young women's descent into sex work, and to be fair, it did go that way for some women.

That wasn't my story, though, and if nothing else, I could set his mind at rest on that point.

"I'm afraid it's simply not that interesting. I moved to LA to be an actress but breaking into film or TV is hard. After a couple of years of not getting cast, I realized I could be more successful in the type of films you could shoot in a day. If you're worried that someone took advantage of me or forced me into it, you don't have to be. I went in with my eyes wide open and I knew my worth from day one. I had an agent and contracts in place before a single frame was shot."

From the way the tension released from his shoulders, I could tell that really did make him feel better. He was sweet to have been worried about it. "What was it like when you did your first movie? I honestly can't imagine taking my clothes off in front of... well, the whole world, really."

"Why not? You've got a great body." To back up my words, I reached over and ran my fingers lightly down his forearm, watching in satisfaction as he shivered at my touch. I could still distract him if I tried.

Almost, anyway. Dorian quickly regained his composure. "You're doing it again, Laina. We're talking about you, not me."

He had a point, I supposed. That time, I hadn't even meant to do it. I'd gotten so used to the men I spent time with outside of work not wanting to talk about my work that I naturally changed the subject without even realizing it.

Leaning back, I answered his question. "It actually didn't feel that strange. The director let everyone know it was my first time in front of the camera, so they were all very supportive. My co-star was a veteran performer, an older man who played my step-dad in that particular movie, and he gave me a lot of tips and encouragement. Honestly, people couldn't have been nicer, and once we started filming, I lost myself in the character. It wasn't me having sex, it was her. Maybe it sounds silly to make the distinction, but to me, it's different. It feels completely different from when I have sex in my personal life."

Dorian considered that for a moment, not giving me any clue what he thought about that. "Have you ever ended up dating your co-stars?" he asked instead.

I shook my head firmly. "People sometimes think actors form a connection because we're intimate with each other, but we don't. We're both just there to do a job. Some of them I like as people, some I don't. The guy I've done the most films with, I actually can't stand off-set, but we keep working together because people think we have good chemistry. But no, overall, the men I work with aren't usually my type."

That last word caught his attention, as I suspected it would. I'd used it on purpose and he walked straight into my trap, leaning forward again eagerly. "What is your type?"

"Is this still related to the work we're going to do together?" I teased, and Dorian immediately blushed, realizing he'd crossed into more personal conversation. I didn't mind, and I liked to flirt as much as anyone, but we'd already talked about me long enough. At least for that morning, I was much more interested in him as an author than as a potential date.

"Sorry, I got carried away. We should get some work done." From his bag, he pulled out his laptop. I'd barely noticed him carrying anything when he came in, his body was such a distraction. "Where do you want to start?"

I knew exactly where I wanted to start, and with a smile, I put the spotlight firmly back on him. "Well, I already know you can write, so let's dive straight into the dirty stuff. Why don't you start off by telling me about the best sex you've ever had?"

Chapter Four

~**Dorian**~

Laina wasn't playing fair. After teasing me for getting too personal by asking about her type, she turned around and asked about my sex life? Technically, that could be considered relevant to what I'd asked her to help me with, but I couldn't sit there and talk to Laina Macintyre about my disappointing sex life. I could barely get through talking about sex in general without my cheeks burning; if we started talking about anything to do with sex and me in particular, I might literally combust.

"I... uh, I don't do well off the top of my head," I admitted, opening the laptop to give myself something to focus on besides those captivating blue eyes of hers. "I can write it down for you if you like."

"You don't talk things out before you write them?" She sounded genuinely curious as she tried to peer around the side of my laptop to see my screen. "I always say things out loud first, even if I'm just talking to myself. I pretty much have to get it all out first before I can put it in any kind of order."

That made total sense to me, based on what I knew of her. "That's because you're an extrovert and I'm an introvert, so we have different ways of working. I need to see the words written down and have a chance to change them or move them around before I feel comfortable sharing them with anyone."

"Huh." Her hum of acknowledgement suggested she respected my method even if it didn't entirely understand it. "So, if I give you a chance to write it down first, you'll read it to me when you're done?"

Fuck. I hadn't anticipated actually reading it to her. I thought she could read it herself while I sat back and tried not to melt into a puddle of embarrassment.

Still, I should try to meet her halfway. It sounded like she preferred to process things through conversation rather than reading and I had to respect that as much as she respected the way I worked. I could give it a shot, anyway.

"Okay, let's try that. But in the meantime, you should be writing something too. How about I give you a scene to write, we can talk it through first, and then you can write it down while I'm working on mine?"

Her eyes lit up, looking pleased that I'd taken her preferred way of working into account. "That sounds great. What should I write about?"

I'd given that some thought already that morning. She said she wanted to learn how to write good dialogue, banter between the characters that showed them building a connection, so we might as well dive right into that, the same way she was having me jump into the deep end by writing a sex scene.

"I want you to write a first date between two people who have previously only been friends, and I want to start to see them building a connection. It doesn't have to be sexual; in fact, it shouldn't be. At this point, they're just sizing each other up as romantic partners and seeing if there's something there between them."

Laina nodded thoughtfully, taking the whole thing just as seriously as I was. "So, there shouldn't be any mention of sex at all? Not even in a flirty kind of way?"

"On a first date? Probably not." I meant it as a joke, but when she flinched, I immediately tried to soften my words, taking any judgement out of them. "Do you usually talk about sex on a first date?"

"It tends to come up," she admitted. "I make sure people know what I do for a living before I go out with them, so I don't waste my time if they're going to be weird about it. That means we usually talk about sex at least in a general way before we even get to the date. I suppose that breaks the ice, and it tends to come up again naturally."

I really hadn't thought about any of that: about men being scared off by her job or about the fact that she'd have to bring it up as soon as someone expressed any interest. In that context, the way that she'd blurted her job out to me at my house the other night made a lot more sense, as did the way she spoke about sex so bluntly, but it didn't really seem conducive to romance.

She must try to scare people off before she got too attached, so that if they stuck around, she'd know they truly didn't have a problem with it. It seemed like a heavy weight to carry into a new relationship, perhaps a bit like people who were extremely famous or wealthy. How many 'normal' relationships had she actually had?

My questions kept multiplying, the urge to know more about her growing stronger with each minute we spent together, but it would have to wait. She wanted to focus on work, and I really should too.

"Tell me about this couple," I encouraged her, having laid out the basic situation. "Who are they? How long have they known each other? How did they meet?"

Laina willingly took up the challenge, perhaps using something she'd already been working on, at least in her head. "Her name is Penelope and she's an animal trainer. Larkin is a stuntman on a movie set. They met when she worked on one of his films, handling the lions that the stuntman had to wrestle with."

"Wow." I hadn't expected anything quite so dramatic, but she had me intrigued. "Alright, that's what they do and how they met. How much later after that meeting is the date taking place?"

Her hand rubbed her chin as she thought about it before moving down her neck and coming to a rest on her chest, just above her breasts while I did my best not to stare.

"It's been six months. He wanted to ask her out before that, but he's shy and she keeps getting called away to deal with animal emergencies."

"The Hollywood stuntman is shy?" That was an interesting character choice.

"Definitely," she confirmed, her eyes not fully focused on me as she came more and more engrossed in the scenario. She wasn't entirely there with me anymore, but seeing the characters in her mind's eye instead; I knew the look. "Nobody expects him to be, all muscles and testosterone, so they all think he's just arrogant and aloof, but he's really just withdrawn. Around her, he feels like he can relax."

She could have almost been describing me. Did she realize that? Did she do it on purpose?

"And how does Penelope feel around him?" I wondered.

"She likes how interested he is in her work. A lot of people get scared away by the animals, but he's not afraid of being eaten alive; it's only people that scare him."

The description made me smile, a wide grin that flashed across my face before I could stop it. "They sound pretty well matched. How do you think the first date's going to go?"

Laina was on a roll. "It'll be awkward at first since Penelope didn't realize he felt that way about her. Maybe he'll say the wrong thing, or she'll just take it the wrong way, but they'll talk it out. She'll use some of her animal calming techniques to get him to relax and just be himself."

"It sounds like a pretty great scene to me." It honestly did; I wasn't just saying that. A whole story for the characters began to unfurl in my mind, the way it always did when I got inspired, but I forced myself to pull it back, recognizing that it would be her story to tell. "Have you got enough to go on?"

"I think so." Laina's eyes came back into sharp focus as she got to her feet. "I'll go work in the living room so I don't distract you. Do you need anything? A drink? Directions to the bathroom?"

Given the size of the house, directions were probably necessary, but I didn't need anything at the moment. "No, I'm good, thanks. Come and get me when you're ready, or I'll come in if I finish first. It's not a race, though; take your time."

She gave me a sweet smile. "This is fun, Dorian. I'm glad you suggested it."

I was too, and though I tried not to stare as she turned to walk away, it proved impossible. I couldn't take my eyes off her until she disappeared from my sight entirely, and only then did I look back down at the blank page on my screen. She'd asked me to write about the best sex of my life, but the truth was, I'd never have an experience worth writing about. I would have to embellish it a little bit and make it sound a little more exciting than it really had been.

Hopefully, Laina wouldn't be able to tell the difference.

~Laina~

Chatting about my fictional characters with Dorian made them seem more real than they ever had before, and I went to the living room to grab my laptop before I could lose that moment of connection.

Glancing back over my shoulder just to make sure I was really alone, I opened up my dictation program and began to speak.

"Penelope: When I got your message today, I thought you must have sent it to me by accident."

"Larkin: Why?"

"Penelope: Well, you've never asked me to go to dinner before, not out at a nice place like this. I didn't think we were the kind of friends who did that."

"Larkin: Maybe I didn't ask you as a friend."

As I spoke, the words appeared on the screen, populating in different colours to indicate the different character's dialogue. A friend had introduced me to the dictation program a few years earlier, and it had been a lifesaver for me. When I finished recording, I could get the program to read it back to me and make any tweaks necessary, all while hardly having to look at the screen at all. I wrote all my scripts that way, and even if the spelling was sometimes a little off, no one seemed to think anything of it.

No one mentioned the word dyslexia to me growing up. In our small town, there wasn't much awareness of any kind of disabilities at all. It probably didn't help that I covered it pretty well. I had a good memory and could remember things I heard, so I did okay on tests even if my spelling was atrocious. The teachers would comment on how I could spell a word correctly one day and not recognize it at all the next day, but nobody put the pieces together about why that might be.

In high school, it became harder for me to ignore or gloss over. Words seemed to move around the page, not helped by thick textbooks with small print, and I could read the same paragraph five times over without understanding it. My grades began to suffer but everyone assumed it came from getting busier with extracurricular activities, and since I could manage a passing grade, no one cared too much. No one expected me to go to university anyway, so what did it matter?

I could read, if I had to, but the idea of reading for fun struck me as completely insane.

When it came to acting, my memory was my saving grace. In high school, I'd ask my friends to read my lines out loud for me while we rehearsed, and once they were in my head, I wouldn't forget them. The truth was that I barely looked at the script at all. If I did, it usually just confused me, so I preferred to leave it behind.

Dorian might have remembered me as not caring what anyone thought about me, but the truth was that I spent half my time in high school terrified that someone would discover my secret. When I graduated, I breathed a strong sigh of relief, thinking the worst of it was behind me.

Unfortunately, I underestimated just how much reading was involved in acting. With a great headshot and a relentlessly optimistic attitude, I got myself an agent pretty quickly, and when she sent me scripts for auditions, I'd have someone read them out loud to me. Men were happy to help if it meant getting on my good side. I could go to almost any bar and find someone willing to give me their time. My first roommate also agreed to do it if I did all the cleaning. I never told any of them exactly why I needed it, I just said it helped me to remember things.

I managed to book some commercials to get a few credits to put on my resumé besides my local high school drama club, and before long, I started getting callbacks to actual films and TV shows. I thought I'd made it; eventually, one of those opportunities would be my big break and all my dreams would come true.

However, almost without fail, I'd show up to an audition and they'd ask me to read something cold, or they'd change a few lines on the script they'd sent me, and dread would take over. I'd blink at the words on the page, willing them to make sense to me, but they stubbornly refused to cooperate. My confidence would plummet and even the words I'd memorized ahead of time refused to come.

My auditions failed, one by one, and soon, the callbacks stopped coming. My prospects that once looked so bright seemed to dry up and my confidence took an even bigger hit. It turned into a downward spiral that I couldn't seem to find my way out of.

After two years of no paid acting work, a casting agent took pity on me at one of the rare second callbacks I managed to get. After I flubbed the lines on the script they gave me, I wanted to get out of there as fast as possible, but he followed me out of the building, stopping me on the street outside. An older man, he looked like he'd probably seen it all.

"You're a beautiful woman, Laina, and your first audition was great. What happened in there today?"

For some reason, the emotions of the day combined with the pressure of the secret I'd been keeping for so long overwhelmed me, and I ended up blurting out the whole story to a complete stranger.

When I finished, he looked me straight in the eye. "Can I be frank with you?"

"Sure." He'd been nice enough to listen to me; I could hear what he had to say too.

"TV is going to be difficult. Between table reads and last-minute script changes, you won't keep up, and directors don't want a project. They'll go with someone who doesn't need their hand held."

That was harsh, but probably true. I just hadn't wanted to admit it before.

"Films, you might have a better chance. There *are* actors with dyslexia, successful ones. They find ways to make it work, but it's going to take a bit of luck and a lot more confidence than you showed in there today to get your foot in the door."

"Dyslexia?" I'd heard the word before, but had never applied it to myself.

He looked surprised by my confusion. "That's what you have, isn't it?"

"I… I don't know." I had always just thought of it as a challenge I had, the same way some people found math tricky.

"Well, step one would be to find out. There are things you can do that'll help, not just in acting but probably in your day-to-day life too. The other thing I'm going to suggest might be completely out of the question for you but I want to put it out there anyway."

"What is it?" My mind was whirling with the information he'd already given me, but I was still eager for any additional guidance he could offer.

"Scripts are a lot less important in adult films. I've got a friend who's one of the best agents in the business and I could put in a good word for you. This isn't amateur stuff, it's real films and real money. Like I said, maybe it's not your thing, but I'll give you his card. You can give him a call if you want, it's up to you."

The white card with raised black lettering looked professional as I took it from him, nothing about it suggesting anything seedy or un-savoury. Like just about everyone in the world, I'd watched porn before, but I'd never imagined myself doing it. Was that even really still acting? The questions swirled around my head but I managed to give him a grateful smile. "Thanks. I'll think about it."

He nodded, not pushing any more than that. "Good luck, Laina."

It took me two weeks to make the call, and the agent had indeed heard about me. He agreed to meet with me, we discussed the pros and cons of the industry candidly, and everything fell into place from there. I never bothered getting an official diagnosis for my reading disability since I didn't see what good it would do, but I'd found a lot of workarounds that helped me in my day-to-day life, to the point where someone like Brock, who I'd dated for months, never had any idea of how I struggled.

Dorian never knew in high school, and I had no plans to tell him at this point either. That was why, when he asked about how I got into porn, I gave him the broad strokes but not the detail. For someone like him, someone who dealt in words every day, it would seem ridiculous, and I didn't want any pity.

He came to *me* for help. He viewed me as an equal and the truth might spoil that. For at least a little bit longer, I'd rather keep up the illusion.

~Dorian~

It took nearly two hours until I had something I was happy with. Well, not entirely *happy* with, but not embarrassed to show Laina, at least. I *couldn't* write a sex scene I was happy with; hence, the whole reason I'd come to Laina for help in the first place.

She still hadn't returned by the time I finished, and despite me turning down her offer of a drink earlier, the warming sun and passing time had made me thirsty. After standing up and stretching out my cramped muscles, I decided to go and find her. She told me she'd be in the living room and I remembered how we got there the day before, so if I retraced my steps, I should be able to locate it again.

As soon as I stepped into the hall, my laptop tucked under my arm, I could hear another voice. Maybe she had company, or had turned the TV on? Maybe she was talking to someone on the phone? I crept closer, trying not to disturb her, and as I reached the door to the living room and heard her character's name, I realized what I was hearing: a computer program was reading Laina's dialogue back to her.

"That's a great trick."

Laina nearly jumped off the couch in surprise and I winced. *Smooth as always, Dorian.*

"Sorry, I didn't mean to scare you. I just meant the computer, the listening, it's..."

"Hang on, wait, let me turn this off." She sounded short of breath as she tapped around on the laptop keyboard until the voice stopped speaking. "I didn't hear you come in."

"Sorry." How many times had I apologized to her in the past two days? My characters never had to apologize; they always said the right thing in the first place. "I was just saying that hearing the dialogue out loud can really help to identify any awkward turns of phrase or words that don't sound quite right. It's a great trick, I use it all the time."

I'd only wanted to compliment her but it sounded condescending as it came out, and Laina's cheeks had flushed a light pink colour. *Fuck.* This was exactly why I couldn't write about any of my own experiences: I always got too much in my head and it got awkward and not sexy at all.

"Right. Yeah, that's why I do it." Laina seemed to regain her composure as she moved over to one side of the couch, patting the empty space next to her. "Are you done? Come and sit down so we can swap."

I would have preferred to sit over on the same chair where I'd sat the day before, especially if she expected me to read to her, but it would have been rude after she invited me to sit next to her. Gingerly, I lowered my body onto the sofa, trying to leave her as much space as I could. "Who's going first?"

"You can read mine first. Put me out of my misery." With a self-deprecating smile, she held her laptop out to me.

"Oh, uh... you don't want to read it to me?" If she wasn't going to read hers, maybe I didn't have to read mine out either. That would be a relief.

"You said you prefer to see the words on the page," she reminded me. "You can consume it your preferred way, and I'll listen to yours since I work better that way."

What she said made sense, unfortunately, and I did appreciate her remembering what I'd said even if the thought of reading out loud to her had my stomach doing all sorts of unpleasant somersaults. I licked my lips to try to ignore the dryness of my mouth, and Laina jumped to her feet.

"I'll go get you some water while you do that."

"That'd be perfect, thanks." With her out of the room, I read through the dialogue she'd written. The beginning felt a bit heavy with exposition, like when the female character said, "Remind me how you ended up in your job?" as a way of sharing a story with the audience even though she would have already heard it, but overall, it really wasn't bad at all. A few lines made me smile, and overall, I could start to feel the chemistry between them.

It really was pretty good.

"I think you're a lot better than you give yourself credit for," I told her when she'd returned and after I'd wet my throat with a large gulp of water. "This isn't bad at all, and the films you sent me had some decent dialogue in them too. You wrote those too, right?"

"That's all leading to sex, though," she pointed out. "This one felt different. They're just talking for no real reason. Is it too vapid?"

Her choice of that word felt significant. Laina had probably had it levelled at her more than once; a beautiful woman who made her money off showing her body was often assumed to be unintelligent, even though the two things weren't in any way connected.

I didn't say that, though, sticking to answering her question instead. "Not at all. I don't know if you've actually listened to people on a first date before, but the conversation isn't usually earth-shattering. Most of the time, both sides are just trying to make sure they don't screw up too badly so they have a chance at a second date."

Her smile could light up any room, even one as nice as the one we were in. "What if they were aware of that and went out of their way to try to scare the other person off by revealing all their most annoying habits and deepest secrets right at the start?"

I grinned back at her. "Now *that's* an interesting premise. I would definitely read that book."

We went through her script in a bit more detail while I pointed out the places I thought there could be some improvements made, and Laina asked smart, insightful follow-up questions, not taking any of the criticism personally. It hardly felt like work at all.

Eventually, though, we had to turn to my work, and my heart started pounding as Laina sat back and waited for me to start reading. I couldn't remember the last time I'd been quite so nervous; it might have even been back in high school, speaking in front of a classroom populated with jerks who disliked me for no good reason other than that I didn't fit the mould they all seemed to have sprung from.

Laina wasn't like that, though. She never had been, and at that moment, she only wanted to help. Clearing my throat, I forced the words out, reading too fast and without any real inflection. Words like 'cock' and 'clit' felt strange in my mouth but I managed to get through them, all the while keeping my eyes glued to the screen so I didn't have to see

Laina's reaction or imagine what she might be thinking. I just needed to get to the end.

When I'd finished, the silence that filled the room felt far louder than it had before. The sofa creaked beneath Laina as she shifted her weight and a bird tweeted outside, each sound magnified by the thumping of my heart as I waited for her response.

Finally, I couldn't take it anymore. "I know it's not great. That's why I'm here," I reminded her. "It's supposed to be sexy and it's not sexy, and I don't know what I'm missing that..."

"Dorian." She cut me off as her hand came to rest gently on my arm, and I closed my eyes, trying to calm myself down. She'd taken all my feedback so well and there I was, losing it before she'd even said anything. "It's not bad, but it's..."

She trailed off, trying to find the word, so I decided to be helpful and supply one for her. "Mechanical? Robotic? Ridiculous?"

"Stop." Her soft voice sounded amused but serious at the same time. "It just doesn't feel like your voice. It doesn't sound like the guy who wrote the story that reeled me in all last night. It almost sounds like you're writing about something you've never experienced before, which is weird because this was your own experience, right?"

I could have lied, but what would be the point? I'd asked for her help and if I wanted to make the most of it, I'd have to be honest with her. "Not exactly."

Laina's brow furrowed as she leaned forward, far enough into my line of vision that I could see her even as my eyes remained on the screen. "Why not? I thought that's what you were going to write?"

She'd asked me to write about that but I hadn't, and once again, my inability to think on my feet came back to haunt me. All I could do was blurt out the truth: "I thought this would sound better."

"Why?" she pressed, still not understanding me.

With a groan, I elaborated further. "Because the best sex of my life really wasn't that great. I don't know what I'm doing, Laina, and if I have to write about it, the whole world is going to know."

Chapter Five

~**Laina**~

Well, I definitely hadn't been expecting that.

And yet, in the context of the scene he just read to me, it made perfect sense. Dorian wrote about sex almost like someone who had never experienced it. He was worried it sounded mechanical, but that wasn't even the real issue; it sounded like someone watching it from the outside with no real knowledge of what it felt like to be the person taking part.

He must have had *some* sex, and he didn't say he was a virgin, but I fully believed him when he said his experience hadn't been very satisfying, if the way he wrote about it was any indication.

I tried to keep my tone as light and non-judgemental as I could. "Have you looked in a mirror lately? You could go to any bar in LA and have a woman willing to take you home and show you *all* the ropes."

He smiled at my teasing, but I could see the pained look in his eyes at the same time. He really was completely serious. How was that even possible? A sweet, kind man like him who looked the way he did? Honestly, when I first saw him the other night, I thought he wasn't my type, but the more time we spent together, the more attractive I found him. And that was even putting aside the fact that to a hell of a lot of women, he would be *exactly* their type right from the first glance.

If it had been his choice not to sleep around, I could understand and respect that, but he sounded so unhappy about it, I couldn't believe it had all been voluntary. So, what was the issue? He had me completely stumped.

"I'm going to be straight with you, Dorian: if you include a scene like that in your book, it's going to stick out like a sore thumb."

He groaned again, snapping the lid of his laptop closed. "So, I'm fucked."

"Not well enough, apparently." The words came out of my mouth before I could stop them, and my eyes went wide as Dorian looked over at me in surprise. Would he take that as the joke I meant it to be?

I couldn't say if his lips twitched first or mine did, but as soon as the cracks began to show, we both broke down in laughter.

"I'm sorry, I didn't mean..."

He didn't let me finish, still chuckling. "Don't apologize. This is exactly what I need: someone who's going to give it to me straight with no sugar coating. Maybe watching more films would help," he suggested, though he didn't sound thrilled with the idea. "You could suggest some more good ones for me."

I didn't think that would solve the problem at all, especially since he'd already watched some the night before. His issue wasn't that he couldn't describe it but that his description felt too removed from the action. Watching more porn wouldn't help with that; if anything, it might make things worse.

"You said you wanted me to give it to you straight, so I will: obviously, watching other people isn't enough. If it were, you'd have figured it out by now."

He winced even as he nodded in agreement. "What if we watched it together? You could explain to me how certain things feel... I mean, if that wouldn't be too weird for you?"

"I think I've made it pretty clear by now that I don't have any problem talking about sex," I pointed out, and Dorian had to concede that point.

"In that case, maybe that's the best solution. It could almost be like an interview and I can really try to get into your head. I need help, Laina. Obviously."

He did, but I didn't think his proposal went far enough. He didn't need to talk to me or ask me questions. What he needed was some actual experience, some experimentation with someone he felt comfortable enough to take risks with.

Someone... maybe a bit like me?

The thought came into my head out of nowhere, but as it settled down and began to take root, I had to admit I didn't hate it. In fact, a pleasant warmth spread through my whole body at the idea. At that moment, I wasn't seeing anyone. I liked Dorian, and I'd just been thinking that I found him attractive. I'd never done a 'friends with benefits' situation before but nothing was stopping me. After all, one thing I definitely knew how to do was keep sex and emotions separate.

Did Dorian think of me that way? I honestly didn't know. He'd been polite and respectful with me up to that point, asking me about my work but never assuming it meant he could be overly familiar with me the way some men did. Would he think it crude if I told him what I was thinking?

Why should he, though? We were adults, not the teenagers we used to be, and if he wasn't interested, he could simply say so and it didn't have to be awkward. We weren't exactly friends yet anyway, just one-time acquaintances and new neighbours. The parameters of exactly what our relationship going forward might be were still being defined, so what better time would there be to throw out a suggestion like the one circling in my head?

With that in mind, I bit the bullet. "What about if we watched some scenes like the ones you'd be interested in writing about and then tried them out afterwards so you could really understand how it feels?"

Dorian flushed so red that the tips of his ears turned scarlet. "Wh-what?"

"You heard me." I had no intention of repeating myself when he'd only asked the question as a stalling technique. "I've got plenty of experience that I wouldn't mind sharing."

"You?" He sounded so bewildered by the suggestion that I couldn't help feeling a little offended. Had he really not thought about it at all?

"Why not me?"

As I tried to guess the reason for his hesitancy, a familiar, sour taste filled my mouth. Was it because of my job? Did he think it made me dirty somehow, or someone he wouldn't want to be associated with? Was he just like Brock after all?

"I'm clean. I'm tested regularly; far more regularly than most people."

Dorian looked horrified at my explanation. "No. God, no, I didn't mean that, Laina. I just meant that... well, I never imagined you being interested in someone like me. Sexually, I mean."

So, he thought I was too good for him rather than the other way around? That made a nice change, and as the tightness in my chest eased, I gave him a teasing smile. "You're a sexy man, Dorian Reid. You should start acting like it."

Although I said that, I kind of hoped he never did. I was growing rather fond of the shy, sweet Dorian.

"So, if that's your only objection, what do you say? Should we give it a try?"

~Dorian~

It had to be a dream. Maybe when I got up from the table by the pool, I slipped on some water and hit my head, and had actually hallucinated the last twenty minutes. That made much more sense than the idea that Laina Macintyre just suggested that we have sex with each other.

She mistook my hesitation for concern over the number of men she'd slept with, but that hadn't even crossed my mind. A person's sexual experience didn't have anything to do with what kind of person they were, good or bad, nor how attractive I found them. I just honestly couldn't believe she'd really suggested it, but she not only confirmed that I'd understood her correctly, she actually called me sexy.

Maybe I'd stepped into an alternate universe when I moved to Malibu, but if that were the case, I hoped I never found my way back out again.

She was waiting for me to say something, so I tried to think about what my characters might do in that situation. They would find a way to make it equally as much about her as themselves, and as my eyes fell on her laptop, still open on the floor where she'd left it, I had an idea that actually might work.

"To make this fair, maybe you should get some hands-on experience too. Let me take you out on an incredibly awkward first date and you'll have more inspiration for your own scene."

Laina's smile faltered just a tiny bit. If I hadn't been paying attention to her carefully, I wouldn't have noticed it. "You want to take me on a date?"

Why did that sound like a bigger deal to her than having sex with me? She suggested that without hesitation, but when I mentioned a date, she got tense. "Sure. You said you're not seeing anyone, right?"

"I'm not, but dating me is different, Dorian, especially in public. I get recognized sometimes."

I hadn't considered that, and when I tried to imagine how the interactions might go, my mind refused to cooperate. "And people actually come up to you? I mean, wouldn't that give away the fact that they were watching... I mean, not that there's anything wrong with it, but... why would they... what would they say..."

I was floundering again, my cheeks starting to turn red, but thankfully, Laina intervened.

"That doesn't stop them, and often, they feel like they can say whatever they want to me because they saw me naked. Dating me means being aware that other men have watched me have sex. Thousands of them. Millions, maybe. It's not like dating the usual girl next door."

Whether she realized it or not, I saw exactly what she was doing: she was trying to scare me off, to get all the negative stuff out in the open so I had an out if I wanted to change my mind.

Apparently, she didn't realize how many good qualities she had to outweigh any negative ones. The woman people thought they knew from watching her movies wasn't *her*, the same way that I wasn't any of my characters, no matter how much I'd like to be sometimes. "I don't care about that, Laina."

She let out a disbelieving scoff, looking unconvinced. "I've heard that before."

The bitterness in her tone definitely sounded like it came from experience and I didn't want to diminish that. However, I didn't think she could judge the way I'd respond based on what other men had done either. "I mean it. I'll be honest with you: I don't like the spotlight. I hide behind my pen name to avoid any kind of publicity and I've never been interested in dating a celebrity, but if the attention is on you and not me, I think I can handle it."

"People will make comments to you too," she warned. "Some guys will congratulate you, others will make backhanded remarks about how they could never trust me not to cheat or how it must suck to know where I've been all day when I get back from work. I'm sure they say even worse when I'm out of earshot. Some people think that because I take my clothes off for a living, I don't deserve common courtesy."

It would definitely be a new experience for me to have people speak to me so candidly, but I truly believed I could handle it. "Consider me warned. I'd still like to take you out."

She shrugged, as if to say it would be my own fault if things went wrong. "When?"

I thought she had meant right away when she mentioned us having sex, so I had assumed the date would be part and parcel of that. "Well, tonight, I guess. And then, if you still want to, afterwards we could…"

Almost of their own accord, my hands made some kind of complicated, completely irrelevant gesture that made Laina laugh. "What was that?"

"Honestly? I have no idea." The way she teased me without making fun of me made me feel more comfortable with her all the time. "But you know what I meant."

"Somehow, I do," she deadpanned. "Alright, I guess we have a plan, then. I have some things I should get to this afternoon. What time will you pick me up?"

Fuck. In my excitement over her agreeing to go on a date with me, I forgot that I had to actually plan a date. So much for actually getting any work done that day. "Seven?"

She smiled again. "Don't ask me, Dorian. Tell me: what time will you pick me up?"

"Seven." I said it firmly that time, like I meant it, and she gave me a nod of approval.

"Great. I'll see you then."

Clearly, I'd been dismissed, so with my laptop in my hand, I headed back down the street to my own house. I'd left my phone behind so I wouldn't be distracted when I should be working, and a couple of messages were waiting for me. One was from my editor, wanting to know how the spicy scenes were coming; that one, I could put off for another day or two. Perhaps by tomorrow, I'd have a lot more inspiration.

The second call came from my mother, simply asking me to call her in her unassuming way. That one, I returned right away, placing a video call to her. "Hey, Mom. What's up?"

As usual, I could only see the top of her forehead. She liked to hold the phone close so she could see me better. "I just wanted to check and see how the move went. How's California?"

She couldn't really understand why I'd moved so far away, but since she still lived within five miles of the house she grew up in, I didn't figure I could explain it to her any better now than I had when I first told her I was doing it.

"It's great. I'm still getting unpacked and settled. The house is perfect, and I've already met one of my neighbours. She came over to introduce herself."

I figured my mom would be impressed with that, and she was. "Well, that's very friendly. Is this a single woman?"

Even from three thousand miles away, she was trying to set me up, but for once, I was actually ahead of her. "Yes, she's single, and we're going out for dinner tonight."

That was pushing the truth, since Laina and I both knew it wasn't a real date, not in the way my mom would think, but I figured the lie would make her happy without hurting anyone, and it did.

"That's wonderful! What does she do?"

I knew the answer to that, but when the simple question came out of her mouth, I froze. Though I didn't think there was anything wrong with Laina's job, I also had no idea how my 60-year-old mother would react to it, not to mention that I didn't know if Laina wanted me to go around telling people. On the off chance my mother ever met her, she might recognize her from my childhood. There were too many variables for me to make a confident, honest response, so I kept my answer vaguely true instead.

"She's an actress. Isn't that what everyone does in LA?"

That made my mom laugh, but she still sounded delighted. "Well, she must be a pretty successful one to live in that fancy new neighbourhood of yours. It sounds like this move is working out just as you hoped, Dorian. I'm so pleased."

I was too, and after promising to update her in a few days' time, I hung up to start researching restaurants in Malibu so I could figure out exactly where to take Laina on our date.

~Laina~

I never expected to be heading out on a date only two days after getting dumped by Brock, but I was glad to have something to look forward to. Despite what most people probably thought about the private lives of people in my profession, I didn't date very much. Finding someone who was actually interested in me for me and not all the other stuff wasn't all that easy.

I didn't have to worry about Dorian sponging off my money. He obviously had enough of his own if he could afford to move in next door. I also didn't have to worry that he only wanted me for sex, since I'd offered it to him without any need for going on a date. He flat-out said he would prefer not to date a celebrity, so he wasn't looking for the rush of fame either. He had no reason to ask me out other than that he genuinely wanted to spend time with me, and for me, that truly was a novelty.

In the afternoon, I had a virtual meeting with Erica, the director of my production company, to go through where we were on all our current projects. Between the two of us, she had the business head while I was the more creative one. She'd started in mainstream films but found it hard to advance in the male-dominated boardrooms, and I preferred to work with another woman who refused to take any bullshit from the pushy men in my industry. Overall, we worked very well together.

When we'd finished going through our entire list, I threw in one more question. "Have you ever heard of the author J.M. Everlee?"

"No, I've never heard of her," she replied sarcastically before realizing I wasn't laughing along with her. "Wait, are you serious? Of course I know her! She's a very big deal."

It seemed Dorian's plan to keep his identity secret was working since Erica believed J.M. to be a woman. I did my best to play along. "You've read her books?"

"Not only read them but I tried to option one back before I joined you. It would have made a great movie, but I didn't get anywhere with it, unfortunately. Apparently, it's impossible to track her down. Why do you ask?"

She was far more invested than I'd anticipated, but I found myself feeling proud on Dorian's behalf that a woman whose opinion I valued so much enjoyed his work. "I met her a few days ago, randomly, and she's going to help me a little bit with my new script."

Erica's jaw dropped as she blinked at me through the screen. I didn't know if I'd ever seen her speechless before. "Are you kidding me?! Laina, if we could get her to accept a co-writing credit, it would be *huge*. The film would get so much free publicity, it would practically sell itself."

That had never even crossed my mind, and it didn't sound like something Dorian would be interested in. "I don't know if she's looking to have her name attached to an adult film, even one that's only 10% sex."

That was the figure we'd decided on; we wanted to do a full-length feature film that included full sex, but not as the primary focus. It just wouldn't cut away right when things were getting good.

"There could be a separate general release cut of it," Erica countered, growing more excited by the second. "A clean version and a spicy version. Some books do that."

Did they? I really didn't know anything about it. "That's interesting, but it's not why I brought it up. I just wanted to let you know that I'm really trying to make sure we have a good script to work with."

"I can meet with her if you don't want to make your relationship about business," Erica offered. "Just set up a meeting and leave the rest to me. We have to at least ask."

She didn't seem to want to let it go, so I simply ended the conversation instead. "I'll think about it. Have a good rest of the day!"

I disconnected the call before she could say anything else.

Getting ready for dinner with Dorian, I put as much effort into my appearance as I would for any other date. Since we probably wouldn't be going anywhere too formal on such short notice, I chose a light, summery dress in shades of orange that showed off my tan perfectly. My hair got piled on top of my head in a casual up-do, and after touching up my makeup, I finished the look with a pair of nude heels.

Dorian would not be disappointed, I could practically guarantee it.

My doorbell rang at precisely seven o'clock, just as I spritzed my perfume on, and I grabbed my small bag with my keys and phone inside. After an overzealous fan tried to steal my wallet once so he could have my photo ID, I stopped carrying anything with me that might give away my real name or address. I couldn't be too careful, and for that reason, I checked the security camera to make sure it really was Dorian at the door, even though I was expecting him.

His already-familiar face looked even more nervous than usual on the screen, and when I opened the door for him, his jaw dropped, just as I'd hoped.

"Wow." His eyes travelled over me in an appreciative but respectful way. "You look amazing."

"You're not so bad yourself." In his light blue polo shirt and khakis, he looked every inch a Californian. The shirt clung to his muscled physique, and a shot of excitement shivered through my body as I remembered I would get to see all of it later that evening. "When did you get into such incredible shape anyway?"

"Since I was a slob in high school, you mean?" he asked with a laugh as he led me to his expensive but sensible luxury car. He wouldn't be the type to own a flashy sports car, and I would have been shocked if he'd shown up in one. Like a gentleman, he opened the door for me before getting in the driver's side.

"Sports weren't really your thing, as I recall," I pointed out.

"That's a very nice way of putting it." He flashed me a grin as he pulled out of my driveway, and my body pulsed with excitement yet again. It shocked me just how much this felt like a real date. "College was an extension of high school in a lot of ways. I had more friends there, found my own little niche, but I still wasn't popular by any stretch, and when I graduated and started writing from home, I realized it would be easy for me to never leave my house again if I wanted to. To avoid becoming a complete hermit, I joined a gym, and surprisingly, I found that I really enjoyed it. Working out gave me a chance to work through any mental blocks I had with my work, and by the time I got home, I'd be full of new ideas. Now, I work out every day as part of my work day. I didn't actually do it to get in shape; that was just a lucky by-product."

Lucky indeed, at least for me.

"And what made you decide to move to Malibu?" I asked curiously. It really was a world away from where we grew up.

"Let's save that story for dinner," he suggested. "I've only got so many interesting stories to go around."

Behind the wheel of his car, he looked calm and in control, far more than in any other setting I'd seen him in to that point. He seemed to forget to be nervous around me and I had to admit it turned me on to see him so confident.

Ever since he'd agreed to have sex with me, I'd become a lot more aware of everything about him.

We made small talk about the neighbourhood and the city in general until he pulled up outside the very same restaurant that Brock had taken me to earlier that week. What were the odds?

"I've heard this place is good," Dorian said as he opened the car door for me. "I should have had you pick since you'll know much better than me."

"This is great," I assured him. Hopefully, none of the wait staff would remember my outburst and I could replace the memories from that night with new ones instead. "So far, so good on the date, Dorian. You promised me awkward and I don't know if you can deliver."

"You haven't even given me a chance yet," he protested, and we both laughed as he opened the door to the restaurant for me. The night really couldn't be off to a much better start.

Chapter Six

~**Dorian**~

I'd never had so many men look at me with undisguised jealousy as when the hostess showed Laina and I to our table. It had nothing to do with her being an actress or anyone recognizing her; she simply looked absolutely stunning that evening and drew everyone's eyes to her, mine included. I'd barely been able to look away since she opened the door of her house, which had made driving a bit of a challenge.

As we got settled at our table and she smiled at me over the fresh flowers and candles between us, I had to pinch myself under the table to make sure it really wasn't a dream.

"So, you promised me a story," Laina reminded me once we'd placed our orders and the waiter had brought over the bottle of wine I'd chosen. She looked like she'd been made for the California sunshine with the ocean sparkling behind her out the restaurant's floor-to-ceiling windows. "What brought you all the way out here?"

I *had* promised to tell her, and though I didn't find it all that interesting, I always kept my promises. "Well, as cliché as it sounds, it all started with a breakup."

Laina smiled knowingly as she picked up her wine glass. "I've had a few of my own, so I get it. How long were you together?"

"Six months."

"Just past the honeymoon stage," she guessed, but that hadn't really been it.

"I don't think I ever saw us together for the long term and that was a big part of the problem. Things were comfortable but not exciting, and if it's not even exciting after that much time, what would it be like in five years? Ten? I don't need drama by any means, but we were just missing the spark, you know?"

The spark I felt whenever I looked at Laina, for instance.

"Wait, *you* ended it?"

She sounded so surprised that I had to laugh. "Is that so unbeliev-able?"

Her sputtered reply sounded a lot like how I'd been tripping over my words around her lately. "No, I didn't mean... I'm just surprised. You don't seem like the dumping kind."

That might have been a compliment but I couldn't tell for sure. "Well, hopefully, she didn't feel like I dumped her. We had a good talk about it and agreed to go our separate ways amicably, and afterwards, I took a long, hard look at my life. Tara was pretty and smart and everything I should have wanted, but I still felt something was missing. It felt like the right time to shake things up, so I did something completely out of character, something no one expected me to, and I bought a house in Malibu online without ever even setting foot in it."

Laina laughed in delight. "Are you serious? Completely out of the blue? That's hard-core impulsive."

"I know," I assured her, still hardly able to believe I'd done it. "My family thought I'd lost my mind, but I just thought if I ever wanted to really live, I needed to get out of my comfort zone, so I decided to not just shake things up, but buy a whole new shaker."

The turn of phrase made her laugh again. "And what was your plan when you got here?"

That was a good question. "Honestly, when I was unpacking the other night, I had no idea. Part of me was panicking, wondering what the hell I was doing there, while another part wanted me to just settle in first and see how it went. There's a chance I would have ended up falling back into a lot of my old routines and turned into just as much of a hermit here as I was at home, but then you showed up at my door and now, I'm out for dinner in a great-looking restaurant with a beautiful woman. I'd say that so far, things have worked out pretty well."

She took the compliment graciously and we chatted more about the neighbourhood and about people we remembered from high school while we ate our dinner.

I'd told her the date would be awkward, but actually, it had to be one of the nicest first dates I'd had in a long time. Maybe that was because we'd spent time together already before we went for dinner. Maybe it was because we both knew exactly what would happen when the date ended, and although my body buzzed with anticipation whenever it crossed my mind, they weren't the nerves that came with wondering whether something would happen or not.

Or maybe it was just because of Laina herself and how easy she was to talk to. How she seemed to find the way I stumbled over my words charming rather than annoying, and how the conversation between us never seemed to flag. In fact, I often found myself returning to previous topics because we let ourselves get carried down some new path and forgot what we had originally been talking about.

Over her protests, I insisted on paying since I had invited her out. We made it out the door and almost to the car, almost making it through the whole date without any major missteps at all, when a couple of men jogged over to us, stepping in front of Laina.

"You're Jenny Vixxen, right?" one of them asked as the other held up his phone to film the encounter, not even bothering to ask Laina's permission.

That must have been her stage name because she flashed a winning smile at the one who'd spoken to her. "That's right. Nice to meet you."

She threw me a quick look, her eyes telling me she had things under control, so I reluctantly took a step back.

"Darren's a big fan," the guy behind the phone said with a smirk. "I haven't seen your stuff yet, but I'll *definitely* check it out tonight."

I thought *I* sounded creepy at times, but he'd practically just told her he was going to go home and watch her have sex, probably with a box of tissues. What the fuck?

Laina smiled over at him as if he'd said something kind. "Hope you enjoy it. Have a good night, gentlemen."

'Gentlemen' was pushing it, and as Laina turned to go, the first one reached out to grab her shoulder. "Hey, how about a quick photo?"

My fists clenched as Laina agreed and he slid his arm around her waist with way too much familiarity. As the guy with the phone snapped the shot, the other man's hand moved lower, brushing over Laina's ass, and I couldn't take it any longer.

Grabbing his hand off her, I quickly twisted his arm behind his back. "She said you could have a photo. That doesn't give you the right to touch her."

"Ow, fuck! Chill out, bro." He grimaced as his friend kept filming, doing nothing to help.

"Dorian. Stop." Laina's voice from behind me was quiet but firm, and reluctantly, I dropped the creep's arm. Laina gave the men one more smile. "Sorry about that."

Why was she apologizing to *them?* The one I'd grabbed shook out his arm, grumbling about it hurting while the other one chuckled. "If you're jealous of that, man, I think you're dating the wrong girl."

My fists clenched again but Laina quickly linked her arm through mine to prevent any further trouble, pulling me towards the car. "Have a good night," she repeated over her shoulder as we walked away.

My hands were still shaking as I opened her car door for her and got behind the wheel myself. Did she really have to deal with that on a regular basis?

"Drive," she instructed, her tone leaving no room for argument, and taking a deep breath to calm myself, I pulled out onto the street and headed for home.

~Laina~

Remembering how in control Dorian seemed as he drove us to the restaurant in the first place, I thought that driving back might help him to calm down after the encounter in the parking lot, and sure enough, his breathing began to even out and his shoulders relaxed as he navigated the traffic along the Pacific Coast Highway.

I hadn't really expected that kind of reaction from him, not when he was reserved and almost shy around most people. Something had obviously touched a nerve for him, but if we were going to continue spending time together, especially in public, he'd have to learn to control it better.

I said nothing as he turned onto the long, winding street that led up the hill to our neighbourhood, waiting to see what his response to the situation would be. I'd learned that I could tell a lot about a man by how he dealt with having lost his temper.

Finally, he glanced over at me. "Alright, I'm guessing I screwed up back there, but I don't really understand why."

As responses went, that wasn't too bad. He seemed willing to hear my side of things, at least. "Those were my customers. You can't go around beating up my paying customers."

"I didn't beat anyone up," he protested. "I could have, but I didn't. Don't I get some points for restraint?"

He turned such a hopeful smile at me that I had to smile back even as I continued to chide him. "What if I went and harassed people buying your books when they knew I was a friend of yours? Especially on video? You don't think that's going to be all over social media later?"

He obviously hadn't considered that, and his shoulders slumped. "But the things they said, and the way he touched you…"

"The touching *was* inappropriate but hardly the worst I've had. As for what they said, what was wrong with it?"

He threw me an incredulous look. "He told you he was going to go home and watch you tonight."

"Which he'll pay to do," I reminded him. "That's what I'm selling. If they were videos taken without my permission, that would be different, but I made those films on purpose, knowing that people would watch them. I'm not ashamed of my movies so why would I be offended that someone wants to watch them?"

Dorian's mouth opened and closed a couple of times on the way to my driveway as he tried to decide what to say, only deciding on an answer when he parked the car and switched it off. "I'm sorry, Laina. I guess I didn't think about it that way. I told you I could handle it and I dropped the ball the first time out."

That apology was a good start, and when all was said and done, I didn't want the incident to spoil the rest of our night. "It's alright. And hey, if it does go viral, people will be talking about me. All press is good press, they say."

He shook his head in a combination of amusement and disbelief. "I can't believe how calm and cool you are about all of it."

"I've had a lot of time to get used to it," I reminded him. "You've had two days. Cut yourself some slack. Now, are you coming in for another drink?"

We both knew I had more than a drink in mind with my invitation, and immediately, Dorian's cheeks began to flush. He didn't hesitate, though. "Yeah. I'd love to."

"Good." I opened my own door, leaving him scrambling behind me as I got to the front door of the house and opened it to let us in. "More wine, or something stronger?"

It would be better if he could relax and not be too nervous, if possible, so it relieved me when he asked for a whiskey. It just so happened to be my drink of choice too, so I poured out two small, neat glasses for us from one of the better bottles in my collection. My fingers brushed against his as he took the glass from me, lingering there for a moment longer than absolutely necessary as I let myself imagine what those hands might feel like on the rest of my body.

Although I disagreed with how he'd handled the man in the parking lot, I couldn't help noticing the ease with which he'd handled him. Those muscles of his weren't all for show; he knew how to use them too, and I couldn't wait to try them out for myself. Usually, big muscles weren't my thing at all, but on him, combined with his overall sweetness, they definitely worked for me.

"So, I think we should start by watching a film for a little inspiration, and then we can try it out for ourselves. Is there anything in particular you want to watch?"

Dorian swallowed hard, as if his mouth were dry despite the whiskey in his hand. "I don't think we need to go too wild. Maybe just something where the characters have been attracted to each other for a while but couldn't act on it for some reason, but finally, they give in?"

I had just the film, but first, I had to take the chance to tease him. He'd given me a few hints already about how he felt about me in high school, but that was the biggest one by far. "Did you have a crush on me all those years ago, Dorian?"

He cast a disapproving look down at his glass, as if blaming the alcohol for his loose tongue, before he offered me a weak denial. "I deal in fiction, remember? I'm just thinking of my scene."

"Uh huh. Sure." The way the blush crept up his cheeks and into his ears told me all I needed to know. "For the record, if you'd asked me out back then, I would have said yes."

His eyes immediately snapped back up to me, his jaw dropping open. "That can't be true."

He seemed so certain of that, it almost insulted me. Did he think of me as one of those stuck-up girls, obsessed with appearances? I hadn't been that way then, and I still wasn't, no matter what my job was. "Why not? You were sweet. I'm pretty sure you still are, just wrapped up in a slightly... *harder* package."

I lingered over those final two words, letting my gaze drop down to the front of his khakis which seemed to have grown a bit tighter since we got back to my house.

Dorian let out a choked laugh. "That's a good line. I'll have to remember that one."

"You can have it," I offered magnanimously. "Now, come on. Enough stalling. Let's go get started."

~Dorian~

Laina's relaxed, laid-back approach to our impending intimacy both confused and relieved me. On the one hand, I didn't know if I should be concerned that she didn't seem even a little bit nervous about what we were about to do. If she felt attracted to me, wouldn't she show it in some way? Or was it one of those things that you simply got less nervous about the more you did it?

On the other hand, I felt nervous enough for the both of us, so the fact that she had a plan helped to take the pressure off. She'd had sex with enough men that she *must* have had worse than me.

At least, I sincerely hoped that would be the case. I really wanted the evening to be memorable for her, as it would no doubt be for me.

Still holding onto my glass of whiskey like a lifeline, I followed her to a room I hadn't seen before, on the other side of the entrance hall. A comfortable living room in monochrome colours with two large sofas, a coffee table, and a large-screen TV mounted on the wall, it had none of the personality and eclecticism of the other living room we'd spent time in. It didn't feel like Laina at all.

I figured out why a moment after we sat down on the couch opposite the TV. "Do you film in here?"

Laina nodded, her attention focused on the TV as she grabbed the remote off the table and scrolled through her digital library. "This whole side of the house is mostly studio space. There's a couple of different bedrooms, bathrooms, a kitchen, an office and this living room. With the pool area outside, it gives us pretty much any setting we want."

That made sense from a financial perspective, but as I looked around again, I couldn't help feeling a tiny bit disappointed that we were in the 'business' side of her house rather than her personal space. It seemed to be a signal, conscious or not, that she didn't consider anything that might happen between us that evening as personal.

Laina noticed me looking but misinterpreted the reason for it. "Don't worry, it's all cleaned regularly."

Why did she always assume the worst? "That's not what I was thinking. Have men really asked you that before?"

She snorted in amusement. "That's mild compared to some of what I've been asked. Here. This one should work."

Having selected a film from her collection, Laina put the remote back down and leaned back, leaning into me with surprisingly familiarity. Her thigh pressed against mine and her head rested against my shoulder as the film began.

It opened with two men in a bar, one sitting at a table looking depressed while the other brought back a couple of beers for them. "What's the emergency?" the one with the beers asked as he sat down opposite his friend.

"Lilly kicked me out," the unhappy man confided.

"No fucking way. I thought you guys were solid?"

As the man explained what happened, his friend listened sympathetically, but at the same time, he pulled out his phone under the table to text the now-single Lilly.

I just heard about you and Brad. You need some company?

It didn't take a genius to figure out where things were heading. I'd requested a story about two people who'd had an attraction but had been fighting it, and there was a guy lusting after his best friend's wife. The slight taboo of it had me shifting in my seat as my pants got tighter. Laina must have noticed the movement just as I was aware of every move she made, and the sweet floral scent of her perfume. All of my senses felt heightened.

When the man in the movie pulled up in front of Lilly's house, the door opened to reveal Laina herself in shorts and a crop top that showed off her toned stomach.

I glanced over at her in surprise. "We're watching you?"

Her hand dropped to my thigh, sending a shiver of anticipation through my body. "Is that okay? You said you wanted to watch me act."

I did say that, during one of my nearly incoherent mumblings, but afterwards, I thought it sounded creepy. However, she said she wasn't offended earlier when the guy in the parking lot said he wanted to watch her. She was proud of her work, so what kind of message would it send if I said I *didn't* want to watch her? And besides, watching it *with* her certainly seemed less creepy than doing it in my house, alone. How many people could say they got to watch her and touch her at the same time?

"Yeah, it's okay." My voice came out thicker than before, and Laina's hand travelled a little higher.

"I'm sorry it had to end like this," the man on the screen said as he and Laina sat down on the very couch that she and I were sitting on at that exact moment. "I know you tried to make it work."

"I did, but there's nothing more I can do," Laina replied in character. She looked amazing on screen, natural and gorgeous, but as I glanced down at the top of her head against my shoulder, I couldn't help thinking the real thing was even better. "Sometimes, it's just time to move on."

The man put an arm around her to comfort her and she leaned into him, just as she was leaning against me right then. Was that intentional? Did she remember what would happen when she chose the film?

"Uh, Bryce?" Laina's character moved her hand along the man's thigh as the real Laina did the same to me, sending another jolt of electricity through my body. "You're not... turned on right now, are you?"

Her hand moved directly onto the bulge in the man's pants as Laina's hand moved onto mine, and I sighed in unison with the man on screen.

"Can you blame me?" he asked, stealing the words out of my mouth. "I've always been attracted to you, Lilly. I just never did anything about it out of respect for Brad. But if you're definitely over him..."

On the screen, Laina's character cut the man off with a kiss, and when I glanced down, my heart racing, to see if she'd continue to mirror the performance, she was ready for me. Her lips landed on mine hungrily as her hand pressed against my groin even more firmly than before.

On her lips, I could taste the whiskey we'd been drinking, and as I pulled her closer, teasing her mouth open with my tongue, the taste got even stronger. It mingled with her own natural taste that intoxicated me even more, leaving me feeling like I could have gotten drunk off her kiss alone.

Laina wasted no time in unzipping my pants and reaching inside them to find my already stiff cock, and I inhaled sharply as her fingers made contact. I'd always considered myself an average size, certainly nothing that would make me a porn star, but as Laina wrapped her hand around me, squeezing my cock as the blood pumped through it, she made a satisfied noise, a little hum of approval that almost made me light-headed.

On the screen, the man was taking his pants off, and Laina encouraged me to do the same, pulling down on the waist of my pants as I raised my hips off the couch. Just as the version of her on the TV did, Laina bent down to take my newly-released cock in her mouth.

"Holy fuck," I managed to stutter as she took me all the way in the very first time, her lips wrapping around the base of my cock as its tip hit the back of her throat.

Sucking as she slowly lifted her head again, Laina grinned up at me once her mouth was free. "You like that? That's a specialty of mine."

"It's... impressive," was all I could get out, losing the ability to speak as she deep-throated me again. My eyes darted to the screen on the wall and the close-up of Laina with her mouth full of cock, and the combination of visual and physical stimuli brought things to a head much, much faster than I'd anticipated. "Oh, shit, stop, I can't..."

My warning came too late. Not even a minute after taking my pants off, my orgasm hit and I came hard directly into her mouth. Pleasure quickly gave way to dismay and humiliation as Laina coughed in surprise, trying not to choke on my cum.

The night would certainly be memorable for her, for all the wrong reasons. *Fuck.* After that, I might have to sell my house and move again. How could I ever face her again?

Chapter Seven

~**Laina**~

Usually, I had a pretty good radar for when a man was about to ejaculate. More often than not, my job involved getting them there, so I knew the signs to look out for: the change in his breathing, the way his muscles would tense and his balls tighten, and often, the way his pelvis thrust involuntarily in a deep-seated reflex.

The signs must have been there with Dorian; I just hadn't been looking for them. I'd been focused on showing him a good time instead. Since he said he'd never had really good sex, I figured I'd start with my mouth, just for a minute or two to get him excited, then back off to give him a chance to calm down by letting him go down on me, just as the characters in the film were about to do. I didn't anticipate that the minute or two I spent with him in my mouth would be all it took, and I'd only just become aware of him telling me to stop when he suddenly released. With my throat relaxed to take him in, the ejaculation seemed to cut off my air just for a second, and I coughed as I quickly pulled back, trying not to bite down on him as I gasped for air.

"Shit," Dorian groaned, quickly leaning forward and rubbing his hand down my back as I tried to catch my breath. "Fuck, I'm so sorry, Laina. That doesn't usually... that's *never* happened... that fast... fuck. Are you okay?"

As I managed to swallow down the mixture of semen and saliva still in my mouth, I nodded my head, not trusting myself to speak until I could be sure my breathing was back to normal. It had definitely taken me by surprise, especially since men didn't usually come in my mouth unless we were in a relationship. For film, we wanted the shot on camera, not hidden away. However, Dorian clearly hadn't done it intentionally based on the horrified look on his face.

"I'm alright," I assured him, reaching over to grab my glass of whiskey and taking a quick sip. "That wasn't part of the script."

I meant it as a joke, trying to get him to relax, but Dorian turned even redder, perhaps the reddest I'd ever seen him. "I'm so, so sorry. You're probably thinking this is why I've never had great sex if I can't even last two minutes, but I swear, this isn't typical for me. I don't know why... I don't know what..."

As he spoke, he pulled his pants back up, as if his softening cock needed to be hidden from my sight, so I leaned closer to him, placing a finger over his lips to stop the flood of words. "It's fine, Dorian. It's not a big deal. If anything, I take it as a compliment."

Since I'd barely touched him, it must have been just the thought of being with me and his own fertile imagination that had him so worked up in the first place, and I had to be flattered by that.

"It's kind of a big deal," he disagreed, inhaling deeply as if he might actually hyperventilate. "You offered to help me and I ruined it."

"Why is it ruined?" I leaned back to take another drink and grabbed the remote to pause the movie on the screen. In the film, my character was still sucking her husband's best friend's cock, so I quickly skipped ahead to the next scene, where he pushed her down on the couch to remove her shorts. Dorian glanced up at the screen before turning his attention back to me. "I told you that movies are shot in multiple parts, right? That was just act one. There's still a lot more to come."

His brown eyes scanned my face, looking for any sign that I might be more upset than I seemed, but I really wasn't. If he got up and walked away at that point, *that* would upset me, but so long as he kept trying, I still intended to have a good time.

"You don't need to be so nervous," I added as gently as I could. "Maybe that's part of why it's never been all that great for you before? Yes, there should be tension and passion and attraction, but the best sex I've ever had usually involved someone I felt comfortable with, someone I could laugh with and be myself with. Someone I didn't feel like I had to perform for. I know you don't expect me to be 'on' tonight, and I don't expect it from you either, so relax. It's supposed to be fun."

There had been a few guys in my past that I'd felt that way about, the sex far more satisfying than even my best on-screen scenes, but eventually, they all went the way of Brock, deciding that my line of work was too much for them to deal with.

"I think you might be right," Dorian admitted, picking up his glass to drain the remainder of the alcohol inside. "I tend to overthink things. A lot."

I had no trouble believing that, but I also thought I might have a solution. "Let's try something. Close your eyes."

By eliminating his vision, I hoped to ground him in his other senses, and it gratified me that he obeyed me without question. He obviously trusted me; he just needed to learn to trust himself too.

"Writers are supposed to engage the reader's senses, right? You describe how things sound and smell and taste and feel, not just how they look. So, tell me: what do you smell right now?"

Right on cue, he inhaled deeply. "Your perfume. It's light and flowery, like being in an English garden after a rain."

That was more poetic than I'd been expecting, painting a rather sweet picture, but he had the idea. "Good. Now, what do you hear?"

Standing up, I reached behind my back to unzip my dress, pulling the zipper down slowly to draw out the sound before letting the dress fall to the floor at my feet.

Dorian's hands gripped onto his knees tighter, but he kept his eyes closed. "You're undressing. It's the sound of my wildest teenage fantasies coming true."

He really could be a charmer when he stopped getting in his own way, and I had to smile. "Excellent. What do you feel?"

Leaning down, I brushed my lips against his cheek.

"Your lips are warm, but the electricity they send through my body feels cool. It makes me light-headed, like my body's overloaded."

"Very good." His words were already miles ahead of what he'd written for me earlier that day. He was letting himself experience it rather than just thinking about the mechanics.

We had one sense still to go, and my heart beat a little faster as I shimmied out of my panties and climbed up onto the couch, on my feet, one leg on either side of him. Dorian's eyes were still closed, waiting until I told him to open them again, and gently, I ran my hand through his hair, cupping the back of his head and pulling him forward until he was mouth-level with my pelvis.

"Time to have a taste and tell me what you think."

~Dorian~

I could hardly believe Laina didn't hold my humiliating lack of control against me, but somehow, she didn't seem to. Instead, she did her best to set me at ease, and as I sat on her couch with my eyes closed, focusing on my other senses as she instructed me to, I started to feel a lot more in control not just physically but mentally too.

We were there to have fun, she said, and I wanted that too. It didn't have to be the best sex I'd ever had. It almost certainly wouldn't be the best for her, but it could still be enjoyable as long as I didn't get in my own way.

I knew from experience that it would take me around twenty minutes to get hard again, but as I breathed in Laina's floral scent, listened to her unzipping her dress, and felt her lips on my cheek, it felt like it might happen a lot faster than that. My blood flowed hot in my veins, my whole body bubbling with excitement, and when I felt the couch move on either side of me, I couldn't begin to guess what she would do next.

Maybe I should have. After all, she'd skipped the movie ahead to a scene where the man went down on her, so when her hand grabbed my head, her touch against my scalp sending fresh tingles down my spine, and pulled my face straight towards her pelvis, it *shouldn't* have shocked me, and yet, when she told me to taste her and describe it, it still came as a surprise.

"Is this position okay?" I asked her, still with my eyes closed. Standing on the couch the way she was, she couldn't feel all that stable. I would have no issue with lying her down and letting her relax.

"It's okay enough for you to get a taste," she confirmed. "Unless you don't want to."

Didn't want to? I could hardly believe my luck. Oral sex was actually the one tool in my sexual arsenal that I felt reasonably confident about. Since I lost my virginity ten years earlier, I hadn't been sitting around hoping for lightning to strike and suddenly make things amazing. I'd made honest efforts to try to improve, figuring that my lack of satisfaction in the bedroom must be at least partly my fault, and part of that involved learning everything I could about how to satisfy a woman. The women I'd dated had been happy to let me practice, and I felt pretty sure I could satisfy Laina in that way if not any other.

As long as I focused entirely on her, things were fine. When I tried to focus on both of us, things got messy.

Keeping my eyes closed as she asked me to, I let my hands find her legs, reaching in the darkness surrounding me until I connected with her calves, her flesh soft and supple beneath my fingers. Slowly, I raised my hands higher up the back of her thighs, resting just below her ass as I used my strength to steady her. Breathing in the enticing scent from between her legs, I leaned closer to her, close enough that my nose bumped up against her skin.

With no other cues to guide me, I used my tongue, lips and nose to figure out exactly where I was. From my brief glance at the screen when she changed the scene, I'd noticed that she kept herself waxed, so it didn't surprise me to find her smooth, and I licked my way down until I reached her clit.

"Mmm," she hummed from above me. "That feels good, but you're supposed to be tasting me, remember?"

I remembered, but I didn't mind the detour. Slowly, my tongue circled her clit, my hands feeling how her hips naturally moved forward, seeking more of my touch. Even without seeing her reaction, I could hear and feel enough to know what worked for her.

My fingers dug into her thighs firmly as I brought my lips lower, travelling along her soft folds until I reached her entrance, and though she wasn't dripping wet, she definitely felt some of the same arousal I did. My mouth watered as I let my tongue slide in deeper, getting my first real taste of her.

"Don't... uh, don't forget to describe... the taste." Laina's words came out breathier than before, and satisfaction surged through me, especially considering I hadn't even really started yet.

"You know how perfect it is when a peach is perfectly ripe?" I kissed her, going back for more, licking and sucking around her hole before thrusting my tongue in again. "Warm, tender, sweet and juicy? On a hot day, when you're both hungry and thirsty, and it melts in your mouth, the sweetness and tartness of it in perfect harmony, the juices running down your chin. That's what you taste like."

"Fuck." Laina's hand gripped my head as I moved back to her clit, sucking it in hard for just a second. "Alright, I think you got it. Now, we can..."

Whatever she intended to suggest, I never found out, since I hadn't finished yet. As my tongue continued to play with her clit, I freed my right hand and brought it around to her front, my left arm wrapping more firmly around her waist to keep her steady. Two fingers pressed into her, drawing a moan from somewhere above me, and her hips tilted forward again, her body responding to me out of instinct.

I actually had porn to thank for teaching me the next trick I employed. During my research, I'd stumbled across a porn star using the technique and the orgasm the woman had when he did looked a lot more real than most of the ones I'd seen on film. I tried it out on my girlfriend at the time and it got rave reviews from her, so hopefully, Laina would like it too.

Maybe she'd actually worked with that particular actor, I realized, but I quickly pushed the thought out of my head. I didn't care who she'd been with before; at that moment, she was with me, and I wanted to make it count.

Twisting my hand so my third and fourth fingers pushed into her, I used my index finger to rub along the side of her clit with each thrust, all while my tongue continued to flick across the top of it. All those workouts to give me stamina came in handy as I increased my intensity, fucking her hard with my fingers as I licked and sucked on her clit. Her wetness increased, her arousal getting stronger and stronger, and still I didn't stop.

"Fuck... Dorian... God." Disjointed words floated into the air above my head as Laina came, her legs trembling around me and her hands clenching against my scalp, but my arm still held her tight. She was never in danger of falling.

I stayed between her legs, lapping up all the sweetness there until she was able to stand on her own again.

"Well, you are full of surprises." With a shaky laugh, she stepped back down onto the floor, my arm still around her waist until she'd fully regained her balance. I'd had my eyes closed for so long that the light in the room felt unnaturally bright as I reopened them and squinted up at her. "I definitely don't need to give you any pointers there."

My cheeks flushed with the compliment and at the sight of her own blush caused by her orgasm. Hopefully, that made up for my premature arrival earlier, and since my cock had already started to show signs of life again, maybe I still had a chance to make the night truly memorable.

~Laina~

All along, I thought I'd be the one in charge, but when Dorian took over, eating me out like very few men had ever done before when they weren't being paid for it, I couldn't bring myself to complain. Where did that skilled, confident lover come from? How could he be the same man who barely made it out of his pants before losing control? Yet again, the contradictions that made up Dorian intrigued me, and more than ever, I wanted to understand exactly what made him tick.

As I took a step back from where he still sat on the couch, he pulled his pants down again, pulling them entirely off to let me know he definitely still wanted to keep going. I could see that while he still wasn't hard, it wouldn't take an awful lot to get him there, and that impressed me too. He must be really enjoying himself, and I loved a man who got turned on by looking after his partner.

"I think you're ready to bring your sight back into it," I suggested, giving him a wink to let him know I still wasn't taking anything too seriously. "If you find yourself getting overwhelmed, though, just close them again and focus on your other senses. I think it will help."

"I do too."

He stood up and stepped close to me as he pulled his shirt off over his head, leaving him completely naked. If anything, he looked even better than I'd expected, his muscles firm and defined, but not overdeveloped. I couldn't stop myself from reaching out to trace over a large tattoo on his shoulder, showing pages of writing fluttering in the wind. I'd never seen one like it before but it suited him.

"Let me get you out of this."

I'd almost forgotten I still had my bra on, but Dorian pulled me closer to his chest as he reached behind me to undo it. As it came loose, he stared down at my breasts in wonder, as if it were the first time he'd seen them even though they were on display on the screen right behind me.

"You don't know how many times I dreamt about this in high school," he admitted sheepishly, making me laugh.

"I honestly had no idea you liked me back then. Whenever I tried to talk to you, you barely said anything!"

"Because I was terrified," he explained bluntly. "I kind of still am, I've just gotten better at pushing through it."

"Good, because I'm very much enjoying getting to know you." Pulling his head down, I kissed him hungrily. My own taste still lingered on his lips and his tongue, turning me on even more, and I grabbed his hand to bring it to my breast, letting him know that he could not only look at them but touch them too.

As we kissed and groped each other, his cock getting stiffer against me, the sounds of my moaning echoed in the background as the couple on screen had moved on to proper fucking, missionary-style.

Dorian pulled back from the kiss, his eyes darting over to the screen. "Is it okay if we turn that off?"

"Sure, if that's what you want." I had thought it would help to keep him out of his head too much, but after his initial mishap, he seemed to be doing a good job of that all on his own. As I bent over to grab the remote from the table, Dorian grabbed hold of my hips, pressing his half-hard cock against my ass. Instantly, my body began to throb again, the idea of him fucking me in that position a definite turn-on.

"Did I distract you?" he teased as the remote hung uselessly in my hand.

His confidence really had grown, and if turning the TV off would help with that, I was all for it. After pressing the button, I tossed the remote aside and leaned forward more, holding onto the edge of the coffee table to steady myself. "Are you all talk or are you going to show me some action?"

His grip on me tightened, letting me know my words were getting to him, but he hesitated. "Do you want me to use a condom?"

Immediately, I tensed. I'd already told him that I got tested regularly, and the question reminded me of one of my exes who refused to go without one since he didn't trust that the tests were good enough. He regarded me as dirty or soiled, I realized after we'd broken up, even if he'd never used those particular words.

However, Dorian already had a habit of surprising me, so I gave him a chance to explain himself before I got offended. "I told you about the tests, remember?"

"Oh, yeah, I know," he quickly stammered. "I just meant: are you worried about me? This is your livelihood, I don't want to mess with that."

Relief flowed through my body as my shoulders relaxed. I'd been right to give him the benefit of the doubt. "I trust you, Dorian. If you say you're good, then you're good."

I didn't put that much faith in all the men I fucked, but it sounded like Dorian hadn't been with anyone in a while. He definitely didn't seem like the kind of guy who slept around for fun.

I was also starting to feel a little silly bent over the coffee table while we talked, but as soon as I said we were good, Dorian's hand moved to my pussy, rubbing his fingers through my wetness and finding my clit again. My legs spread wider almost without me meaning to do it, my body craving more of his touch, and he gave me exactly what I wanted, his fingers slipping inside me, slowly at first and then faster, fucking me with his hand while he got himself the rest of the way ready.

By the time the head of his cock pressed against my entrance, I couldn't have been much more ready myself. "Yes, Dorian. Show me what you've got."

With a grunt of pure need and satisfaction, he pushed into me, his cock still not fully erect but close enough, giving my body exactly what it craved.

I liked sex; I always had. I certainly wouldn't have gone into my profession if I didn't, and there weren't many things I hadn't tried by that point, but for some reason, hearing the sweet, sexy man behind me whisper, "Holy shit," with his cock inside me, knowing he'd dreamed about it long before I became rich or famous, might have been one of the sexiest things I'd ever heard.

Since he seemed to respond well to my encouragement before, drawing on his senses, I tried it again. "What do you feel?"

"Like the luckiest man in the world."

My laugh got choked off as he slid out of me and back in again, already feeling harder. Talking seemed to help him from overthinking, so I encouraged him to keep going. "Describe it to me."

"It feels like..."

Another thrust, his fingers digging into my hips as he pulled me back towards him at the same time that he pushed in.

"...at the end of a long day..."

Moving quicker as his erection became more secure, he thrust harder, his length filling me perfectly.

"...when every muscle in your body is aching..."

One hand drifted away from my hip, reaching down to my clit and sending a shiver down my spine as my body clenched.

"...and you lie down on the softest, warmest, most perfect bed in the world..."

The rubbing on my clit combined with the deep, throaty sound of his voice, his own need pulsing through every word, drove me even closer to the edge.

"...wrapped up in the covers like a cocoon..."

He showed no signs of slowing down as my body began to tremble.

"...and you feel like you could stay there forever and never need anything else in the world. That's... what it feels like."

"Fuck," I gasped as my orgasm built, seeming to swell inside my body until, in a rush of pleasure, it burst.

Somewhere in the murky haze, I could hear him swearing softly too, his movements slowing as he pumped inside me, still not lasting very long, but significantly better than the first time.

Now, *that* had been something worth writing about.

Chapter Eight

~**Dorian**~

The buzzing of my phone pulled me out of my pleasant dreams. As soon as I opened my eyes, blinking in disorientation at the new surroundings of my bedroom, the dream disappeared, leaving no details behind but only a vague sense of contentment.

Or perhaps, the contentment was left over from the night before.

Despite the rough beginning, in the end, my encounter with Laina had been pretty damn good after all. She helped me get out of my head in a way no one ever had before. I couldn't say if her actions did it, or simply the fact that it was *her*, but it had been, far and away, the best sex of my life.

For a second, I hoped it might be her getting in touch with me that morning even though she told me she'd be working all day.

Unfortunately, as I managed to grab the phone off my bedside table, squinting in the bright sunshine coming through my window, the call display showed my editor's name instead. Since I hadn't returned her call the day before, I would have to bite the bullet and answer.

"Good morning, Emily, how are you?"

My rather cheery greeting took her by surprise since she usually liked to tease me that I sounded like a man awaiting sentencing for a crime every time I picked up one of her calls. "I'm fine, thanks. Can I take your good mood to mean that you've finished the draft that you promised me?"

Normally, I'd feel bad about missing a deadline, even an unofficial one, but that morning, I felt too good to let it bother me too much. "Not yet, but I'm feeling a lot more inspired at the moment. I'm going to be working on it today and I'll get it to you as soon as I can."

"You certainly sound chipper," Emily pointed out once again, making me wonder exactly how morose I usually sounded. "California must agree with you. I hear you're making friends already too."

Instantly, my mood turned a bit more wary. "What have you heard?"

"I had a call from Erica Chilton at the end of the day yesterday. She's the producer who tried to get the movie rights to All My Best Heartaches a few years ago, if you remember?"

"Vaguely." I didn't pay much attention to the business side of things, preferring to let my publishing company and agent handle that. Emily and my agent, Claire, happened to be best friends, so they frequently worked in tandem on my account.

"Anyway, she's currently director of a company called Illiana Productions, and she said her creative manager has been chatting with you over the last few days. She wanted to know if that meant your interest in making films had changed, and if so, she wanted to put their hat in the ring to work with you."

A lot of information had been packed into that statement, and I tried to lay it all out again and figure out what it meant. The name Illiana Productions didn't mean anything to me, but Laina was a short form of the name Illiana, so I had to guess the production company belonged to her. Since Laina was pretty much the only person I'd been spending time with since I arrived in Malibu, that all made sense.

What confused me was why Laina would have told her company's director about us spending time together, or why she would have then been in touch with my editor. How much did Laina tell Erica? My gender? My real name? What I'd asked her to help me with?

Did she know what Laina and I had done the night before?

All the lightness in my chest seemed to evaporate, replaced with a large lump that sat uncomfortably somewhere around my heart. Maybe I'd been too quick to open up to Laina about everything. I had assumed she was still the girl who stood up to the bullies and defended me, but she'd told me herself that she had a shrewd head for business. Was she actually just interested in my writing career all along? Had this all been some kind of ploy to trade in on my name and my fan base?

My thoughts grew wilder and more fantastical with each passing second, and though logically, I knew the most outrageous scenarios probably weren't true, I couldn't entirely silence the little voice in my head that said it made a lot more sense that she saw a business opportunity in me rather than that she had genuinely been attracted to me.

Had I been fooling myself all along?

"Dorian?" Emily's voice in my ear reminded me that I was still in the middle of a conversation, and that I'd probably missed several more things she'd said.

"Sorry, I think I lost you for a second," I stammered, trying to cover for my distraction. "Can you repeat the last bit?"

Emily sighed. "I said that I'm all for adding in some spice to your books but partnering with a porn company is probably a step too far."

"Yeah, of course. I mean, no, that's not what I'm doing. I'm just..." I trailed off, having no idea what to tell her that wouldn't invite more questions, but finally, I settled on something near the truth. "The owner of the company is an old friend of mine from high school and it turns out she lives in my new neighbourhood. It's a purely personal connection. No business at all."

"I'm glad to hear it." She did sound genuinely relieved, making me realize she must have been holding her true feelings back before, waiting to see how I'd respond. "Our marketing team would have had a heart attack."

My laugh sounded hollow to my ears. "It's nothing to worry about. Erica must have gotten the wrong idea."

Had she, though, or what had Laina said that made Erica decide to call my publishing company?

"Well, I won't keep you from your writing." Having accomplished what she called me for, Emily was ready to move on, which I usually appreciated. We kept our relationship professional, and though I'd worked with her for years, I didn't really know her very well at all.

"Can I ask you something before you go?" The words were out of my mouth almost before I realized I meant to say them, and I blurted out my question before she could say no. "Do you watch porn?"

The silence on the other end of the phone was so profound that for a moment, I thought she might have hung up.

"I'm not sure that's really relevant to anything," she finally answered.

"No, you're right. I'm sorry." I didn't know what I'd been thinking in asking, honestly. "Forget I asked. I'll update you on the new chapters as soon as I can."

When we'd hung up, I tossed the phone back onto the table and looked around my new bedroom, my good mood vanished just like the dream I'd had before waking.

Maybe the night before had been a dream too, in its own way. The situation had seemed one way to me, but I knew very well that things could look quite different from a different point of view. I thought we were just two people reconnecting and maybe even finding something in common, but perhaps, the plot twist was yet to come.

~Laina~

"Cut!"

As the director's call rang out, I led the crew in a round of applause. "Great work, everyone. Let's pack it all up and move inside."

With the sun shining brightly earlier that afternoon, we'd been shooting in my backyard for a few hours, but clouds were beginning to gather. Thankfully, we just got the last shot we needed so we could move all the equipment back inside before any rain started to fall. The production assistant gave the actors bathrobes to put on and directed them to the bathrooms where they could shower and clean up.

My role on this particular film was entirely behind the camera. Though I still acted regularly, the scripts often called for a younger woman, and I had to admit that I couldn't pass for an 18-year-old anymore. The film we just wrapped featured a stepfather/stepdaughter situation, and nobody was hiring me for those, not even my own company. Those days, I was more likely to be playing the step*mother*.

After helping move the last of the equipment inside, I went to the kitchen to pull out the food I always had delivered for the actors. Having sex on camera for a couple of hours was hungry work, and I knew how much I appreciated being looked after when I worked for other companies. I had just brought it back to the same living room where Dorian and I had sex the night before when Rylan, the star of the film, came out of the bathroom, dressed in his jeans and t-shirt, his hair still damp from the shower.

"Thanks, Jenny, this is great." He flashed me a smile as he grabbed a plate and helped himself to a sandwich and some carrot sticks from the platter I'd just placed down on the coffee table.

Everyone in the business called me by my stage name. Very few people actually knew my real name, or that the Laina Macintyre listed on the company documents was actually me.

Rylan cracked open a diet soda to go with his food. "How're things with you and... what's his name again? Brick?"

Rylan and I had worked together many times over the years and we got along really well. Unlike a lot of the other actors I worked with, we actually chatted about our personal lives, and he loved to tease me about the kind of guys I dated, calling them uptight corporate bores.

He might have been onto something. "It's Brock, as I'm sure you know, and there are no 'things' anymore. We're no longer together."

He winced before taking another bite of his sandwich. "Ah, shit. Sorry. What happened?"

"The usual. Is it me, Ry, or is it just men? I mean, Shelby accepted your job, but every single guy I've dated ends up having issues with it."

Shelby was Rylan's wife and they'd been married for almost three years. I'd met her a couple of times and from what I'd seen, she dealt with his career and everything that came with it like a pro.

He quickly disabused me of that notion. "She accepts it now but it hasn't been without its challenges. She gets jealous, not so much about the work, but with the fans. For a while, I gave her access to all my accounts and DMs so she could check them whenever she wanted. She'd say she trusted me but not the other women, which doesn't make a lot of sense in my book. Eventually, she figured out how to deal with it in a way that works for her. If you're thinking you're ever going to find anyone who's not already in the industry and won't stumble over some part of it, I think you're heading for disappointment."

I knew that, and some small stumbles, I didn't mind. Things like Dorian sticking his foot in his mouth, adorably, more than once, for example. As those memories crossed my mind, I couldn't help smiling, and Rylan took notice.

"Hang on, is there someone new already you're not telling me about? Who's that smile for?"

"No one," I quickly covered up, waving to Janelle, the other actor, as she came into the room. "Come and have something to eat."

I'd never worked with her before that shoot, but she'd done a great job that day, and she sank onto the couch next to Rylan, looking exhausted. "What're you guys talking about?"

Rylan answered with his mouth full. "Keeping a relationship going in this business. Are you seeing anyone?"

She snorted as she leaned forward to grab some carrot sticks off the plate on the table. "No. The last guy I dated wanted me to quit working. He said he considered my job as a form of cheating."

"You see?" I threw Rylan a triumphant look. "It's not just me. Men are the problem."

We laughed and chatted for a bit longer until my phone began to buzz. The first time, I ignored it. After the third, Rylan and Janelle were both glancing down at my pocket, and by the fifth one, I had to pull it out.

"Sorry. I better see what this is."

The first message I saw came from Erica, who just sent me two question marks with a link to a video. When I opened the link, it took me no more than a second to realize what I was looking at.

The guy from the night before had posted the video of Dorian confronting my fan, just as I thought he would, and it was blowing up, at least in the porn community.

"Who's that?" Rylan had leaned over my shoulder while I'd been bent over my phone, and watched with me as Dorian twisted the fan's arm behind his back, neutralizing him with hardly any effort at all. "Is he the one who had you smiling before?"

"Is he an actor?" Janelle asked. Somehow, she'd already got the video up on her phone too, and she held it up to show me. "Is he one of yours? I'd love to work with him."

Why did that make me feel both proud and a little bit uneasy all at the same time? "He's not an actor. Just a friend. I... shit. I better go deal with this."

They both understood, so I left them there with the food and drink as I returned to my own half of the house. My phone continued to buzz and I quickly put it on silent before giving Erica a call.

"How could you not tell me about this?" were the first words out of her mouth. "We could have had a response prepared and now we're scrambling. I've got the team working on it."

"I'm sorry, it slipped my mind." She tutted at me in disbelief, but it honestly had. Between the rest of the evening with Dorian back at my house and the film shoot that day, I'd completely forgotten about it. Even when I'd been thinking about him during the conversation with Rylan just a few minutes earlier, it hadn't clicked that I should probably let Erica know about the parking lot encounter. "It's not that bad, is it?"

"That depends on how we play it. Who's the guy?"

"An old friend from high school who'd prefer to stay off the radar. We're not naming him." Dorian definitely wasn't ready to have his name publicly linked to a porn star. "He's from the same small midwestern town I grew up in, and it's his first time in California. He got a little overzealous about defending me. That's all it is."

I'd left out quite a bit, but I hoped it would be enough to satisfy her.

"You're just full of surprises this week," she admonished me. "First, you're collaborating with J.M. Everlee and now, you've got a drop-dead gorgeous muscle man looking out for you."

My breath caught as she listed those two things together, and my grip around the phone tightened as I waited to see if she'd figured out the connection between them.

Thankfully, it didn't seem she had. "Any other secrets you want to let me in on?" she asked instead.

"I think that's all of them." I tried not to sound too relieved as I laughed. "Sorry to give you extra work today. Let me know if you need me to do anything."

She promised she would and hung up to get back to managing our official response to the video. Erica fell firmly into the camp that believed that people talking about you was always a good thing, no matter what they were saying, but I felt a little more cautious. The more mainstream this went, the greater the chance that someone might recognize Dorian.

He'd come to California for a new start, but somehow, I doubted this was what he'd had in mind.

~Dorian~

By the time the rain started falling, I had a serviceable spicy scene for my book. I couldn't call it 'good' for sure; I would need an independent opinion on that, but it felt more authentic than anything I'd written before. Reading it back, I could feel the male character's excitement and uncertainty, how much he enjoyed the experience but how unclear he was about what it all meant. The female character, on the other hand, felt like an enigma, her motivations buried deep beneath the surface, only to be discovered by him at a much later date.

The first few raindrops on the window, I barely noticed. The sky had gotten cloudier while I'd been absorbed in my laptop, and when I glanced outside, I thought it must be quite a bit later than it actually was since it had grown so dark. Only a few moments later, with hardly any warning, the skies opened. Fat, heavy raindrops plummeted to the ground, bouncing off the flagstone patio in my backyard, the sound like a stampede of tiny little watery invaders surrounding my house.

Among the sudden din, I almost missed the sound of the doorbell.

If the weather had been nicer, I might have ignored it since I wasn't expecting anyone or anything, but given the state of the downpour, I didn't want to leave anyone standing outside for longer than necessary, even if they were trying to sell me something.

I certainly didn't expect to see Laina at my door, her drenched clothes clinging to her body, her hair plastered to her head and her makeup running down her face.

"Oh, shit." I nearly tripped over my feet trying to get out of the way. "Come in, quick."

As soon as she stepped inside, I closed the door behind her. Even in the brief time it had been open, a small puddle had managed to accumulate in the entrance way, and the water dripping off Laina's soggy form only added to it.

She could only laugh as she held up her hands sheepishly. "It wasn't raining when I left my house."

Since I'd seen for myself how quickly it came on, I believed her. "You've got to be freezing. Let me get towels…"

I started to head for the linen closet but quickly realized her clothes would still be soaked through, so I spun back around.

"No, wait, I'll grab you some new clothes."

I headed in the opposite direction but soon stopped short. She couldn't just change right at my front door, though. There had to be a better solution.

"On second thought, hold on."

Without giving her a chance to argue, I scooped her up, holding her tight to my chest as I carried her down the hallway to my bedroom. The ensuite bathroom had a large walk-in shower where she could remove her wet things, and in the meantime, I could grab her something warm and dry to wear from my closet.

"Dorian, I'm leaving a river behind me," Laina protested along the way, but I didn't stop until I'd deposited her safely into the bathroom.

"You can change here, let me get you something to put on."

It only took a couple of minutes to find one of my old college sweat-shirts and a pair of cotton pants with a drawstring. They'd be big on her but at least they wouldn't fall down. With the replacement clothing in hand, I returned to the bathroom, only to stop short as I caught sight of her standing completely naked in the middle of the room, drying her hair with a towel.

Somehow, she looked even better than she had the night before. Maybe because I stood further away and could see the whole of her at once? Maybe because the way she held her arms up over her head showed off the curves of her breasts and hips to their best advantage. I couldn't say for sure; all I knew was that the sight mesmerized me.

"Oh. Sorry. Uh, I didn't mean to... I didn't think you'd be... I just wanted to..."

No complete sentences wanted to come out, but Leila smiled at my rambling anyway. "You already saw me naked yesterday, remember?"

I could hardly forget, but it didn't mean I expected to see it again right then in my bathroom. Exhaling, I tried to get over my surprise and focus on the practical. "You can wear these for now. I'll throw your clothes in the dryer."

Trying not to stare at her, I handed her the clothes I'd picked out and wrapped her sopping wet things in another towel to take down the hall to my laundry room. By the time I got them in on a delicate dry cycle, Laina had found her way to my living room, my clothes almost comically large on her, and her hair twisted up in a towel, turban-style, on top of her head.

"Well, that wasn't exactly the way I expected this visit to start out," she said with a laugh as I came to sit down next to her. "Thank goodness my phone is waterproof."

She held the device in her hand, and immediately, I was reminded of the phone call I'd had that morning. I'd been wondering when I would get a chance to ask Laina about it, not expecting her to simply appear at my door unprompted. She must have had her own reason for coming, though, so I asked her about that first. "What brought you over this way before it started to rain?"

The smile slowly faded from her face. "Well, I'm afraid it's not great news. You remember the guys in the parking lot last night?"

That had to be a rhetorical question; of course I remembered, and she must know I did.

"Well, they posted the video just like I thought they might. It's been tagged as 'porn star's jealous boyfriend' and it's taking off online."

A range of emotions flew through me at the same time, everything from shame at mishandling the situation and putting her in an awkward position to pride over the fact that people assumed Laina and I were a couple. "I'm sorry," were the first words out of my mouth. "Are they saying bad things about you?"

Laina's face brightened again. "Actually, most people are on your side. Half the comments are women wishing they had someone like you protecting them or men saying they'd do the same if someone tried to grope their girlfriend. The people who think you overreacted are vocal, but they're few and far between."

That sounded like good news to me, and I couldn't figure out why she'd felt the need to come and tell me about it in person. I didn't mind that she had, I just didn't understand it. "So, what's the problem?"

"Well, it doesn't look like it's going to be a problem for me, but I'm concerned about you. If it stayed in the porn community, that would be fine, but it's starting to go viral and getting picked up in other places, including in the romance book groups. I'm afraid that someone might recognize you."

That confused me more than it cleared anything up. "But no one knows who J.M. Everlee is."

Laina shook her head. "No, that's not what I mean. They won't know that it's you, the author, but they'll know that it's *you* you. Your family could see it, for example, if someone recognizes you, and there you are out for dinner with a porn star. You'll have some explaining to do."

At last, I understood why she was worried. It certainly would make my next phone call with my mom a little awkward if she saw it, but I could deal with that if it happened. To be honest, the conversation I'd had with my editor that morning concerned me a lot more.

"You're sure that no one will make the connection between me and my pen name?" I clarified.

Laina gave me a funny look. "Of course. Why?"

I might as well come fully clean with her as she'd just done with me. It seemed the quickest way to get the answers I needed. "Someone from your production company called my publisher yesterday, saying that I was working with you, and that they wanted to discuss a possible collaboration."

Laina's mouth dropped open in what looked to me like genuine surprise. Yes, she was an actress, but it didn't look fake to me in any way. "I had no idea, Dorian. Honestly. I told her I was working with you but I never said anything about us doing a film together. I knew she was interested but I told her to stay out of it. I'm sorry, that must have been a surprise."

It certainly had been, and I appreciated that she recognized that. "So, you're not just being nice to me to try to get the rights to my books?"

I tried to make it sound like a joke, but real insecurity lingered behind the question, and frustratingly, I knew Laina could hear it too.

She leaned closer to me in her towel headdress and my oversized sweatshirt, somehow looking just as appealing as ever despite the ridiculous clothing. "I'm 'being nice to you' because you're nice to me. Because I like you, Dorian. Can you trust that?"

I wanted to believe it, I truly did. "It kind of felt that way last night," I admitted.

"Kind of?" She raised an eyebrow at me, feigning insult. "It sounds like I didn't make it clear enough. Maybe I need to try a little harder."

With that, she closed the rest of the distance between us and kissed me, as if all my doubts could be wiped away with her lips.

To be fair, she just might be onto something.

Chapter Nine

~**Laina**~

I hadn't gone over to Dorian's house with the intention of kissing him. I went to warn him about the video and I wanted to be able to see his reaction when I did, since I had a feeling if I told him over the phone or by text, he would say it was fine when he didn't actually feel fine about it. He seemed like the kind of guy to try to spare my feelings to the point of hiding his own, but if he was sitting right in front of me, he wouldn't be able to conceal his reaction so well.

His eyes always gave him away.

I also didn't anticipate getting caught in the sudden downpour, but the way Dorian came to my aid, nearly spinning in circles as he tried to decide on the best course of action only made my feelings of affection for him grow stronger. He really was a sweet man and I hadn't known an awful lot of them in my life.

He reinforced that opinion when I finally got to tell him why I'd come. From the way he swallowed, his jaw clenching and unclenching nervously, I could tell he wasn't thrilled about the video being out there or the attention it was getting, but he didn't lose his temper or lash out at me. Not even close, actually. He discussed it with me calmly, and the contrast between him and the other men I'd dated grew even stronger. If Brock had been filmed in a video with me that went viral, he would have gone into a full meltdown, bemoaning the blow to his precious 'respectability'.

Dorian didn't care about any of that. Practically the first words out of his mouth were asking about *me*, wondering if people were saying bad things about *me*, how this would affect *me*.

For himself, he was far more concerned about the fact that Erica had been in touch with his publisher, and that didn't please me either. I'd specifically told her to back off and let me handle things. We'd need to have a conversation about that, but first, I wanted to reassure Dorian that I had no intention of using him. As someone who had been treated like a commodity many times in my life, I knew exactly how it felt, and I didn't want him to think for even a second that I would betray his trust that way.

So, I kissed him.

Maybe it wasn't the smartest thing to do. I couldn't even say for sure why I did it, other than that I felt close to him, sitting in his living room, wearing his clothes, and talking about things calmly and rationally like two adults. In my drama-filled life, that felt pretty novel.

Or maybe I just did it because he looked ridiculously sexy in his long-sleeve t-shirt and sweatpants. Obviously, he hadn't been planning to go out or expecting company, but I liked the casual version of him.

Whatever my motivation had been, as soon as our lips connected, any doubts I might have had about whether it was the right thing to do went out the window. His kiss felt even better than I remembered from the night before, probably because his confidence had increased since then. He knew he could satisfy me, so his nerves were a little more under control, and it showed. Although I initiated the kiss, it didn't take long for Dorian to take control of it.

One hand slid over my cheek, cupping my face, while the other wrapped around the back of my head beneath the towel, his grip firm and decisive. One hand suggested tenderness and the other promised passion, and the way they seemed to coexist in him along with all of his other contradictions had my body throbbing in anticipation.

Taking a shuddering breath, Dorian broke the kiss, resting his forehead against mine. "Are you hungry? Is there anywhere else you need to be tonight?"

I had a good idea why he was asking, and I had exactly the same thing in mind. At that moment, I only felt hunger for him. "No, and no."

"Good." I only got a glimpse of his heart-stopping smile before he picked me back up again, lifting me like I weighed nothing as he got to his feet and carried me back down the hall to his bedroom.

What were we doing? Was it just an extension of what we'd done the night before? Was it just a matter of opportunity with the rain still pounding down outside, pinging off the panes of glass on his bedroom window in a way that made me shiver in thanks for being inside and warm?

It didn't mean anything more than experimentation or passing the time, I tried to convince myself. When he undid the drawstring of the pants he'd given me and slipped his hand inside, finding me wet and aching for him, the shiver that ran through my body was left over from the chill I'd received earlier. When I reached down to trace the outline of his cock, hard and ready in his sweatpants, it would have only been because he saw me naked earlier. That would turn any straight man on.

We were two people who happened to be in the right place at the right time, wanting the same thing, and unlike the night before, I didn't worry about whether he was getting inspiration from it and he didn't worry about whether he made any mistakes. We just let the desire and need lead us, acting as our silent director as we stroked and kissed and murmured words of praise and wanting to each other.

I could barely even remember how our clothes came off, I only knew they had when his firm body pressed down against mine, face-to-face this time as my legs wrapped around his waist and he lined his cock up against my entrance. He kept his eyes on me as he pushed into me, watching me in awed appreciation. My expression must have looked pretty similar; hovering there above me, he looked like a daydream I might have had back when I truly believed in romance.

No premature ejaculation cut into the rhythm that time. He fucked me slowly, almost languidly, in no hurry at all. His lips stayed parted, as if he were about to say something, or as if he simply lacked the strength to close them, and his brown eyes stayed fixed on my face whenever he wasn't kissing me.

It felt like it would never end and he never wanted it to. It felt like there was nowhere else in the world he would rather be.

Eventually, his hand drifted down my body and between us, finding my clit as he increased his pace.

"Fuck, Dorian," I panted. "Somehow, you made getting caught in the rain the best part of my day."

"If this is what happens on a rainy day, I hope the sun never shines again." His fervent declaration would have made me laugh if I weren't so close to my orgasm already.

Instead, I only vaguely recognized the sweet, witty remark while my body reacted to the fiercely possessive tone of it. My mind drifted back to the comments I'd read on the video, all the people wishing they were the one Dorian was protecting instead of me, and how strong he'd looked in the video as he pulled the man away from me, and my brain and body combined to bathe me in the bliss of my orgasm.

"That's good," he praised me, still focused on the task at hand, not letting up on me for a second. "I think I can do it again."

"I think you can too."

With a groan of appreciation, he propped himself up, hooking my legs up over his shoulders as he began driving into me harder and faster. The unsure man of the night before was a distant memory as Dorian lost himself in the moment, a thin sheen of sweat sparkling across his skin as he fucked me just as well as half the porn stars out there.

Even though we'd been going for ages already, it still felt too soon when my second orgasm hit, and Dorian's followed almost immediately after. He'd obviously been waiting for me, showing far more control than he had the night before.

That was the Dorian he should be far more often. Hopefully, he thought so too.

~Dorian~

I thought I'd done all right the night before, in the end, but looking at it objectively, what just happened between me and Laina put my previous efforts to shame. While the night before had felt scripted and scrutinized, even with all of Laina's encouragement, that afternoon evolved naturally, a consequence of the rain and proximity and good old-fashioned lust, neither of us having planned it but both eagerly seizing the opportunity.

"Are you hungry *now?*" I asked once my breathing had evened out, while I was still on top of her.

Laina laughed as she looked up at me, her blonde hair still a bit damp and beautifully tousled on my pillow. "Actually, yes. It doesn't look like the rain's letting up anytime soon, does it?"

We both glanced over at the big windows in my bedroom where raindrops continued to wind their way down the panes, less forcefully than before but no less frequently. "I think you're stuck here for a while," I agreed, assuming she'd been asking to determine whether she could go back home yet. "I can cook something for us if you like. Any allergies?"

"None. You cook too? Is there anything you don't do?"

I loved the way she went right back to teasing and flirting with me, even while I was still inside her. She made it feel like having sex with each other was something we did all the time. Maybe that came with the sheer number of times she'd done it and partners she'd had? It didn't have to be a big deal each and every time, and that took the pressure off me even more.

"I hate cleaning," I admitted as I slid out of her and got to my feet, gathering up the clothes we'd discarded on the bedroom floor. "As soon as I could afford it, I started hiring a housekeeper."

"Me too," Laina laughed, taking the clothes I offered her and heading to the bathroom to go and clean up. "So if you're looking for a woman to clean up after you, you've got the wrong one."

She meant it as a joke and I took it that way, smiling at her as she closed the door behind her, but I also couldn't help thinking about how it almost sounded as if she were thinking about what a relationship between us would be like.

I'd been thinking about it too but trying not to get ahead of myself. So far, she hadn't said anything about wanting more from me than some professional help. I'd written enough romance novels to know the problems that came from two people having different expectations, so I wouldn't let myself hope for anything more until she made it clear if this meant more to her than just fooling around.

Laina found me a few minutes later in the kitchen, having redressed and washed up already, pulling out some pots and pans to start on supper. "Put me to work," she instructed. "What can I do to help?"

I gave her some vegetables to chop while I prepped the fish, and we talked about the weather in California versus where we grew up and the worst storms we'd ever been in, the conversation coming easily and flowing smoothly.

"Tell me about Erica," I prompted as we sat down with our meal and a bottle of white wine. Thankfully, I'd had some groceries delivered earlier that day and could actually pretend like I regularly had people over. "The publisher said she tried to get the rights to one of my books a few years ago?"

"She really gave you the hard sell, didn't she?" Laina rolled her eyes before taking a bit of her fish, at which point her eyes closed completely as she let out a groan. "Shit, Dorian, this is really good."

I shifted in my seat as the sound she made reminded me of the noises she'd made in my bedroom not that long ago. "I'm glad you like it. And yes, it sounded like Erica was pretty enthusiastic."

"That's one word for her." Laina laughed as she leaned back in her seat, picking up her wine glass. "I hired her because she doesn't take no for an answer, but when she uses that tenacity on me, it can be pretty annoying. I only told her that you were helping me with my new script and she flipped out. It sounds like she's a pretty big fan of yours, but she called you 'she' the whole time, so your identity is still totally safe."

"And you don't think she'll put it together from the video that it could be me?" I wondered out loud.

"I don't think so," Laina assured me. "It did cross my mind too, but the more I thought about it, the more I realized how big of a leap that would be. She thinks the author is a woman, so why would she jump to any conclusions about the man I went for dinner with?"

I agreed that it wouldn't be the most obvious connection, and that relieved me a great deal. Being in the spotlight with Laina would be one thing; having that spotlight connected to me as an author would be quite another, and a step that I definitely didn't feel comfortable taking.

By the time we finished eating, the rain had petered off and the dryer had finished its cycle, but Laina still didn't seem in any hurry to get going. "What have you been working on today?" she asked instead as we made our way back to the living room with our leftover wine.

I decided to tell her the truth since there didn't seem to be any point in being shy about it. "Actually, I've rewritten that scene from yesterday, based on last night. After today, I might need to rewrite it again."

Laina's eyes twinkled in amusement. "Well, now you've got me curious. Would you read it to me?"

"You don't want to just read it yourself?" Although I understood she generally preferred to hear things out loud, I really didn't consider myself a great narrator.

Laina disagreed. "I like hearing your voice. It's pretty sexy. It might even turn me on again."

Well, fuck. With that incentive, she didn't leave me much choice. Only the slightest bit of encouragement from her would be needed to have me ready to go again too.

Grabbing my laptop, I had just pulled up the document when my phone rang on the table beside me. A quick glance at the screen showed that it was my mom again, calling on video, which seemed odd. She didn't usually call again so soon after a chat unless she had something to share.

"Do you mind if I take this?" I asked Laina, and she quickly shook her head, telling me to go ahead. Trying to look as casual as possible, I hit the answer button. "Hey, Mom. What's up?"

"That's what I'm calling to ask you. Why are people calling to tell me that you're in a video with a porn star, Dorian?"

Oh, shit. That had gotten to her way faster than I could have anticipated, and just hearing the word 'porn' out of my mom's mouth made me cringe.

"This really isn't the best time," I told her, trying to get her off the phone before she said anything else in front of Laina. "I'll call you later, okay?"

"No, it's not okay! You've only been out there for a few days and you're already hanging around with people like that? What am I supposed to tell people? What am I supposed to tell your Nana?"

I cast a quick, furtive glance over at Laina, whose face had gone rather stony. Desperately, I tried to salvage the situation. "You can tell them that I had a nice dinner with a beautiful woman, and she got harassed in the parking lot afterwards so I stepped in. That's the truth."

My mom looked both unconvinced and perplexed. "A beautiful woman? She's practically a prostitute! You can't honestly believe that there's nothing wrong with it?"

Laina got to her feet while I scrambled for something to say that would satisfy them both. "It's her job but it's not who she is. Since when do you judge someone based on what they do for a living?"

Laina had started to move to the hallway, and I was torn between going after her or finishing the conversation with my mom. If I hung up on her, I'd never hear the end of it.

"This isn't just any job," my mother argued. "You're not actually dating her, are you?"

Technically, we weren't dating, but I couldn't help asking the question: "What if I am?"

"Then that sea air has gone to your head already. Seriously? You're going to date someone who will be sleeping with other men all the time? That's not you! You're a romantic at heart, Dory, you always have been. I know you said you wanted a change, but this isn't the kind of change you need."

While she'd been talking, I heard the front door close, and I ran my hand down my face in frustration. "I have to go."

Without waiting for a response, I hung up the phone and dashed to the door, hoping I could still catch her before she got to the end of the driveway. Unfortunately, when I yanked the door open, she'd already disappeared, but undeterred, I grabbed some shoes and headed out into the street after her.

~Laina~

My sandals slipped across the wet grass as I cut across my lawn, trying to get to my front door as quickly as possible before any of my other neighbours could see me hurrying home in clothes that clearly didn't belong to me. As I power-walked, my heart pounded in my chest, feeling like it might burst all the way out, and my reaction honestly bothered me just as much as anything that had been said.

Most days, I couldn't give a flying fuck what anyone thought about my profession. They could moralize all they wanted while I sipped champagne in my Malibu mansion. However, once in a while, someone still found a crack in my armour, a tiny hole in my self-defense that I somehow hadn't noticed, and that was how it felt when Dorian's mother called me a prostitute.

What she was really saying, in not so many words, was that I wasn't good enough for her son, that someone who sold their body must not have any other redeeming qualities that could make up for the baseness and crassness of that professional choice.

From where I stood, there was a big difference between what I did and prostitution, but I wouldn't look down my nose at anyone who chose to do that with their life either. Everyone had their own path in life and their own choices, and as long as they weren't hurting anyone, it didn't make them bad people.

That was the basic concept that people like Mrs Reid just couldn't seem to understand.

"Laina! Wait!" I heard Dorian's voice right as my fingerprint unlocked my front door, but I didn't look back. Before he could reach me, I slipped inside and closed the door behind me. The energy I needed to deal with his apologies and explanations felt beyond me at that moment. I just wanted to sink into a warm bath and forget about viral videos and movie deals and sexy, reclusive romance authors.

I was still slipping my sandals off as he reached the front door and knocked on it firmly, as if I just hadn't heard him outside. "Laina, open up, please. I'm not leaving until you do."

Maybe he knew I'd heard him after all, but I still didn't have to open the door if I didn't want to. Of all people, he should understand how it felt when you just wanted to be alone. Eventually, he'd take the hint.

Leaving him knocking at the door, I went down the hall to my room and pulled off the clothes Dorian had given me. My ensuite bathroom had a large soaker tub, and I added some of my favourite mango-scented bubble bath to help me relax. I'd turned the notifications on my phone off after speaking to Erica, so I left it in the bedroom as I climbed into the tub, groaning with pleasure as the warm water enveloped me.

In my mind, I put my own worries aside and focused on the script I'd started writing instead. People didn't like my character Penelope's job as an animal trainer, condemning it as too risky for her and cruel to the animals, no matter how much she tried to convince them otherwise. As a stuntman, Larkin understood how it felt to have people judging him, and he stood up for her whenever anyone tried to make her feel stupid for how she'd decided to spend her life.

After solving Penelope's problems in my head, my own felt a little more manageable, even though nothing had actually changed. When I'd dried off, I pulled on a comfortable pair of flannel pajamas and headed to the kitchen to see if I had any ice cream in the freezer. On the way, I passed the security panel for the house right as it flipped to the camera focused on my front door, and I stopped in my tracks as I saw the figure sitting on the ground with his back to the door.

Changing course, I headed to the door instead and yanked it open without warning, making Dorian flail as he tried to keep himself upright. "What are you doing out here?!"

He got to his feet, wiping the seat of his jeans off. At least where he'd been sitting wasn't wet from the rain, but it still must have been hard and cold. "I told you I wouldn't leave until you let me in."

Was he actually serious? "What if I hadn't heard you?"

That let him know that I *had* heard him, but he didn't seem concerned about that because he simply shrugged. "Then I would have waited longer."

That had to be one of the most ridiculous things I'd ever heard, but it was also rather sweet, in a strange kind of way. "I honestly didn't know you were still there."

"Then you've underestimated me," he pointed out, giving me a sheepish smile. "I can be pretty stubborn when I want to be. Can I come in now, please?"

I supposed we didn't have to keep talking at my front door, so I stepped aside and let him in, still trying to decide how I felt about him sitting out there for almost an hour, waiting for me. "What was so important that it couldn't wait?"

"You are," he answered simply. "Can I have something to drink?"

With a sigh, I led him to the kitchen and got him a glass of water as we both took a seat at my kitchen table. "I'm sorry I ran off," I said once he'd drained three quarters of the glass in one gulp. "Usually, I don't let stuff like that bother me, but every now and then, it touches a nerve."

"I can understand that," he assured me. "What she said was completely out of line, Laina. She didn't know you were listening, obviously, but it's still no excuse."

"It was honest *because* she didn't know I was there," I pointed out. "At least now you know for sure how she feels."

"And you think her feelings are going to change whether or not I want to spend more time with you?"

A challenge lay in those words, and I answered it with one of my own: "Aren't they?"

He didn't answer my question any more than I'd answered his. Instead, he leaned forward, his elbows resting on the table. "Tell me about the times it did."

My breath caught, a lump forming in my throat that I tried to push back down. He wanted to know why I felt so certain? I had plenty of experience to back me up. I'd dealt with disapproving mothers before and it never worked out well.

If he wanted examples, I could give him examples.

"My first serious relationship after I started in porn was with a guy named Tad." Dorian grimaced at the rather douchey-sounding name, but I let that slide. "He found my job exciting and he actually loved to watch me with other men. He even joined me on set a few times and it really turned him on. I thought I'd hit the jackpot."

"It does sound kind of perfect," Dorian admitted, rubbing his fingers across the glass in his hands in a way that made it abundantly clear that he didn't share that same fetish.

"Until I met his mother," I added bluntly. "I guess Tad didn't expect me to answer honestly when she asked me what I did for a living over lunch at her country club."

"She wasn't impressed?" Dorian guessed.

"She had me escorted off the premises."

His mouth fell open as he blinked at me in disbelief. "What did Tad do?"

"Oh, he came and apologized to me afterwards, but I could tell it wouldn't work out. We broke up shortly afterwards. With Jeff, I never even met his mother. As soon as he told me she volunteered on her church's council, the writing was on the wall. When I asked point-blank to meet her, he refused."

"You've never dated someone whose family accepted you?"

He sounded shocked by that, but he'd hit the nail on the head. "It's partly my fault, I guess. I tend to date people who are successful and ambitious, and often they got to that point through the ambition of their parents. No mother has dreams of her son marrying a porn star. It just doesn't happen."

Dorian winced at my proclamation but he couldn't deny it, not after what I'd heard his mother say. "What about your own parents?"

"My dad died just after I moved out here, before I got into the industry. My mom called me a whore when I told her about my first film, and said not to bother contacting her until I repented for my sins. Needless to say, I haven't been in touch."

I tried to keep my tone light to avoid any pity on his part, but his brown eyes shone with sympathy anyway.

"Well, I can't speak for any of them, but I can tell you that my mom's reaction doesn't change anything about the way I feel about you, Laina. I'd still like to work with you, and I'd still like to do... well, whatever you call what we did today."

He didn't know how to label it and truthfully, I didn't either. It had been entirely unexpected and genuinely nice, but perhaps, it would be better to leave it at that. We'd both had a nice time, and though he said he'd choose me over his mother, men didn't really ever mean that. Even if they did, I didn't want them to have to make the choice.

"I think for now, we're better off sticking just to work. It's been a long day, Dorian, and I'm tired now, but if you'd like to come back over tomorrow, you can read me your chapter then, alright?"

In his eyes, I could see his reluctance to go, but he accepted my request anyway. "If that's what you'd like. Have a good night, Laina."

I walked him back to the front door, closing it behind him, and once he'd gone, I leaned onto the door for a moment, trying to quell the disappointment inside me. We'd never even said we liked each other, and yet, I felt almost as upset about our dalliance coming to an end as I had about my six-month relationship with Brock. Clearly, my equilibrium had been thrown off somehow. Maybe I needed a break from all men, other than the ones in my script.

At least they could never let me down.

Chapter Ten

~Dorian~

So many times after high school ended, once I went to college and Laina moved away and I had no way of getting in touch with her, I wondered what would have happened if I'd just been brave enough to tell her how I felt. It usually came back to the same conclusion: she would have let me down gently, but let me down all the same.

Since reconnecting with her, she'd challenged that idea, saying that if I'd asked her out, she would have said yes. I had no way of proving if that were true, but I wasn't about to let history repeat itself. After she sent me away, I could slink back to my house and nurse my disappointment, or I could try to be proactive and show her that no matter what other men might have done or how she'd been let down before, it didn't mean things would be the same with me.

I didn't want to spend another ten years wondering what might have been, and if I wanted more than the professional relationship she offered, I'd have to prove to her that I meant it.

My plan started with a phone call.

My mom answered on the second ring, sounding flustered. "I hope you've got good news for me because the phone is ringing off the hook here. Everyone has seen that video."

"How did you see it in the first place?" In our truncated conversation earlier, I hadn't had a chance to ask her.

"Your cousin, Mark, sent it to me."

That didn't shock me. Mark practically lived online, and if it really was spreading as fast as it seemed to be, it seemed entirely possible that he would have come across it. Why he decided to share it with my mother was a whole other question.

"Listen, Mom, we need to talk about what you said before. Lai..."

I started to say Laina's name before remembering that my mom didn't know anything about Laina. She'd only seen the name Jenny Vixxen on the video, and she had no idea that Laina and Jenny were one and the same. Very few people knew that, and I understood, probably more than most, how important that distinction could be. Thankfully, I caught myself before the word came out all the way and I quickly coughed to cover it up before carrying on.

"The woman in the video was here in the room with me when you called before. She heard every word you said."

To her credit, my mother looked a little chagrined at that news. "Well, you could have told me that at the time."

"You didn't really give me a chance," I pointed out. "And besides, you shouldn't be saying anything about a person that you wouldn't say to their face anyway. Isn't that what you always taught me?"

I had her there and she knew it, but she still tried to find a loophole. "This is different, though. She's..."

"She's what? A celebrity? A porn star? Neither of those things changes the fact that she's still a person with feelings."

"She's probably heard worse, I was going to say," my mom corrected me weakly.

"And that makes it right?" Anyone listening to our conversation would have thought I was the parent rather than her, lecturing her on right and wrong.

"No, it doesn't," she conceded. "But what did you expect my reaction to be? Especially out of the blue like that. You could have given me some warning..."

I didn't cut her off that time; she trailed off all on her own with a loud gasp.

"It's your neighbour, isn't it? You told me you were going out for dinner and that she was an actress. Did you know what kind of actress she was when you asked her out?"

"Are you implying that she lied to me?"

It felt like talking to a stranger. I'd never known my mother to be so judgmental, and as I thought back to my conversation with Emily that morning and how jumpy she'd gotten when I asked her if she watched porn, I had to conclude that something about the word made people uncomfortable. In a way, it was strange; sex was in our faces in so many parts of our lives, from advertisements to TV shows to the news to romance books, and yet, as soon as the word 'porn' got mentioned, it became something unsavoury and something to be ashamed of.

My mom, however, shot down that assumption. "I'm not implying anything of the sort. You're just looking for something to be offended about now, Dorian. Let's stop accusing each other and just tell me how it came about."

With a sigh, I gave her an abbreviated version of the truth. "I knew what kind of films she acted in, she never hid it from me. We did a writing exercise together since she's also a scriptwriter and I asked her out. There's a lot more to her than just that one thing."

"It's kind of a big thing," my mom pointed out, but her tone had definitely softened. "You didn't mention it to me when you told me about her, so I think you know that."

She had a point, unfortunately. I hadn't felt comfortable telling her, and I could see now that had been the wrong move. "I didn't know how you'd react," I admitted.

"Well, I might have been a bit calmer if you'd told me about it yourself rather than finding out from Mark! It came as a shock."

I had to concede that point as well. "And he told everyone else too, huh?"

"Everyone," she confirmed. "But you have no problem with that, apparently?"

Honestly, I didn't, not in the long run. "It might be awkward to begin with, but I'd rather have her in my life and deal with a little awkwardness than lose out on getting to know her better. She's really something special."

My mom sighed, the sound of her breath echoing in my ear across the miles. "I haven't heard you say that about any woman in a really long time. Have you told *her* that?"

The memory of my last conversation with Laina made me wince. "Not exactly. After the video and overhearing you and everything else today, she basically blew me off. She doesn't think I can handle being with her. I think she's had some pretty shitty experiences in the past and she's afraid I'll be the same."

That was what I'd taken from the conversation we'd had, and it was why the next thing I had to ask my mother was so important to me.

"This is where I need your help, Mom. What do you think about getting on a plane and coming to see my new house?"

My mom picked up on my intentions immediately. "You want me to meet her?"

"It'd kill two birds with one stone; you could get to know her, and she could see that I'm not embarrassed to be with her. Besides, you wanted to come see my new house anyway."

"And you told me I'd have to wait until you'd had a chance to settle in," she reminded me, but from the way she laughed, I knew we were close to an agreement. "When do you want me to come?"

Having a good-sized bank account came in handy in several situations, and booking last-minute flights was one of them. "How about tomorrow?"

~Laina~

After my morning swim and shower, I sat down at my desk to start my work day. Each morning, I would click through the numbers from our websites and take a look at the subscriber and download numbers, just to make sure nothing had taken an unexpected turn. That day, when I hit refresh on my browser and the new numbers popped up, I could only stare at them in disbelief.

"That can't be right." Muttering to myself, I hit refresh again, but the numbers didn't change. They were almost ten times higher than usual, and our usual days weren't too bad at all.

An app on my screen connected me to Erica in a matter of seconds. "Are you seeing these numbers?" she asked gleefully as soon as her face appeared. Working out of her home office didn't stop her from dressing up just in case she needed to be seen. While I had on my yoga pants and a t-shirt, she wore a white suit with a yellow camisole beneath it, looking suitably sunny for the bright California morning. All traces of the previous day's rainstorm had blown away and the skies were blue and full of promise.

"I thought it must be a glitch with the website," I admitted, taking a sip of my herbal tea as I clicked back over to the screen with the numbers on it. "It's for real?"

"Very real," she assured me. "Your big-budget full-length film just got a lot more real too."

The budget for my new film had been a constant bone of contention between us. I wanted it to look just as good as any Hollywood film but Erica wanted to keep costs down. With this sudden influx of income, my arguments just got a lot more compelling.

I could only think of one thing that had changed from the day before to that morning that might account for the difference, but it seemed so unlikely that I had to ask for verification. "Is this really all because of that video?"

Erica nodded as I switched my view back to her. "People are eating it up! I spent fifteen minutes scrolling through my social media apps this morning and I must have come across it twenty times with different people reposting it and commenting on it. That means people who have never seen you before are looking you up and ending up on our site. This isn't even the half of it, Laina. We won't find out about increases in our films on other sites until the end of the month, and even on our site, those numbers only go to midnight Eastern time last night. Tomorrow morning, be prepared for an even bigger spike."

What would Dorian think of that, I wondered? Inadvertently, he'd given me a ton of free exposure, which meant even more people would be watching me have sex.

What would his mother think of it?

Not that I cared about that, I reminded myself as soon as the thought crossed my mind. Impressing mothers didn't make my priority list at all, especially not when we had to capitalize on this newfound interest in me. "Is it worth making a quick new short to have a new release?"

Erica's eyes lit up. "I was hoping you'd suggest that. I think it would make an absolute killing. Any chance you could get the hunk from the video to film it with you?"

The tea I'd just swallowed nearly came back up again as I choked on it in surprise. "He's not an actor," I managed to sputter before turning away to cough as I tried to get my breath back.

"He doesn't have to be with a body like that," Erica countered. "Besides, for a short, there won't be much dialogue."

She did have a point. 'Shorts' were usually just that: a short film, no more than ten minutes, with very little setup before clothes started coming off. They were for the people who wanted to get right to the action, and we could pump one out in a few hours.

"I'll ask him if you're too embarrassed to," she added with a grin. "I'm not shy."

That reminded me of the other thing I wanted to talk to her about. "You mean like the way you went to J.M. Everlee's publisher after I asked you not to?"

Erica simply shrugged, looking unrepentant. "She told you about that, did she? Did she say if she was tempted?"

Luckily for her, I couldn't throttle her through the computer screen. "You're missing the point! I asked you not to get involved. You might not be shy, but he is, so just let me handle it."

"He?"

Only when she repeated the word back to me did I realize the mistake I'd made. For a second, my heart seemed to pause at the idea that I'd given away Dorian's secret, but thankfully, in the next second, a simple reason occurred to me to explain away my slip. "The guy from the video. That's what we're talking about, isn't it?"

"Oh. I guess so." She sighed, leaning back in her chair while I breathed a secret sigh of relief. "Unfortunately, I don't have any way of getting in touch with Dorian Reid, so at least where he's concerned, you'll get your wish. I won't talk to him."

"How do you know his name?" Maybe I should have played dumb, but hearing it from her lips caught me completely by surprise. I knew for certain I hadn't told it to her.

"People outed him in the comments on the video ages ago. I haven't been able to find much about him online other than some old high school and college photos. You said you knew him in high school, right? Talk about a glow-up."

Shit. Dorian's mother seeing the video was bad enough, but if people were going to be researching him and trying to track him down, like

Erica already had, I'd need to give him a further heads-up. If he wasn't already regretting that he'd decided to get involved with me, he would be soon.

Shaking my head, I tried to push all that to one side and focus on business. "Look, we're wasting time here. Dorian's not an option, so start making some calls and see who's available. I'll need two camera operators, lights and makeup as well as the actor. The rest we can improvise."

She agreed and we hung up so she could get a crew together and I could go get a space ready for filming. I'd been hoping to work more on my script that day but it would have to wait. When opportunity came around, you had to seize it. That philosophy had gotten me to where I was, and I saw no reason to turn my back on it.

I'd worry about Dorian later. Chances were he'd probably be coming up with an excuse not to see me again anyway after the chaos I'd unleashed in his life. I'd seen men withdraw time and time again when the full scope of my world came into view, and after the conversation I'd overheard with his mother the day before, I'd be shocked if I even heard from him again.

~Dorian~

Although I wanted to text Laina first thing that morning, I forced myself to wait and play it cool, even though 'cool' had never really been an attribute of mine. My mom's plane touched down just before noon, so by the time I picked her up, we had some lunch, and I showed her around for a little bit, Laina should be finished work. If she got in touch about working together on our writing that day, I would make an excuse, but otherwise, I planned to surprise her later that afternoon. If she didn't know my mom would be there, she couldn't come up with a reason to avoid her, and I felt confident that once they met face-to-face, they would actually really like each other.

It turned out I didn't need to worry, because I didn't hear from Laina at all. Maybe she was waiting for me to make the next move. Maybe she had only said she'd see me that day to be polite. Or maybe she just got busy, which I could definitely understand. Sometimes, I got so caught up in my writing that hours passed without me realizing it.

Whatever the reason might be, I didn't let it bother me too much since it played into my plans anyway. She thought I was like all the other men who had let her down, but by doing something completely unexpected, I might be able to convince her otherwise.

The sun had already dried away any traces of the previous day's rainstorm as I drove along the coast to the airport. My mom couldn't have chosen a better day to get her first impression of California. Along with lunch in Santa Monica, I'd already made a reservation for three that evening at one of the fanciest restaurants I could find, paying a premium for the last-minute booking. I didn't generally splash my money around quite so much, but I wanted to send both Laina and my mom a clear message that I wasn't embarrassed to be seen with Laina anywhere or by anyone.

First, though, I still had to let my mom in on one more secret, which I did once we were seated at our restaurant for lunch, overlooking the pier and the ocean.

"What I'm about to tell you can't leave this table," I warned her to start with. "Nobody can know about it, *especially* Mark."

"You can trust me," she promised. "I've never told him about your books, have I?"

My mom *had* kept my pen name a secret all these years, which gave me the confidence to tell her the truth about Laina too. "Actually, this has a lot in common with that. The woman you're going to meet also uses a stage name."

"You mean Jenny Vixxen *isn't* her real name? I'm shocked."

"Fair enough." Her sarcasm made me smile, especially since she seemed to be comfortable enough to be teasing me about the situation. "There's more, though. She's actually someone I knew before I moved in next door to her, though I didn't know she lived next door when I moved in."

With a sigh, my mom placed her fingers on her temples. "For someone who has such a way with words, Dory, you can make things much more complicated than they need to be. What are you trying to tell me?"

"She's someone I knew in high school. She's from our town."

She certainly hadn't expected *that*. Her jaw dropped, quite literally, as she blinked at me in surprise. "Are you serious?"

"Completely. So, you can see why it's important that this stays quiet. Whether she wants to share that information with anyone else is her decision, not mine, but I thought you should know. This isn't just some week-long infatuation. We have a history, as limited as it might be."

My mom gasped so loudly that people at the neighbouring tables turned our way to make sure she hadn't choked on something. "Oh my God. I know who she is! It's... what was her name? Laura? Lana?"

Furtively, I glanced around to make sure the other diners had all gone back to their meals. "Laina. Laina Macintyre."

"And she's a *porn star*?" Those last words came out in a high-pitched squeak that had people looking our way again while I tried not to groan.

"She's an actress," I corrected her in a whisper to remind her to keep her voice down too. "Can we call her that, please?"

"Laina Macintyre." My mom was still in such a daze over that she barely registered what I'd said. "Didn't you have a crush on her back when you were kids?"

That time, I was the one who drew attention as I choked on my reply. "How do you know that?" I had never told *anyone* about it, and certainly not my mother.

"A mother knows these things," was all she would say, relishing my surprise. "But this is interesting, Dorian. Do you think that maybe those past feelings are influencing how you feel about her now? I'm not saying she's not a lovely person, but..."

"But you don't think I would have been interested in dating any *other* adult actress," I guessed. "Well, to be honest, yes, I do think my past feelings are playing a part, but not in the way you're suggesting. I think so many people only see the persona she's made for herself, but because I knew her before any of that, I think she can be herself with me. I really hope so, anyway."

"It's even more serious than I realized," my mom mused. "I'm glad I came."

"I am too, but I wanted to tell you all of this and get it out in the open before you meet her so that you go in with an open mind. She's more than just her job."

"I'll be on my best behaviour," she promised.

After lunch, we walked around Santa Monica for a while before heading to my new home. My mom's jaw dropped again as she got her first look at my house in person, and as much fun as I had showing her around, I couldn't stop glancing at the clock every now and then, the butterflies in my stomach getting stronger as the afternoon grew later.

Finally, my mom couldn't take it anymore. "Why don't we go and get the introductions over with before you have a heart attack?"

It should be late enough in the day that Laina wouldn't mind the interruption, so grabbing my keys and wallet, we headed out the door.

As we rounded the bend in the road to Laina's house, I could see a couple of cars parked outside her house that weren't usually there. If she had company, that could put a damper on my plans, but I didn't want to overthink things. The new Dorian took control of the situation rather than reacting to it, so I walked up to her door as confidently as I could with my mother at my side, and rang the bell.

A few moments later, the door opened to reveal a short woman in jeans and a ball cap, her brown, curly hair just barely contained beneath it, holding a clipboard in her hands. "You're late," she greeted me, looking me up and down without making any attempt to hide it. "Who's this?"

She gestured at my mom while looking down at her clipboard, and despite my confusion, I answered the question. "This is my mother. Is, uh, Jenny expecting me?"

At the last moment, I remembered to use her professional name, since I suspected this woman, whoever she might be, probably wouldn't know her as Laina.

"Half an hour ago," she retorted. "Come on, don't waste any more time. They're all in the back."

She pointed toward the door opposite the one we stood at, the one that led to Laina's backyard, and though I still didn't have a clue what was going on, I still wanted to speak to Laina. I could at least extend the dinner invitation, and if she needed more time to finish up her work, we could leave again.

"This is lovely," my mom had to admit as I opened the door for her to go out into the backyard. Laina's pool and yard sparkled in the afternoon sunshine, the water reflecting the light and the white stone gleaming. Just as I was just about to explain how the decor had all been inspired by Laina's travels in Italy, my mom suddenly came to an abrupt stop in front of me.

It didn't take me long to see why, and as the full scene came into view, my stomach dropped violently.

At the side of the pool, beneath some portable lights and with two cameras aimed at them, stood a very handsome and completely naked man, groaning in appreciation as his cock disappeared into the enthu-siastic mouth of a bikini-clad Laina.

Chapter Eleven

~Laina~

The director swore under his breath in frustration as my doorbell rang. "That must be Jeremy, finally. Ava, get the door."

"Got it." The director's assistant headed to the door while I got back to my feet.

Earlier that day, as I wrote and blocked the scene for the day's short, I decided that two men would be better than one. I wanted something a little racier than a standard poolside fuck, but nothing too kinky to scare off anyone dipping their toe into porn for the first time. A threesome would work quite nicely.

When I called Erica back to request a second actor, she told me she had the perfect guy in mind. "His headshot literally just came across my desk this week. He's pretty new, but he looks a lot like this Dorian Reid of yours. At first glance, people might think it's him, and that'll spark interest."

Normally, for an actor, a headshot would be a picture of their face. In our world, it had a double meaning, as actors submitted both the standard shot and one of their naked body if they didn't have any professionally-shot work for us to review.

"Fine, whatever." I didn't want to waste time arguing with her or pointing out that Dorian was hardly 'mine'. The rest of the crew would be arriving soon and time was money. "As long as he's vetted and can be here quickly, we'll give it a go. He won't have to say much."

"I'm on it," she promised.

By the time everything got set up, Jeremy still hadn't shown up and we couldn't wait any longer to at least get started. I showed Ava his headshot - the one of his face - and told her to let him in when he arrived. No one else should be admitted while we were filming.

We had just got to the point of the script where my character got the first man's cock out, and no sooner had I put it in my mouth than the doorbell rang, ruining the take.

While Ava went to get the door, the director instructed us on where to pick up to allow for a good edit. "Just go from undoing his pants. We can skip the dialogue."

Victor, the other actor involved, winced as he shoved his hard cock back into his jeans and zipped them back up. "I should've worn sweats."

"I won't keep you waiting too long," I promised.

"Action."

The director gave us our cue, and I immediately dropped back to my knees, unzipping Victor's pants as I looked up at him adoringly, licking my lips in anticipation. In the scene, he played my gardener who I decided to reward for his good work with an extra treat. When his partner arrived, things would get even hotter.

Eagerly, he pulled his jeans off, again, and I grabbed hold of his cock, a fairly large one even by industry standards. I'd done a film once where they wanted me to do anal with him, and though I didn't have many things on my refusal list, that time, I said no.

"Oh, shit." Victor's groan was in character, but probably not entirely faked as I took him into my mouth again. My thong bikini didn't hide much, and the image of me down on my knees, focused on his pleasure, would be a winner, I knew.

Unfortunately, the take was interrupted again, that time by a loud gasp from over by the door.

"Cut," the director groaned. "What was that?"

I had no idea, but with the cameras stopped, I turned around to take a look. At first glance, I thought I must be looking at Jeremy, the actor Erica had sent. *He really does look like Dorian*, I thought as I laid eyes on him, but a moment later, as I took in his expression and the middle-aged woman standing next to him, the two of them looking like deer caught in the headlights, I realized it wasn't Jeremy at all.

"Dorian?" I got to my feet again, wiping the saliva from my lips that had just been wrapped around another man's cock. Maybe I should have been embarrassed, but his appearance was so unexpected that I didn't feel much of anything other than surprise and confusion.

"I... I'm... I'm so sorry." His stuttering uncertainty returned in full force as his face went beet red. "I didn't know you were... busy."

Obviously, he hadn't realized we were filming, but how had he even got in? And who was the woman with him? "What are you doing here?"

His eyes dropped to my breasts, barely covered by my bikini top, for just a second, but enough that I became aware of them too, especially in front of the woman I still didn't know.

"I... I came to invite you out for dinner."

He sounded utterly defeated as he offered his explanation, which still made little sense to me. Why did he have to come over to do that? Why not just send me a text? He'd ignored me all day and then showed up? Why?

"Jenny, we really don't have all day," the director called out, not trying to be rude but reminding me that the clock was ticking.

"Yeah, sorry, just one second." As I glanced back, I realized everyone was watching us, and this was one time I preferred not to have an audience. "Come with me."

Heading back towards the entrance hall, I grabbed one of the dressing gowns off a pool chair, getting it tied up just as I stepped into the hall. Once inside, I spun back to face Dorian.

"This really isn't the best time, and I meant what I said last night. We should stick to work, and a dinner doesn't sound like work."

"I know you said that, but I thought... oh, fuck." He covered his face with his hands, as if he could disappear so long as he couldn't see me, just like a little kid. "Laina, this is my mother."

It took a second for the words to sink in and for my eyes to move over to the woman who still stood beside him, looking just as shell-shocked as Dorian did, if not more. I could see the resemblance in more than just their expressions too; she had the same brown eyes, but where Dorian's were usually warm and kind, hers looked much cooler.

His mother. His mother who lived six states away and had insulted me on the phone just the previous evening was somehow standing in my house, having just walked in on me in the middle of a scene.

He had to be fucking kidding me.

"Mrs Reid." It took all my self-control to force the words of acknowledgement out and cover up the humiliation that surged through my body. That small crack in the walls I'd built around myself, the ones that kept out the feelings of shame and inadequacy, grew wider, and my defensive instincts kicked in. "Well, I'm sure that was much more than you wanted to see, but I suppose that's your reward for coming over uninvited."

Dorian winced as his mother's lips tightened. "I'm sorry, Laina," he apologized again. "It's entirely my fault."

"Not entirely. Ava!" I shouted out the assistant director's name and she came running in from outside, her face gone pale. "This isn't Jeremy."

"I know. I'm so sorry, Jenny, he just called to say he's stuck in traffic and won't be able to make it. I didn't realize... he looks just like him."

To be fair, I could see how she'd made the mistake, but it didn't fully excuse it. "Did you ask for his name? Did you ask for *her* name?"

I gestured at Dorian's mother, and Ava grimaced. "No. He just said she was his mother."

"Have you ever met an actor who brings their mother to a shoot?" The words came out so sharply that they could have cut glass. "Show them out. Now."

"Laina, wait..." Dorian tried to protest, but I didn't stop. With the other actor not coming, we had to reshoot the whole opening, and we couldn't waste any more time. Dorian wouldn't follow me; his manners were too good for that, so as soon as I stepped back outside, I knew I was safe.

After all of that, he certainly wouldn't want anything more to do with me. My life could go back to the way it had been before his unexpected reappearance in my life, before I started caring what anyone else thought of me again. Mrs Reid would go back to our hometown with enough to satisfy the town gossips for a month, Dorian could go back to writing his sex-free novels, and I'd make the film I wanted to make, thanks to the extra publicity he'd helped me get.

Maybe I'd give him a small footnote in the credits, but at that moment, I honestly couldn't see how there would ever be anything more between us than that.

~Dorian~

If that could have gone worse, I couldn't imagine how.

In hindsight, my error couldn't be clearer. The cars outside the house and the person I'd never seen before answering the door should have told me immediately that Laina was working. If she worked in an office building, I wouldn't have thought I could just walk into the boardroom and ask her to dinner, so why would it be okay for me to do it in her home office either? The whole thing happened so fast, and I supposed

I assumed that the woman at the door recognized me from the video or that Laina had told her I'd be coming, but in retrospect, neither of those scenarios made much sense.

She'd mistaken me for someone else, apparently, and now Laina thought I had no boundaries or common sense, and I couldn't really disagree, particularly with the latter.

My common sense seemed to disappear every time I got near her.

Both my pride and my heart felt bruised as my mom and I walked silently back to my house, neither of us saying a word until I'd closed the door behind us and we could be completely certain we wouldn't be overheard.

"I'm sorry," were the first words out of my mouth. My mom deserved an apology as much as Laina did. She'd been doing her best to try to come to terms with Laina's profession and give her the benefit of the doubt, and I'd just unintentionally shoved it straight into her face. Would my mom ever be able to look at Laina again without that very vivid image of her on her knees cropping back up?

"That was an experience I could have lived without," she replied in understatement.

"Let's get a drink."

With a glass of wine in hand, we sat down in my living room. I forced the liquid down, pushing it past the lump in my throat, and gave my mom the closest thing I could to a smile. "Well, I guess dinner isn't happening."

"After what just happened? No, I don't think so."

From writing my books, I knew better than most how things could appear completely different from different perspectives, and I tried to always remember that in my own life. With that in mind, I asked my mom to share her thoughts on the entire situation. "What did you take away from that encounter?"

"Well, she's not afraid to tell you what she's thinking. There's no beating around the bush."

From her tone of voice, I couldn't tell whether she thought of that as a positive or negative, but in my view, it was a good thing. I actually really liked that Laina told me straight out when I did something to upset her, whether it be after the confrontation in the parking lot with her fans or what happened that afternoon. When I had to try to guess what someone else felt, my tendency to overthink could send me into a spiral. Having her tell me straight out helped me, even when it wasn't what I wanted to hear.

"I also think she was embarrassed, maybe even more than you or I were," my mom added.

"Really?" Embarrassment didn't really factor into the emotions I picked up from Laina; I'd only see indignation and annoyance. On the other hand, I felt truly awful about it, and I could tell how shocked my mom had been. "I find that hard to believe. She's proud of her job."

"I think she can be proud of it and also be embarrassed that we walked in on it," my mom countered. "She heard what I said last night, and she doesn't know that you and I talked it out afterwards. In her head, I went in there ready to judge, and what I walked in on only made things worse."

Maybe she was right. My intention had been to prove to Laina that I didn't have a problem with the people I cared about knowing what she did, but *she* didn't know that. All she knew was that I'd suddenly turned up to invite her out for dinner with the same woman who had insulted her the night before.

Fuck, I'd completely messed this up.

The only good thing I could see at all was that my mom seemed to be defending Laina and trying her best to see things from her point of view. "It sounds like you think her reaction was understandable?"

She took a long sip of her wine, leaving me in suspense for several painful seconds. "Honestly, I understand her reaction but I think there are red flags there too. Her instinct seems to be to push you away rather than talk things out."

Frustratingly, I had to admit she had a point. Though Laina did tell me how she felt at times, she also closed herself off at others, like the first night we reconnected, for instance, or after hearing what my mom said on the phone. If everyone had a 'fight or flight' instinct, Laina's seemed to be flight, at least some of the time.

Still, I couldn't entirely blame her for it. "She does that because of the way people have treated her in the past, other men in particular."

My mom acknowledged that with a nod of her head, but her tone didn't change. "Again, that's understandable, but not especially conducive to a healthy relationship. It creates drama and you're not someone who does well with drama."

I couldn't argue with that when she knew me so well. "You don't think we're right for each other?"

The little doubts in the back of my head had been trying to tell me that for days, that I was fooling myself, that I'd never be exciting or confident enough to fit into Laina's world, but to hear my mother say the words out loud punched me in the gut anyway.

My mom's expression softened at the disappointment in my voice. "I don't know her well enough to say that yet. All I'm saying is that you need to be careful, Dory. I don't think *you* know her well enough either. Don't fall too hard until you do."

We might be a little too late for that, but I would try to keep it in mind anyway.

"I have to admit, you're taking this better than I expected." When I first realized exactly what we were looking at in Laina's backyard, I thought my mom might have a heart attack.

A Mona Lisa smile graced my mom's face. "Believe it or not, I'm not a total innocent. I have had sex before; how do you think you were born?"

Of course, she had to wait until I had just taken a drink of my wine to say that, nearly making me choke on it.

Her grin grew wider. "There. Now we've both got visuals we'd rather not have."

"Thanks for that." Shooting her a pained look, I took another drink to ease the burning in my throat and to try to wipe the memory of that comment from my brain.

"Did it really not bother you to see her with another man, though?" she asked curiously.

Since she asked it so genuinely, I took a moment to think it over. "Honestly? No. I was surprised, but not jealous. She doesn't feel anything for him, I know that. It was just work."

Laina gave sex away freely; for her job, and to me too. Her heart, on the other hand, she kept much more firmly locked up. I'd have been much more upset to walk in on her kissing someone in private than seeing her being much more physically intimate in front of the camera.

"I'm going to guess not a lot of men are so understanding about it," my mom pointed out. "It's too bad she's too caught up in her own narrative to notice."

Her choice of words gave me a sudden flash of inspiration. Narratives were my bread and butter, but so far, I hadn't done a great job of showing Laina my side of the story. Heartfelt speeches had never been my forte. Maybe if I wrote it down instead, it would come out better.

Maybe the time had come to write myself into the story.

~Laina~

By the time I signed off on the edited version of the short to go up on the website and escorted the last of the crew out of my house, exhaustion had crept up on me. Normally, the excitement of releasing a new film invigorated me, but after the stress of the shoot, the actor not showing up and needing to rearrange everything, I just felt relieved to get it all finished.

As soon as I was on my own again, though, my fatigue was joined by another, unwelcome feeling.

Frustratingly, it felt a lot like guilt.

No matter how I tried, I couldn't erase the image of Dorian's regret-filled eyes as I ordered him out of my house. He accepted it, didn't fight or argue with me, and even took responsibility for the situation. If he had been belligerent or shouted at me, it would make it a lot easier to stay angry with him, but in his quiet acceptance, he made me question my actions and my feelings about the whole thing, and I couldn't say I particularly liked what I saw.

The first guy I really fell for after I started making adult movies stormed onto my set once. Long before I had my own production company, with someone else paying for studio time and all the fees, he humiliated me as he pushed his way past security and brought the entire production to a halt, demanding that I pull out of the film. Somehow, he'd been under the mistaken impression that just because we'd started sleeping together, it meant that I wouldn't be having sex with anyone else. In front of the rest of the cast and crew, he called me a slut when I explained how it was part of my job.

Obviously, we broke up, and after that, I made sure to have an explicit conversation at the start of any new relationship to make it clear that I would continue to work while we dated, and that my work involved having sex with other men. Or women. Sometimes both. Those sexual encounters didn't mean anything to me emotionally. They called it acting for a reason, and if the guy couldn't understand the difference, I could put an end to the relationship before it even began. I also never allowed any of the men I dated on set after that, even if they swore they could handle it. I didn't want a repeat of that demeaning, embarrassing experience, ever.

So, even though we weren't technically in a relationship, Dorian's unexpected appearance on set that afternoon triggered a lot of those memories and emotions in me, especially when he explained he had his mother with him. I assumed they'd come to pass judgement on me, just as my boyfriend had on that long-ago day, and I struck first before they could cast any stones at me.

However, in the quiet left behind when the shooting finished, I had to admit that didn't seem very likely. Dorian had seemed genuine in his apology to me the night before when I overheard his mother's comments. We still had plans to work together. Why would he bring his mother over simply to humiliate me?

And they hadn't pushed their way onto the set either. They were admitted by error, plain and simple, and though I still wasn't happy about it, even at the time, I recognized that Dorian wasn't entirely to blame.

I still couldn't imagine what he'd been thinking in bringing his mother over to my house in the first place, but if I wanted to be fair, I had to admit I had no reason to jump to any negative conclusions about his intentions. He'd only shown me kindness and consideration to that point, and I probably should have given him the benefit of the doubt.

In the movie script I was working on, my female character misunderstood the love interest's motivations when he prevented her from getting a job on a film she'd put in a bid for with her animals. She took offense, assuming he'd ruined her chances because he didn't trust she could do a good job, when in reality, he knew from working with the director of the film that he didn't take safety seriously, and he'd done it to protect her animals. She only figured it out after she'd already chewed him out for it, by which time she owed him a rather significant apology.

As much as I hated to admit it, I suspected I owed Dorian an apology too. I'd gotten so used to being the one who got wronged that I'd forgotten how it felt to be on the other side.

This would all be so much easier if we just had a script to follow.

As I tried to decide on the best way to build back the bridges I'd burned, especially while his mother was still over at his house, I kept coming back in my head to the apology scene I'd written for my movie.

Maybe I *did* have a script after all.

Dorian liked the written word. He'd told me that he often felt more comfortable reading and writing than saying things out loud, so maybe if I sent that scene to him, it would charm him just enough that he'd consider accepting my apology.

Grabbing myself a glass of wine, I pulled out my laptop and sat down in the kitchen to have my computer program read the scene out loud to me again. A few lines, I tweaked, based on my own feelings and the things I wanted to say to Dorian, but overall, the sentiment was already there. With a deep breath, I composed a single-lined email: *Does this sound like the kind of apology you might accept?* After attaching the scene, I hit send before I could change my mind.

No sooner had I raised my glass to my lips than an email hit my inbox with Dorian's name on it.

"There's no way he read it that fast," I muttered to myself, frowning as I clicked the email open, my heart beating faster in the seconds it took for the email to load.

If I were a braver man, I would have done this.

Those were the only words, his email just as brief as mine had been, also with a document attached. Still confused, I opened the document and found a completely different scene to the one I'd just sent him, obviously written by him.

It didn't seem to be in reply to my email in any way. He must have just sent it at almost the exact same moment I sent mine, both of us thinking of each other, both choosing the same method of reaching out.

My heart still racing, I loaded the document into my dictation program and pressed play.

It started out with an almost word-for-word reenactment of what happened that afternoon, from the moment he and his mother arrived in my backyard, through our conversation in the hall, until I told them to go. Hearing my words repeated back to me in the computerized voice made me wince. I certainly didn't come across very well, and I was pretty sure Dorian hadn't taken any artistic license. If anything, he probably made me sound more reasonable than I'd actually been.

However, after I gave the order for Ava to show Dorian and his mom out, the events turned from memoir to fiction.

"I'm not going anywhere," the Dorian on the page said. "You're short an actor. Let me help."

A surprised half-gasp, half-laugh came out of my mouth as I covered my mouth with my hand, trying not to laugh. He hadn't really written that, had he? Would he really go there?

Apparently, he would. The scene kept going, and over his mother's protests and mine, he convinced me to let him try. I'd only gotten to the point where he returned to the set with me, ready to get started, when my phone buzzed with a text from the man himself.

Can I come over?

I kept my answer short and to the point.

You better.

Chapter Twelve

~**Dorian**~

As soon as the idea came to me for the scene I wanted to write, I excused myself from the living room. "There's something I need to do. We'll have to take a rain check on dinner, so why don't you go online and find somewhere to order in from? Get whatever you want."

My mom rolled her eyes back at me. "I'm perfectly capable of cooking something for us, we don't need to waste money."

"You're on vacation," I reminded her. "Even if it hasn't been much of one yet. Please, relax, go outside, order something special, and I'll come out and eat with you as soon as it gets here."

With a shrug, she agreed, and I headed to my room. After cancelling our dinner reservation and swallowing the forfeited deposit, I grabbed my laptop and started writing. For the first time ever when writing a sex scene, the words flowed easily. With very little effort at all, I could put myself in the scene, imagining exactly how I'd feel, what I'd see and touch and taste, and I described it all in vivid detail.

Maybe *too* much detail. When I finished, I hesitated, wondering if I'd gone too far, but in the end, the point of sending it was to see if Laina and I could find a method of communication that worked for us. If she found the gesture inappropriate or cringey, then obviously, we weren't meant to be. But if, on the other hand, she was charmed by it, we might just be able to find our way back from the cliff edge we were walking along.

Steeling my nerves, I typed a short message and sent the document, hoping with everything I had that she'd take it in the spirit I intended it.

With that done, I started to get to my feet to go see how my mom was doing with dinner, when a new email from Laina suddenly popped up in my inbox.

For a moment, I thought it must be an automated reply since she couldn't possibly have read the scene so quickly. A second later, I wondered if she'd decided she just wouldn't read it, and had responded to simply tell me to back off. My stomach felt like lead as I opened the new message, and my brow furrowed as I read over the single sentence it contained.

It didn't seem to have anything to do with the email I'd just sent her, and as I started to read through the scene, one from her new script that she hadn't shown me before, it gradually hit me: she must have sent it before she got my email. She sent it as a way to test the waters, just as I'd done with her.

We were speaking the same language after all.

The scene was short, but sincere, and told me as clearly as any direct words could have that she wasn't angry with me. In fact, she took responsibility and apologized.

With new hope rising, I grabbed my phone and sent her a text, asking if I could come over. It would be better to talk this out face-to-face now that the timing was better, and thankfully, she agreed. Slamming my laptop shut, I headed out to my backyard, where my mom had taken my advice and was lying in the sun with a book.

"Dinner will be here in about ten minutes," she told me as she caught sight of me. "We could eat out here, it's such a nice night."

Given what I had to tell her, her offer made me wince. "How angry would you be if I left you alone for dinner?"

After inviting her out to visit, leaving her on her own that night would be a dick move, but Laina and I really needed to talk and I didn't want to put it off.

My mom caught on immediately. "You're going to talk to her?"

She didn't need to say who she meant by 'her'. We both knew. "She emailed me to apologize."

"Make sure that she actually says it in person, too," my mom advised. "Don't let her off the hook just because she's pretty."

"Do you really think my self-esteem is that low?" I'd tried to become more sure of myself over the years, and worked damn hard at it, actually, even if it didn't always show.

"I think that sometimes when we're around people from our past, we tend to revert to the people we were when we first knew them," she theorized. "You're not that shy boy from high school who didn't have a date to the prom. You're a handsome, kind, wealthy, successful man, and she'd be damn lucky to have you."

My mom's words made me blush as if I *were* that awkward teenager all over again. "Thanks, Mom. This is... getting weird. I'm going to go."

Her laugh followed me back through the door as I grabbed my keys and headed out the front door, jogging down the street to Laina's house.

The extra cars from earlier had all disappeared as I walked up the driveway, and the front door opened even before I reached it. Obviously, she'd been waiting for me.

"Wine?" Laina asked as soon as I stepped inside.

"I probably shouldn't. My mom and I already had some." We were still on shaky ground and I needed to keep my wits about me. Getting drunk wouldn't help.

She winced before turning towards the kitchen. "In that case, I'll have another for the both of us. How's your mom coping?"

"A lot better than I thought she would be, actually."

"Really?" Laina sounded genuinely surprised as she picked up the half-full wine glass sitting on the counter next to her laptop. That must have been where she'd been sitting when she emailed me. "She didn't get on the next plane back home?"

She took a seat in front of the laptop so I sat next to her, my cheeks heating up as I saw she had the scene I sent her still open on the computer. She hadn't given me any hint yet about what she thought of it.

Averting my eyes, I focused back on her question. "No. In fact, she's lounging in my backyard right now, waiting for her dinner to be delivered. She might end up getting used to this life and never want to leave."

That was a joke, and Laina took it as one, smiling as she took a sip of her wine. "Well, I'm glad she's still around. I owe her an apology too, assuming that you're accepting mine?"

Swallowing uncomfortably, I tried to follow my mom's advice and ask Laina to say the words to my face. "What exactly are you apologizing for?"

Her eyes widened in surprise at the question, but she didn't try to pawn me off with a vague answer. Instead, she took a moment to really think it over. "Well, I'm sorry about jumping to conclusions about why you came, and I'm sorry for letting my past dictate the way I responded to you."

That matched up exactly with why I thought she'd reacted the way she did. "Why did you think I came?"

Her hand rested on the counter, tantalizingly close to mine. If I moved forward just a few inches, we'd be touching. "In the moment, it felt like you'd brought your mother there to judge me, but I realized afterwards that probably wasn't right."

The fact that she'd thought that for even a minute sent a pang of sadness through my chest. If her past experience had taught her to expect that, the men she'd dated were even worse than I thought. "Actually, I really just wanted to take you to dinner so my mom could get to know the real you, not the one in the video or the one in your films."

I thought she'd appreciate that sentiment, but Laina shook her head. "Don't do that, Dorian. Don't divide me into separate people. They're *all* the real me, just different parts. If you accept one, you have to accept them all."

"I do," I quickly assured her. "I'm sorry, I phrased that badly. I think what I actually said to her was that there's *more* to you than what she'd seen, not that you weren't those other women."

"Okay." Her smile of acceptance told me she believed that, and I appreciated that she'd corrected me on it. Words mattered; as someone who made my living from them, I understood that. "Now, tell me more about this scene."

She gestured towards the computer screen as the blush stole up my neck again. "I don't think it really requires any further explanation, does it?"

"Well, I'm not sure. I didn't finish it yet."

"Why not?" She seemed to be teasing me but I didn't understand why.

Laina arched an eyebrow at me, her weight shifting on her chair very subtly, but enough that it drew my attention. "I thought you could read it to me. Your voice is much better than the computer."

"You had the computer read it to you?" The idea made me grimace, imagining the words I'd tried to make sexy being read in a monotone, robotic voice. "Why not just read it yourself?"

For some reason, Laina's lips pursed. "I told you: I absorb things better by hearing them."

"I get that, but surely..."

"No." Her forceful refusal seemed to take us both by surprise, and Laina took a breath before closing the laptop lid. "Never mind. It's not important. You don't understand."

I didn't, but I also didn't intend to let her shut me out again. "Explain it to me, Laina. I'm right here, listening. I want to know."

Her teeth dragged across her lower lip, pulling it into her mouth in uncertainty. "You'll think it's stupid."

"I can promise you that I won't." She'd already shown a bit of vulnerability in apologizing to me, and it felt like we were on the verge of some other kind of confidence, if she could just take that step and open up to me. "Laina, you were kind to me back in high school when no one else was, and you've been generous with your time and your... expertise over the last week. I've trusted you with my biggest secret. Anything you tell me, it's just between us, and I won't judge you for it. I promise."

Those pretty blue eyes of hers looked up into mine, searching them for any hint of a lie, but she wouldn't find one. I meant every word, and she must have seen that because, with a deep breath, she answered me.

"I have the computer read it because I can't read very well. I've always struggled with it. We're not exactly a good match: you're brilliant with words and I've never even read a book. That's why I didn't want to read for you. Because I can't."

~Laina~

When Dorian came over, I certainly never thought I'd be blurting out my deepest secret to him. Hardly anyone knew about my dyslexia, far fewer than those who knew my real name. Erica knew because she needed to for our work. My agent knew, the same agent I'd been with since I first started in the industry. Though I rarely needed him anymore, I was still technically his client. Aside from them, no one really knew the full extent of it. I'd certainly never told *any* of the men I'd dated before.

Why did I tell Dorian, then? Maybe because it was simply getting tiresome to keep it a secret with the way we were working together. Maybe because of how well he handled everything that happened between us that day? Or maybe I did it out of some self-sabotaging instinct, because he seemed to have some rose-coloured version of me in his head, one who was worth all the trouble I'd unintentionally brought him in the mere week we'd been spending time together.

Once he knew my secret, he wouldn't think I was so perfect anymore, and maybe I wanted to shatter the illusion and show him the real me before I got too attached to the way having his respect and support felt.

His brown eyes blinked at me slowly after I blurted it out, his brain obviously trying to process what I'd just said. "What do you mean you can't read? You graduated from high school. I was there."

He sounded so confused, almost like he was doubting his own memory, that I had to smile. "I *barely* graduated. Mr Ferguson let me do a special oral exam in English after I failed the final. If he hadn't, I wouldn't have gotten my diploma. And before you ask, that's not a euphemism: he really just asked me the questions out loud."

"I wasn't going to ask that." In contrast to my smile, Dorian's expression remained serious and still rather bewildered. "You're an actress, though. You have to read and remember all your lines."

"I have to remember them all, yes, but I came up with all kinds of ways to get around *reading* them. I got pretty good at developing ways of coping and masking my problems. I've had a lot of practice."

"But... you text me. You email me. I've seen you texting other people."

He didn't mean it in an offensive way, so I did my best not to be offended. "I *can* read, obviously. Short sentences are fine, but when there's a lot of text, things start to get muddled."

Dorian leaned forward, looking slightly less confused but more curious. "What do you mean? What happens?"

No one had ever really asked me to explain it before. "The words just kind of jumble together. They move on the page, or pieces of them do. Or sometimes, I can see the words just fine, but they just don't make sense to me no matter how many times I read them. It can physically make my head hurt. It's... annoying."

That was an understatement, and Dorian obviously understood that. He still seemed to be struggling with the scope of the issue though. "So, all the books in your living room…"

"I told you: I haven't read them. They're just for decoration."

"And the script you've been working on?"

"I use a dictation program on my computer. It types out what I say and then reads it back to me. I barely have to look at the words at all."

"Wow." Dorian leaned back, swallowing in a way that made me think he was regretting not taking me up on my offer of some wine. "That's really clever."

"Clever?" I repeated the word out loud without really meaning to; it just took me by surprise so much that I couldn't help it. Of all the words I thought he might use to describe me, that one had never crossed my mind.

Dorian nodded emphatically. "Yeah. I've tried to do dictation and I just can't do it. My brain doesn't work that way, I get all tongue-tied when I try to speak the words out loud. Kind of like real life."

He said it in such a charmingly self-deprecating way, as if his occasional awkwardness could be put on the same level as my reading disability, that neither was any more embarrassing than the other, that I could hardly believe it. Brock would have been horrified if I told him I had trouble reading. Nearly all the men I'd dated would have been, or used it as a reason to look down at me.

Dorian didn't seem bothered in the least. He simply wanted to understand it.

Who *was* this man?

I'd thought my announcement would be the end of our conversation, but it didn't seem that way, and so, I reached over and opened up the laptop again. "So, that's why the computer was reading me your chapter, but it's not ideal, as you can hear."

As I pressed play, the tinny, monotone, robotic voice echoed from the speakers: "I'd never been naked in front of another man before, but it didn't feel as strange as I thought it would. Maybe because I didn't care what he thought, or the director, or any of them. Laina's opinion was the only one that mattered."

"Okay, stop," Dorian groaned, nearly drowning in the heavy blush that washed over his cheeks. "That's awful."

I smiled over at him sweetly. "I agree, which is why I think you should read it to me instead."

He couldn't argue with me when he'd just proved my point, so reluctantly, he reached over and pulled the laptop closer to him. "You're sure about this?" he asked, his eyes showing both embarrassment but also a touch of desire. He knew what might happen if he started reading it, and so did I. We were entirely on the same page.

"Positive."

Clearing his throat, Dorian began to read. "As Laina got down on her knees in front of me, everything else around us seemed to disappear. Her eyes stayed fixed on mine, like I was the only person in the room, even though she held another man's cock in her hand. She made me feel like I was the only one who mattered. She always had. Even though somewhere in the back of my head, I knew this was all for the cameras, I didn't really care. At that moment, it felt real."

I leaned closer to him as he read, his deep voice rumbling through the words, and my hand went to his thigh as he said it felt real.

Dorian's breath caught as his eyes left the screen, glancing up at me curiously. "Keep going," I encouraged him. "I'm listening."

His voice sounded shakier than it had before when he resumed, but he did his best to keep going. "Leaning forward, her movements exaggerated for the sake of the camera that followed her every move, Laina wrapped her sweet, warm lips around the head of my cock."

My fingers found his cock through his pants, teasing him as he breathed in deeply.

"I'd never been someone who felt entirely comfortable being on the receiving end of oral sex. All the attention being on me had never been my comfort zone, but in that situation, although I was definitely the one getting the better deal out of the situation, the cameras didn't care about me. They were trained on the gorgeous blonde at my feet, the one who hummed in pleasure and took my cock down her throat so far that her nose brushed against my pelvis, encasing me in wet, perfect warmth."

The sound of his zipper as I pulled it down added some sound effects to his reading, enhancing it even more.

"It felt so good that no one would have blamed me for coming on the spot."

That line made me laugh, an obvious reference to what had happened between us the first time we got intimate, and he flashed me a quick smile of his own before continuing.

"Thankfully, I didn't. Looking over at the other man helped to bring me back to reality, especially as Laina pulled back off my cock, rubbing her hand along my shaft, now covered with her saliva, and turned back to take the other man's cock into her mouth instead."

Reaching into his pants, I pulled out Dorian's cock, noting with satisfaction that he was just as aroused by his chapter as I was. My body throbbed just as much as it would if I were watching the scene play out in front of me. More, even; I'd become almost desensitized to seeing porn, but hearing it and letting my imagination create the pictures instead felt even sexier.

"She shared her attentions between us equally, fucking one of us with her mouth while she stroked the other with her hand, and then alternating, never making either of us feel left out. When I accidentally caught the other guy's eye over Laina's head, he gave me a nod as if to say, 'Are we the luckiest bastards in the world, or what?' and I couldn't find a single reason to disagree."

I'd waited as long as I could, but his words combined with the sight of his hard cock proved too tempting. Leaning down so my face was in his lap, I licked my way up his exposed shaft as Dorian panted above me, trying to catch his breath.

"Don't stop," I murmured. "Keep reading."

My tongue flicked over his head in both encouragement and distraction, and exhaling loudly, Dorian carried on.

~Dorian~

Nothing had ever been more purely erotic in my entire life than reading my words to Laina about her sucking my cock while she actually did it. The images in my head combined with the ones in front of me, each of them amplifying the other, making me impossibly hard, impossibly fast. But unlike the other night when I came so embarrassingly quickly, this time, I didn't feel out of control. She was feeding off my words, so if I stopped, she would too. The power belonged to both of us equally.

I was, however, finding it increasingly difficult to stay focused on the words on the screen as her tongue pressed down against my cock. She knew exactly what she was doing, just how to tease me and exactly which spots would get me most excited.

Maybe that was kind of how it felt for her when she tried to read: the words right in front of her but refusing to make sense.

Her explanation about her reading difficulties had truly taken me by surprise. I'd had absolutely no indication that she experienced anything like that. She hid it very well, but learning how she'd adapted and found ways around it made me admire her even more. People already judged her based on her looks, not expecting her to be nearly as business-minded as she was, and each new thing I learned about her only made her seem more incredible to me.

Maybe we wouldn't ever be a couple who curled up and read books together, but I would happily read to her, especially if occasionally, I would get rewards like the one she was giving me.

My mom had warned me not to fall too fast, but with every moment, our future together seemed clearer and more defined to me. I could practically write it all down already.

With great effort, I focused back on the words on the screen, squinting at them to try to make sense of them while Laina's tongue slid over my head. "From the corner of my eye, I could see the director making a hand signal, like a baseball coach, and though I had no idea what it meant, Laina seemed to. Without turning towards the camera at all or showing that she'd noticed the director, she got to her feet and led me and the other man over to the gazebo in her yard, the camera trailing after us."

I stopped reading as Laina took my cock in her mouth, just the head, sucking on it hard enough that my whole body shuddered.

"Is there a problem?" she asked as she released me, grinning up at me mischievously.

I didn't know how much more I could take, but thankfully, we were getting to the next part of the scene, which she wouldn't know yet since she hadn't read that far. When we reached it, I could take control of the situation. I just had to make it that far.

"Shimmying out of her bikini bottoms, Laina climbed up onto the bench that ran around the gazebo's perimeter, her perfect, pink pussy on display not only for me, but for the camera as well."

"Perfect, huh?" she teased, her tongue still drawing lazy patterns on my cock, but a second later she gasped when I reached down and tilted her head up, two firm fingers beneath her chin.

"Maybe I should take another look, just to be sure."

From her heated expression, I could see she liked that idea just as much as I did, and she quickly got to her feet, removing her pants in no time at all. I didn't stay idle either, getting up to take my pants fully off, since I didn't need them for the next part of the scene.

Her kitchen had a bench on one side of the table, and we both headed for it, me carrying the laptop so I could continue to read. My body ached for her, and I could guess by the way her thighs pressed together as she walked that she could feel it too, but I wanted to give her more than just the physical pleasure. I wanted to stimulate her mind and her imagination first, making her come with my words just as much as my actions.

"Directing us without any words, Laina brought the other man in front of her so that she could take his cock back into her mouth, and from my position behind her, I could see her spread her legs wider, letting me know silently but undeniably that her pussy was mine to do with as I pleased."

Laina let out a soft sigh at those words, spreading her legs for me just as she had in my scene. My eyes left the screen to take in the gorgeous sight, just as wonderful as I'd remembered it.

"I was right," I murmured, my tone making it clear I was no longer reading from the screen. "It's perfect."

A moan left her lips as my cock rubbed against her, sliding through the wetness between her legs, close to her entrance but not going in.

I didn't need to look at the computer for the next lines. I remembered them perfectly well. "In the moment when I entered her, the world around us disappeared once more. The cameras, the crew, the lights, the other man, all of it faded away, until all that remained, all I could see and all I could feel, was the gorgeous woman in front of me who made me feel sexier than anyone ever had, who made it safe for me to be honest, and who had the best fucking pussy I'd ever had the pleasure of sliding into."

Laina laughed in surprise at the final words, a laugh that quickly got choked off by her groan as I pushed into her, just as I'd described. Her wetness left me in no doubt that she had found the whole experience just as stimulating as I had, and though the chapter continued, I didn't read any more. It couldn't compare to the real thing. Nothing ever could.

"You'd be... a great... actor," Laina breathed out between my thrusts, her hands balling into fists as I reached around her to find her clit.

"No, I wouldn't," I disagreed with a laugh. "I could never do what you do, but that's okay. We all have different strengths."

"You've got a few," she groaned in appreciation. "Fuck, Dorian. I'm going to come."

"Good." I wouldn't be far behind her, she'd worked me into such a frenzy already. "I want to feel it, Laina. It's the best fucking feeling in the world when you come on my cock, and I can't find the words to describe it. Maybe if you do it more often, I'll figure it out."

She wanted to laugh, but she couldn't, not with my fingers pressing down on her clit and my cock stroking her walls, hard and fast. Instead, she seemed to almost melt before my eyes, relaxing just before her body began to shudder around me.

"God, yes, just like that." The words came out as a grunt as I kept thrusting, feeling her contract around me until my orgasm hit too. My fingers left red marks on her hips as they dug in tightly, holding on for dear life as pleasure flooded my entire body.

For a long moment, neither of us spoke, or moved, neither of us wanting the moment to end. Naked in her kitchen, the laptop on her table, my cock buried fully inside her, I had to admit it felt even better than the other times we'd have sex.

Would it continue that way, getting better every time, the more we got to know each other? Where would it end? I both wanted to know and didn't at the same time.

Laina moved first, shifting her body forward so that my cock slid out of her, slick with our combined arousal. "Well, maybe you should get home to your mother. She shouldn't have to eat alone."

She was right, but I would have rather stayed there with her, talking with her and maybe, eventually, getting to see her bedroom for the first time. I certainly hadn't been thinking about my mother until she brought her up.

However, I wouldn't push it. We'd gotten over our earlier argument and made up in rather spectacular fashion, and for that night, I would have to be satisfied with that.

"Can I take you to lunch tomorrow? With my mom?" It hadn't worked out that day, but it didn't mean I planned to give up. I wanted her to know that, even in light of everything that had happened today, I was serious about her and my mom getting to know each other.

To my delight, Laina agreed without argument. "Sure. I'll make a reservation for us. Any preferences?"

"Whatever you choose will be great." I went over to grab my pants off the floor. I'd clean up at home since she seemed ready for me to go. "I really liked your scene, by the way. I didn't get a chance to say so. It felt real."

"Thanks, Dorian." She gave me a warm smile that didn't feel in the least like acting. "I liked your scene too."

A wink accompanied those words, making me flush all over again. If I wanted to leave there in a state fit to see my mother, I better leave soon.

"Goodnight, Laina." I gave her a kiss on the cheek before letting myself back out the front door.

Chapter Thirteen

~Laina~

As soon as Dorian left, I picked my clothes up off the kitchen floor, closed my laptop, and headed for my bedroom. A long, hot soak in the tub was exactly what I needed to try to make sense of the whole crazy, unexpected day.

Not just that day, even. Ever since Dorian had reappeared in my life, things felt different. Off-balance. Unsettled. The break-up with Brock might have contributed to it, but I really didn't think so. To be honest, he'd barely crossed my mind since I left him at the restaurant, whereas Dorian kept popping into my head, over and over again, whether I wanted him to or not.

In his eyes, I saw a whole other version of myself, one that was softer and kinder and more open than the woman I'd become in the years since our paths had last crossed. I didn't think there was anything inherently wrong with the woman I was; I'd merely become who I needed to be to survive and thrive in my new life. Still, something about Dorian's version of me appealed to me, perhaps the same way it appealed to him too.

But I *wasn't* that woman, not really, and when I turned around as he finished fucking me in the kitchen, flush with the pleasure of a truly satisfying sexual experience, his words and his actions combining to set off a whole new fire inside me, I saw the look in his eyes and it stopped me cold.

No one had ever looked at me with quite that much *adoration* before, and I didn't feel entirely comfortable with it.

Neither of us had said anything about a relationship. We were simply supposed to be helping each other out with our writing, and an undeniable physical attraction existed between us, but nothing further than that had been suggested on either side. For that reason, I sent him on his way as soon as we'd finished, to give me a chance to think things over before things got any more complicated.

Sinking down into my bathtub, the warm water melting into my skin and the scent of my coconut bubble bath instantly making me feel a bit calmer, I tried to sort through what I felt first. It wouldn't do me any good wondering what he might be thinking or wanting until I knew exactly what I wanted.

Normally, I didn't jump right from one relationship into another. Not short of sex whenever I wanted it, I had no need for physical intimacy to keep me satisfied. When I *did* decide to actually date someone, it would be because I saw the potential for someone to offer me more than just sex.

I wanted someone who challenged me, who enjoyed my company and conversation but also encouraged me to expand my horizons, someone successful in their own right who wouldn't rely on me for anything material but who would be supportive and proud of what I'd achieved.

Dorian fit all those criteria and more besides. Sinfully gorgeous but not arrogant about it: check. Talented but humble: check. Sweet and sensitive to my feelings: probably more than any man I'd ever gone out with before.

Honestly, I couldn't think of many flaws at all. Yes, he could be a bit awkward at times and unsure of himself, but the more time we spent together, the less that seemed to be an issue. His sexual confidence had certainly grown. And although he made some mistakes, like man-handling my fans or bringing his mom to my shoot, none of them had been intentionally disruptive. He meant well, he simply needed a better understanding of the world I lived in, and on that point, he had been nothing but open and willing to learn.

All in all, he seemed like an ideal partner for me, and as I let that realization wash over me, I sank down into the tub further, submerging my head beneath the water to try to dampen the giddy excitement that bubbled up inside me.

I couldn't let myself get too carried away yet, because even if I accepted the fact that there might be something there worth exploring on a deeper level than we'd done so far, I still had to look at things from his point of view. Even after everything he'd seen of my life, and even after learning that I could barely read, he still seemed to have an almost idealized picture of me in his head, a picture that he'd started to build many, many years earlier.

What had been so special about me in high school that he'd developed feelings for me strong enough to still be there more than a decade later?

I couldn't come up with an answer in the bathtub, so I pulled myself up, the water dripping from my skin and from my hair while I grabbed one of the big, fluffy white towels folded neatly nearby. The coconut scent lingered on my skin as I patted myself dry, and wrapping the towel around my body, I headed to my closet where I kept a few boxes of random mementos from my childhood.

Inside the box on the very bottom of the pile, I found what I was looking for: my senior year high school yearbook. It had been years since I'd looked at it or even thought about it, but as I flipped through the pages, the memories rushed in thick and fast. The squeak of sneakers on the polished hallway floors and the sound of lockers slamming closed.

The smell of bread baking in the Home Ec room that always made my stomach grumble and the sticky sweetness of the berry lip gloss I wore.

The drama club page brought even more memories, slightly bitter-sweet as I remembered how certain I'd been in those days that I would become a big Hollywood star. Closing my eyes, I could see the bright lights blinding me as I stepped on stage and hear the applause of the crowd. As I took my bow, my heart swelling as I basked in the adoration and appreciation of my fellow students, friends and family, I caught a glimpse of a slightly overweight boy in the front row, clapping even louder than the rest.

My eyes popped open in surprise as I realized exactly who it must be. Did I really remember Dorian being there, or had my imagination just put him in that seat? I honestly couldn't be sure. Flipping through the pages, I looked for Dorian in the group photos, but he wasn't there. Once or twice, I thought I could see him in the background, but never at the front of the picture. The only photo I could find that I knew for certain was him was his individual photo.

As I already knew, the years had certainly been kind to him. Staring back at me from the page was a young man who looked supremely uncomfortable in his own skin. He offered the camera an apologetic smile, as if he felt bad for taking up the photographer's time, and beneath his photo, the words offered little insight.

Dorian Reid

Future Plans: College

Clubs & sports:

Friends:

It felt unfinished, giving no indication of the man he'd been then, or the one he would become.

By contrast, my section filled all the possible space beneath my photo, and I stared at the past version of myself, trying to see that girl through a young Dorian's eyes. To me, she looked just as unsure of herself as Dorian did, except that she hid it better. She hid the fact that every class, every assignment was a struggle, and the fact that she felt stupid most days. From her smiling face, no one would have guessed that she just wanted to get out of that town and disappear into a world where she could be anyone she wanted to be.

Had the facade fooled Dorian too, or had he recognized somehow, even back then, that deep down, we were more alike than anyone else guessed?

As I closed the cover of the yearbook and put it back in its box, I didn't feel any closer to the answers, but I did feel more certain about one thing: if I wanted to know exactly how he felt and what he wanted, I would need to ask him, and lunch the following day should be just the opportunity I needed.

~Dorian~

My mom and I had a quiet evening together, catching up on things and enjoying each other's company. She didn't ask me how things went with Laina when I returned, and I didn't offer any explanation other than to say we'd be having lunch with her the next day. I didn't say anything more than that mostly because I really wasn't sure what to say. The sex had been incredible, but afterwards, it felt like a switch had been flipped and she just wanted me gone. However, she'd offered to go to lunch with us the next day, so she wasn't shutting me out again. It felt like something different, but I had no idea what it might be.

At breakfast the next morning, Laina texted me with the name of a restaurant she'd chosen.

It's my treat, her text added. *The short I shot yesterday had an incredible response overnight. That video of you defending me is paying huge dividends. Lunch is the least I can do.*

That was a welcome outcome, but she didn't owe me any thanks for it. Nothing about that video had been intentional, and it could have just as easily backfired as she'd been worried it might.

However, I wasn't about to argue with her over lunch, since I really just wanted to see her and couldn't care less about which of us picked up the bill.

She hadn't offered for us to travel together, and I suspected she wanted the option to leave separately if things didn't go well. For my part, I preferred to think more positively, but I wouldn't push her on that either. She was giving lunch a chance, and I would take it.

We'll see you there at noon, I texted her back, which earned me a thumbs-up emoji in reply. Not exactly a declaration of love or desire, but at least she hadn't changed her mind.

I'd take it.

At the restaurant, a chic but casual place overlooking the beach, we arrived first, and the hostess showed us to the table Laina had reserved while I tried not to look concerned. We were a little early, I reminded myself. My anxiety never let me arrive anywhere late, but Laina didn't share the same compunction, and that was fine. She didn't have to be there early, as long as she came.

"I haven't seen you look this nervous in years," my mom observed as she leaned back with a glass of the sparkling wine Laina had already ordered for the table. "Are you expecting a disaster?"

"They seem to be following me," I admitted. "Not very much has gone smoothly with Laina so far."

"And yet, here she is. It can't be all that bad if she keeps coming back for more."

My mom's eyes had wandered to a spot somewhere over my shoulder, and immediately, I twisted around to take a look for myself. She hadn't been teasing me; Laina really had just walked in and was heading to-wards us, looking as absolutely stunning as always in a white blouse and tan capris with strappy sandals. Just as they had at the other restaurant we went to, all the other diners turned to watch her go by.

That level of attention would still take me a while to get used to, but when I stood up to greet her and she leaned in to kiss my cheek, I felt like the luckiest man in the whole damn world.

"Mrs Reid." Laina moved from me over to my mother, who had also gotten to her feet, and she held her hand out confidently. "I'm glad to see you again under slightly better circumstances."

It didn't surprise me that Laina addressed their previous meeting right up front. If something could be dealt with head-on, that seemed to be her preferred way of handling it.

For her part, my mom shook Laina's hand politely. "You can call me Ruth. This is a lovely place you've chosen."

Even though Laina had seemed confident before, I could still see her shoulders relax at my mom's reply, making me realize she must have been a little nervous after all, though I didn't initially see it.

"Have you ordered yet?" she asked as she sat down.

"No, not yet." I pulled my own chair back in as I got settled again. "We were waiting for you to…"

"Excuse me?" A couple of young women, no older than twenty, cut me off as they walked up to our table, giggling nervously. "You're the couple in that video, right?"

My mind blanked, and for a moment, all I could think of was the scene I'd written the day before and how Laina and I had acted out parts of it afterwards. There wasn't a video of *that*, was there?

Thankfully, before I could get into a full-blown panic over something that didn't even exist, I realized what they were actually talking about: it had to be the viral video from the parking lot. They'd recognized the two of us from that.

"That's right," Laina answered with a smile, but that time, I *could* see her tenseness. She really did care about making a good impression on my mom, and she was worried this kind of interruption wouldn't help. "We're actually just about to order, so if you don't mind…"

"How did you get into porn?" one of the women asked, loud enough that people at the next table gave us a startled glance. "My boyfriend and I post videos but they don't get a lot of views."

"Get an agent," Laina advised her bluntly, keeping her voice down as she tried to bring the conversation to a close. "Amateur videos won't get you anywhere. Now, if you'll excuse us..."

"Do you do movies too?" the other woman asked me. "I tried to look you up but I couldn't find anything."

The idea that she'd been trying to find videos of me naked, and bluntly told me so in front of my mother had my cheeks flushing yet again. "No. Sorry. It's nice to meet you but..."

Neither of us seemed to be making any headway at getting them to leave without causing a scene, but thankfully, the waiter turned up at just that moment. "Is everything alright here?" he asked, looking between the women and our table with a firm authority that had the women soon retreating. When they'd gone, he turned to my mom with a smile. "Sorry about that, ma'am."

Laina and I both turned to my mom in surprise, and she shrugged as she took another sip of her wine. "While you two were both trying to be polite, I called the waiter over."

I'd missed that entirely, and so had Laina, apparently. She gave my mom an appreciative smile. "Thank you. I suppose I should have anticipated getting recognized after that video, but I thought in a family place like this, we'd be alright."

"You have to deal with this all the time?" my mom asked sympathetically, and I could see how much even that small amount of empathy meant to Laina.

"Should we order?" I suggested, and as we talked over the menu together, it felt like things were off to a pretty good start. One disaster had been averted, and hopefully, no further ones were on the way.

~Laina~

Talking with Dorian's mom felt surprisingly natural. Since she still lived in the town where I'd grown up, we knew a lot of the same people, and she caught me up on the latest dramas in town while we sipped our sparkling wine and laughed together over the craziness of small towns. Dorian didn't say much, just throwing in the odd off-hand remark that made me laugh, and looking between me and his mom with what looked like satisfaction on his face.

If he wanted to make it clear to me that his mom hadn't meant the things she'd said about me on the phone, he was doing a pretty good job, but I'd never been one for sweeping things under the rug, so as we finished up our meals, I leaned back with my glass of wine and brought the subject up directly.

"So, you must have questions about my job. I can explain the ways that it's different from prostitution if you like, but if you have any more specific questions, I'm happy to answer those too."

From the corner of my eye, I could see Dorian tense, but I kept my eyes on his mom instead, waiting to see how she'd respond. That would be the real test; would she be one of those people who didn't mind spending time with me so long as I hid everything about my career, a rather large part of my life, or was she willing to learn and hopefully, eventually, accept it? Dorian had already proven himself to be the latter, so the question simply remained: how much did he and his mother really have in common?

She didn't flinch, or tense up. Instead, she leaned forward, looking me straight in the eye. "I'm sorry for the things I said on the phone the other day. I was very surprised about the video, and about the whole situation, and I didn't take the time to process it fully before I called Dorian."

I could understand that, and I appreciated that she not only apologized for me hearing her, but for saying those things at all. "I've been known to say things before fully thinking them through too."

"I think we all have," Dorian interjected, but neither of us looked at him. This was between me and his mother, and she understood that as well as I did.

"But I'm curious, Laina," she continued. "You took offense at me comparing you to a prostitute, and you just brought it up again. Why would you look down on those women when you're essentially selling the same thing?"

"Mom." Dorian's tortured groan distracted me enough that I did look over at him that time. His cheeks were red, the same way they always got whenever he was embarrassed over something. He couldn't hide his feelings even if he tried, and I found it rather adorable.

"It's okay, Dorian. It's a valid question." Shooting him a quick, reassuring smile, I turned back to his mother. "I certainly don't look down on them, but from the tone of voice you used when you compared me to them, it seemed pretty clear to me that you did."

Her lips tightened, but she didn't argue with me, letting me continue my explanation.

"The reason I said there's a difference between what they do and what I do is because there is. First of all, prostitution is illegal in this state, but even if we ignore that fact, they're selling sex, plain and simple. What I'm selling is the *fantasy* of sex. My customers, the people who watch my movies, get to watch a carefully staged and edited version of a sexual encounter featuring me. They never get to see me or touch me, and they certainly don't get to have sex with me. That's the difference."

"But the men in those movies get to have sex with you," she pointed out.

"Yes, but they're not paying me for it. They're working and getting paid, just the same as I am. We're equals."

"And you don't feel it's inappropriate to have sex with other men while you're in a relationship?"

That was really the key question, and the one I knew most people didn't or couldn't understand. They thought that I couldn't truly be committed to a relationship if I had sex outside of it, but that philosophy had never made sense to me. "Different people have different ideas about what constitutes cheating. I don't judge how anyone else defines it, but to me, what I do in front of the camera has nothing to do with my personal life. It's simply a job and there are no emotions involved. If I were to have sex with that same man in private, it would be a completely different scenario."

"So, you only have sex off-camera with people you have feelings for?"

That question came from Dorian, rather hesitantly, and I glanced over at him in surprise. Did he really want to talk about our own situation right then?

I answered him as honestly as I always did. "Casual sex when I'm not in a relationship is a whole other category, but once I've agreed to be exclusive with someone, I am, in all the ways that count to me."

Mrs Reid sighed, drawing my attention back to her. "I can't say I fully agree, but then, it's not my life. If it works for you and the man you're with, I suppose that's all that matters."

I couldn't agree more. "I've never understood why people take what other people decide to do in their private lives quite so personally."

Some people might have taken offense at that, but Mrs Reid smiled. "I suppose because it makes them question their own lives, and that makes them uncomfortable. Life is easier when you think you have all the answers."

That sounded rather wise, and Dorian's mother overall struck me as a thoughtful, intelligent woman. I could certainly see where his consideration came from. "Do I make you uncomfortable?" I asked her straight out. If I did, I would prefer to know it up front.

"Surprisingly, no." She delivered that answer so drily that all three of us had to laugh. "I can't say I'm entirely comfortable with what I saw at your house yesterday, but it's made me think about why not, and the rather misogynistic view of pornography that I grew up with. Those ideas are probably due to be revisited anyway."

I couldn't ask for more than her willingness to look at things from a different perspective, and Dorian seemed pleased with how the conversation had gone too. "That sounds great, Mom, but if you're planning to revisit it on a more personal level, I don't think I need to hear about it."

Another round of laughter circled the table, and the waiter came over to clear our plates away. "Can I tempt anyone with dessert?"

Mrs Reid shook her head. "Not for me. I'm going to head back to the house now, but you two can stay and have some if you like."

Dorian's brow furrowed in confusion. "Go back? What do you mean? You came with me."

"And I can take a taxi back," she assured him. "Laina, it was nice to get to know you a little better, and I have a feeling I'll see you again before I go. Dory, take your time."

With that, she walked away, leaving the man across the table from me blushing again. "Sorry. That wasn't very subtle."

"Subtlety isn't really my thing anyway." His mom's actions actually felt like a seal of approval to me, like she knew that by leaving us alone, things might get more serious between us, and by giving us that space, she'd given us her blessing. Maybe I read too much into it, but it felt that way to me. "I'm not really interested in dessert, but a walk on the beach sounds nice."

Dorian quickly agreed, and after I'd paid, we headed out the door together, neither of us quite sure what came next.

Chapter Fourteen

~Dorian~

I remained vigilant as we walked out of the restaurant, ready for any other photo-seekers or fans who might have been waiting to approach Laina until we left, but it proved unnecessary. We walked out unimpeded and made our way down to the sandy expanse of Zuma Beach where a few surfers were out in the water while sunbathers lounged on their towels, soaking up the rays. It looked exactly like I'd expected California to look, and having Laina there beside me made it exceed even the biggest expectations I'd had for my move.

"Are you going to be okay to walk in those?" I asked her, looking down at the pretty sandals she wore.

"No, but there's an easy solution." Putting one hand on my shoulder to steady herself, Laina reached down and slipped the sandals off, one after the other. "There. That's better."

She wiggled her painted toes in the sand to emphasize her point, making me smile. She seemed to be in a good mood, which relieved me since I really didn't know how the conversation with my mom had made her feel.

I decided to ask her straight out rather than wondering about it. "I'm sorry if that got uncomfortable for you at all back in the restaurant. My mom can be pretty blunt at times."

"I didn't mind at all." Laina sounded completely sincere as we began walking down the beach, the straps of her sandals looped over her fingers, making them swing gently as she walked. "I'd much rather have someone ask me questions and try to understand than sit there quietly, judging. I'm glad you got us in the same room, Dorian. I like her."

That meant so much to me, since I was pretty sure my mom liked Laina too, despite the misgivings she had. If Laina and I were going to have a relationship beyond merely friendship, it would be important to me that the two most important women in my life respected each other, even if they didn't always see eye-to-eye.

Next, I just had to find out if Laina and I were on the same page at all when it came to moving the relationship between us to the next level. Usually, I had that talk with a woman before I had sex with her, not after, but nothing about the last week with Laina had been typical, so why should that conversation be any different?

"In that spirit, do you mind if I ask you a question?"

Her eyes darted over to me for just a second, and I wondered if she guessed what I wanted to discuss. After all, I hadn't been entirely subtle with my question back in the restaurant either. "Go ahead," she invited. "I'm an open book. Or an open movie, maybe? There should be a version of that phrase for those of us who don't read very well."

That reminder of what she'd shared with me the night before reinforced to me that she felt comfortable around me, which had to be a good thing. I'd certainly started to feel more comfortable around her, and that didn't come easily for me with anyone. Though I still stuck my foot in my mouth occasionally, it seemed to be happening less and less often.

After glancing around to double check no one else could overhear our conversation, I got straight to the point. "The first time we had sex, it was part of our agreement. We did it to help with my writing, but the other times, it sort of just happened."

Laina didn't disagree with that, but she didn't say anything either. When I also paused, waiting for her to reply, she raised her eyebrows at me. "That's not a question."

I supposed not. "Well, I guess my question is: what did those other times mean to you? What do you think the situation between us is?"

My shoes dug into the sand, my legs feeling more leaden than usual as I waited for her response.

When it came, a smile accompanied it. "Honestly, I wanted to ask you the same thing, but since you got there first, I suppose I have to answer."

I appreciated that. Going first in those kinds of situations was never easy.

Her next words were as blunt as ever. "I like you, Dorian. However..."

The pause she took there, inhaling the ocean air deeply, nearly killed me. However what?

"I just got out of a relationship and I wasn't looking to jump into another one right away."

"I get that," I quickly assured her. "Breakups affect people in a lot of different ways. I already told you that mine led to me moving out here."

As the words came out of my mouth and I heard how self-absorbed they sounded, I winced. We were talking about her and *her* feelings, not me.

"When did your relationship end?"

Laina looked over at me with an almost sheepish smile, an expression I hadn't really seen on her face before. Usually, she looked so confident and in control. "The night you moved in."

"What?" I definitely hadn't been expecting that answer, and it made my stomach twist uncomfortably. Was I just a rebound for her? A distraction? I hadn't gotten that impression at all, but the fact that she hadn't even mentioned it to me left me wondering if I'd misread everything. She'd had plenty of opportunities to bring it up.

"That sounds so much worse than it is," Laina groaned. "I didn't set out to hide it from you. It's just that we didn't really know each other that night, so it would have been an odd thing to mention, and then, as the days have gone on, I honestly haven't even thought about it that much. My thoughts have had a completely different focus instead."

From the way she smiled at me, it seemed clear that she meant she'd been thinking about me, which gave me a little more hope, but I still felt thrown off. "Were you serious with him?"

"Yes?" The word came out as a question, and Laina groaned again. "I don't know, actually. We were together for six months, but just when I thought we were getting closer, he pulled away."

"Why?" Six months wasn't nothing. I couldn't imagine spending that much time with Laina and then walking away.

"The usual," she replied with a shrug. "My job got too much for him. He thought he'd be okay with it, but he wasn't. I've heard that break-up speech so many times that it's an instant and permanent turn-off for me now. I have absolutely no desire to get back together with him. I don't even miss him. He's dead to me."

That sounded quite extreme, and my face must have reflected my concern, because Laina laughed.

"I mean that in a very non-violent way, but life is too short to waste pining over someone who never deserved the chance they got. So, I'm not grieving the relationship, but I also wasn't looking for anything other than to say hi when I saw you moving in and came over."

That gave me a lot of new information I hadn't had before, but she still hadn't actually said a word about her feelings for me, if she in fact had any. "And now? What are you looking for now?"

"Now..." She trailed off again before throwing the ball back into my court. "Now, I'd like to hear what your thoughts are. What do you think is happening between us?"

~Laina~

Dorian gave me a penetrating look when I asked for his opinion on the situation between us. He'd already called me out once before on how I deflected from discussing myself, or anything too personal, and he seemed to have noticed I did it again. I didn't mean to; I just didn't know exactly how to explain how I felt.

"Well, my break-up happened a lot longer ago than yours did, so I don't have qualms about getting into a relationship in general. How I feel about getting into one with you specifically depends a lot on how you feel about it. So, what are you looking for now?"

He repeated his question, refusing to let me off the hook, and I had to admit I kind of admired that. I knew my strengths and weaknesses, and sometimes, I needed someone to hold me to account and not let me get away with glossing over things. The Dorian I met outside his moving truck hadn't seemed like that kind of man, but with each passing day, he'd grown more and more confident, to the point that he wouldn't back down when I didn't tell him what he wanted to know.

"Well, I still wouldn't say I'm *looking* for a relationship, but sometimes, things just find you, whether you're looking for them or not."

The tentative smile I offered him was returned sincerely, but he didn't say anything, still waiting for me to elaborate further.

"In some ways, you're not like the men I usually date. They're often extroverted, with flashy jobs and flashy lives. They like to be seen, and I know that's not you."

Dorian nodded thoughtfully. "No, it's not, but those other relationships haven't worked out, right? So maybe you actually need something else?"

"I was getting to that," I teased him, smiling as his cheeks began to turn red again. "The flip side of their confidence and love of attention is that they care a lot about what people think. You're not like that, either. You're an incredibly successful author, but you hide behind your pen name, not taking any of the accolades for yourself. When the video got out, you didn't care what people said about you, only about how it would affect me. I've misjudged your motivations at times, like when you showed up at my house, because I didn't understand where you were coming from. A man like you, concerned more about me than about yourself, is a bit of a foreign concept to me."

Expressions ranging from hopefulness to confusion to concern flitted across Dorian's face. "I honestly can't tell if you mean that as a good thing or not."

On that point, I could reassure him. "It's a good thing, Dorian. Definitely a good thing."

He let out a breath in relief. "Okay, so..."

"Wait. I'm not done yet." Now that he'd gotten me started, I wanted to get it all out. "It worries me a bit, though. You're a private person, and I respect that. You like your anonymity, but as you've already seen, my life is just the opposite. People love your work but don't know your face, while my face is the most recognizable thing about me. If this movie that I want to make does well, it might even get more of a mainstream audience. Do you really think you can handle that kind of scrutiny for the long-term? Just the last few days have been a lot."

Men had a tendency to assure me they could handle any challenges I warned them about, and then failing to do so, but Dorian didn't immediately promise me it wouldn't be an issue. He took a moment to really think it over as we kept walking, my feet sinking into the warm sand that pushed its way between my toes and the sun gently baking my skin.

"It's a whole new world for me," he finally admitted. "I can't say that I'll love it, and I can't say that I'll ever get used to people thinking they have a right to you just because they've seen you on a screen. But you've learned to live with it, and I think I could too, as long as you're patient with me."

Again, his thoughts were primarily about me rather than himself. That protective instinct of his was another new thing for me in a man. I'd had plenty of possessive ones, but never someone who so naturally wanted to shield me from anything unpleasant. He would have to learn that wouldn't always be possible, but at least he seemed willing to learn, and willing to acknowledge he didn't already have all the answers.

There was more to think about, though. "What if being associated with me hurts your business?"

His lips tightened into a frown. "Why would it? No one knows who I am."

"Not at the moment, but sometimes, secrets get out. I've taken precautions so that if my real name ever became public knowledge, no one would be able to track me down, or at least not without some impressive computer hacking skills. I don't think it will happen and I take a lot of care to make sure it won't, but sometimes, things just go wrong. So, think this through with me: imagine that tomorrow, the world wakes up to the news that J.M. Everlee and Dorian Reid are one and the same. They already know that Dorian Reid has been seen with Jenny Vixxen. Suddenly, your readers know that they're reading books by a man who's dating a porn star. What does that mean for your business?"

Dorian fell silent again, leaving only the sound of the surf washing onto the beach lingering in the air.

When he spoke again, he didn't answer the question. Instead, he asked one of his own. "Why are you trying to scare me off? If you're not interested, Laina, just say so. I can handle it, but right now, it feels like you're trying to make me be the one to walk away."

"I'm not trying to push you away."

He didn't look convinced. "Really?"

"Really." Taking a deep breath, I lay it all on the line for him, as openly and honestly as I could. "I just want you to go into this with your eyes open, because if we do this? If you say you can handle it, and we get together, and you make me fall for you even more than I already am, and then you say that it's too much? *I* couldn't handle that. Not again. Not from you."

His face looked uncharacteristically tight as we came to a stop, turning to face each other, both of us doing it naturally, as if it had been planned.

"So, before you say you want something more with me, I want you to be completely, totally sure, that you know what you're getting into. If you walk away right now, there'll be no hard feelings, I promise. I'll understand. We can still work together, if you want to. We can still lend each other sugar, or whatever the hell neighbours do these days. But if you say you want to try, then you need to be okay with *all* of it."

His kind eyes looked down at me, as conflicted as I'd ever seen them, while I forced myself to stop talking and wait to hear what he would say in response.

~Dorian~

In the last minute, Laina might have told me more about herself than she had in the whole week before that. I heard so many different things in what she'd said, things I needed a second to absorb as she looked up at me with her beautiful blue eyes staring straight at me and those gorgeous pink lips of hers slightly parted, waiting for a response.

First, she said she was falling for me. It got tucked away in the middle of her sentence, trying not to draw any attention to it, but I heard it anyway. *If you make me fall for you even more than I already am.* That had to mean she'd already started to, and the thought made my whole body feel lighter as my heart tried to float out of my chest.

The first girl I'd had a crush on, the one I judged all other women against, the one I never in a million years dreamed would be back in my life in any way, just admitted she had feelings for me. I wished I could go back and tell my teenage self that, to give him something to hold onto when things got rough.

That wasn't all she said, though. I'd accused her of trying to scare me off, but the more she explained, the more I understood why she did it. It wasn't because she didn't want me, since she'd just admitted that she did. The worst-case scenarios, all the doom and gloom, talking about my identity being exposed and all the rest of it, came from a place of self-defense. Previously, she'd told me about men who let her down, and it sounded like the guy she'd just broken up with had been the same. She didn't want to go through that again, and I could understand that completely.

What I heard clearest of all was that she wasn't invincible. She got hurt, just the same as anyone else did, no matter how beautiful or successful or confident she might be. Even at that moment, with the bright California sun shining down on her, reflecting off her blonde hair like a halo, making her look almost angelic, she was still a woman like any other, and at the very essence of everything she'd said, I could hear her very simple request.

Don't break my heart.

I had absolutely no intention of it, and I laid that out for her as clearly as I could.

"Laina, I can't see the future. I can't say for certain that nothing will ever come between us, but I can say this: I accept your job and everything that comes with it. I understand that if we start dating, you'll continue to have sex with other men in front of the camera. I understand that when we go out in public, people will want to talk to you. Sometimes, I'll think they're wildly inappropriate and you won't, but I'll work on understanding where the line is for you. And I understand that, even if you have trouble reading, you're a damn good businesswoman and a talented writer. Have I covered it all?"

The appreciation in her eyes would have been answer enough, even if she hadn't spoken out loud. Her words, when they came, were gently teasing. "That speech deserves a place in one of your books. I guess people don't write romance stories about porn stars, though, do they?"

I'd never read one, but it didn't mean she didn't deserve a real romance. "They should. And even if they don't, it doesn't matter. We can write our own."

That actually sounded like something one of my characters would say, and Laina seemed to agree as a smile slowly spread across her face. "Are you for real, Dorian Reid?"

"I think so?" I patted my chest as if I were checking, hoping to make her laugh, and it worked. "You can touch me yourself to make sure."

Instantly, her expression turned more heated, her laughter turning into a sigh of contentment. "I might just take you up on that."

She leaned forward, her hand reaching up to wrap around my neck and pull me down to her, but just before our lips connected, someone shouted at her, using her stage name.

"Jenny!"

We both turned to look, expecting another of her fans, but instead, a man with a professional-looking camera stood there, his pants rolled up and his feet bare as he snapped photos of us without saying another word.

"Someone from the restaurant must have posted about us being there," Laina muttered under her breath before smiling over at the man. "Hey. How about we pose for a couple of pictures and then you can go on your way?"

The man gratefully accepted her offer, while I once again marvelled at how calmly she handled everything that came with her fame. When the photographer said he'd like one of us hand-in-hand looking at the ocean, Laina turned to me to see if I'd agree, speaking quietly again so he couldn't hear.

"If you do this, everyone will know we're together."

"That's fine with me if we really are together. Are we?" She still hadn't actually said the words, but once again, I read it in her eyes before she said it.

"I guess we are. Now, pretend you're happy."

I didn't have to pretend at all, smiling genuinely while we posed for the pictures, trying to act as if we didn't know the camera was there. The photographer kept his word; as soon as he had the photos he wanted, he wished us a good afternoon and left us alone, and Laina turned back to me.

"Is your mom expecting you back anytime soon?"

Although I'd invited my mom out to California, I couldn't bring myself to feel bad about ditching her, not if I got to spend time with Laina instead. "It didn't really sound that way. She can take care of herself, and if she runs into trouble, she's got my number."

"Good." Laina's pleased smile told me she'd been hoping for that answer. "In that case, I think we should head back to my place where we can have a bit of privacy."

That sounded perfect to me. Still holding hands, we turned back towards the restaurant, our cars, and the promise of the rest of the day together.

Chapter Fifteen

~Laina~

Dorian's hand in mine as we walked back along the beach seemed both surreal and perfect at the same time. For me, that small gesture of intimacy almost seemed like a bigger deal than sleeping with him had. It suggested that we trusted each other not only with our bodies, but with our hearts too.

We were still only at the very beginning. Maybe in a week's time, or a month's time, we'd find we weren't compatible after all. As he said, neither of us could see the future, but that possibility didn't really bother me, so long as he didn't go back on what he'd just said about accepting the professional part of my life completely. Every breakup I'd had in recent memory came back to something about my job. If Dorian and I broke up but had a normal breakup, over the kinds of things that people usually broke up over, I would consider that a welcome change.

I didn't want to think about breakups at that moment, though. We still had so much to learn about each other, and that afternoon would be the perfect time to start.

Since we'd driven separately, he followed me back up the hill to my house, his car behind mine, staying close behind but not too close. Supportive but not interfering, it felt like a good representation of his general approach to me, and I could definitely get used to it. I'd taken my own car to lunch just in case things got awkward and I wanted to leave. I didn't want to be reliant on anyone else, and where some of my boyfriends found that frustrating, Dorian seemed to understand it.

Just one more way he'd proven himself to be different from all the other men in my past. Maybe I've just needed a slightly awkward, shy guy all along.

After parking my car in the drive, I shook my head at myself, trying to stop myself from getting carried away. We'd only agreed to date each other. From the way my stomach fluttered as he stepped out of his car, big and strong and handsome with a sweet, excited smile on his face, people would have thought he'd asked me to marry him or something.

"You don't have to do any work today?" Dorian asked as I let us in through the front door. His hand wrapped around mine again naturally once we'd kicked our shoes off and headed to the living room.

"There's plenty of work I *could* be doing, but nothing that urgently needs to get done. If I didn't make myself take some time off, it would be easy to work all day, every day."

As we went to sit on the couch, I planned to sit next to him, but Dorian pulled me into his lap instead, his strong arms wrapping around me in a way that made me feel safe and protected and needed, like he didn't want any distance between us at all.

"I get that," he assured me. "It's the same for me. Part of the reason I moved out here was to try to find a better work/life balance. If I didn't go to the gym, I wouldn't have left the house at all for the past six months."

"Well, I definitely appreciate the results of that dedication to your health." My fingers trailed across his shirt, their tips pressing against the firm strength of his muscles even through the fabric. "But I'm sure we can find some other ways to keep you in shape now that you're here."

"Oh?" His voice took on that tighter quality that happened every time he started to get turned on. He had several adorable little quirks like that, and there were probably more I hadn't even noticed yet. I couldn't wait to learn them all. "Like what?"

He shifted beneath me, as if I wouldn't feel his cock starting to get harder if he adjusted his position, ignoring the fact that I *wanted* to feel it. Pretending to be getting more comfortable, I wiggled my ass on his lap, pressing down directly on his cock as Dorian inhaled sharply. "Well, there's my pool, for one. I do laps most mornings, and you're always welcome to join me. Sometimes, I even swim naked."

He groaned as I moved my hips again, applying just a bit more pressure to his groin. "Do you really?"

"Of course. It's my pool, I can do what I like. If I want to go skinny dipping, I will."

As soon as the words were out of my mouth, Dorian's expression changed, his cheeks starting to redden again, not in arousal, but in embarrassment. "I've never been skinny dipping on purpose. The closest I ever came was in high school when Cody Morrison stole my trunks during gym class."

I'd forgotten all about that, but as soon as he mentioned it, my memory took me straight back to that day. The strong smell of chlorine in the school pool and the afternoon sun streaming in the high windows, and the sound of laughter as Cody held up Dorian's swimsuit. The teacher had left early for some reason, trusting a bunch of 18-year-olds to get out of the pool and changed on our own, but the jerks from the football team had other ideas.

"Give them back, please." Dorian's voice could barely be heard above the shouts of laughter, his face bright red as he tried to cover himself with his hands and stay afloat in the water at the same time.

"Oh, you want them?" Cody taunted, placing the trunks down about six feet from the pool's edge, tantalizing close, but not close enough for Dorian to reach. "Come and get them."

In conversation with some of my friends, it had taken me a minute to figure out what was going on. I had no idea how they'd gotten his trunks off in the first place, but as I took in the whole scene, I knew I had to step in. Always happy to pick on someone further down the school's food chain from him, Cody would back off when someone from an equal social status challenged him. Only a few days remained in our senior year, and I couldn't wait to get out of that school and out of that town. I'd had enough of all of that bullshit.

"Hey, Cody." All eyes turned to me as I walked over to him, still in my swimsuit, patting my chest dry to call his attention to it, not that it took much. "Are you busy tonight?"

He glanced over at me in surprise and obvious interest; surprise because we'd never really gotten along, and interest because he was shallow enough to think he actually had a chance with me. "No, I'm free. You want to do something?"

I smiled at him sweetly. "No, I'm busy."

A scowl immediately darkened his face. "Then why did you ask?"

"Because you're going to need some time to recover."

Before he could ask me what that meant, the question that was obviously on the tip of his tongue, I stepped closer to him, grabbed hold of his shoulders, and kneed him hard in the crotch. Gasps and even a couple of screams echoed in the large, airy room as Cody doubled over in pain, swearing like a sailor. Meanwhile, I bent down to pick up Dorian's trunks off the floor and tossed them back into the pool.

"Grow up, all of you," were my parting words as I headed to the girl's change room with Dorian's grateful expression lingering in my mind.

That same man, older but still just as gentle and sweet, held me even tighter as I gave him a sympathetic smile.

"I'd forgotten all about that.

"I thought you might have," he admitted. "I'm sure it meant a lot more to me than it did to you, but things like that were why I thought you were the coolest girl in school by far."

"You don't still let that crap bother you, do you?" I hadn't thought about high school in a long, long time, and I hoped Dorian didn't dwell on it either. He'd accomplished so much since then, and those other guys had never been worth losing sleep over anyway.

"I try not to, but sometimes, it just pops into my head anyway."

That, I could understand. "Well, how about we replace it with a new memory instead? We could go for a swim right now, and whenever you think of skinny dipping from now on, *that* will be the memory that comes to mind. You'll never have to think of the other one again."

That time, rather than trying to shift his hardening cock away from me, he pulled me down onto it even harder instead. "I'd fucking love that, Laina."

With a grin, I got to my feet, pulling him up after me, and we headed outside into the warm afternoon sun.

~Dorian~

Laina's idea to create a new memory couldn't have been more perfect. The sharp edges of that long-ago humiliation had already been dulled with time, but with Laina at my side, grinning at me, as she pulled off her shirt and threw it onto one of the deck chairs beside her pool, I knew I'd never think of that day again without thinking of this one too.

She'd been my hero on that occasion, among others, even though she hadn't known it. To her, it hadn't been anything out of the ordinary, nothing she felt she deserved accolades for, but she did, and I had never had the chance to thank her properly. Hopefully, I could remedy that omission that afternoon.

Both of us eager to get in the pool, we raced to see who could strip down the fastest, laughing as we fumbled over our buttons and zippers.

Laina beat me in the end, but only because my already-stiff cock slowed me down, getting caught in my underwear as I tried to pull it down. Laina's eyes dropped to my cock in appreciation, lingering there for just a few seconds, before she gave me a wink, and stepped over to the pool, diving in gracefully, her naked body shimmering below the surface that twinkled in the afternoon sun.

"What are you waiting for?" she asked with a laugh when she resurfaced, seeing me still standing there beside the pool.

"Just enjoying the view," I told her honestly. With her hair slicked back and droplets of water shining on her face and shoulders, she looked like a mermaid or some kind of siren, beckoning me to join her.

"Mine's not bad either," she teased me back. "But if you want to touch rather than just look, you'll have to get in."

I didn't need any further incentive than that, but with my erection, jumping in after her seemed potentially dangerous. I took the steps instead, making Laina laugh again.

"That's a rather large flotation device you've got there. I might need to hang onto it if I get in trouble."

Her words sent a rush of heat through me, counteracting the cooling effects of the water. "Don't worry, it won't slow me down. I bet I can still catch you."

Swimming was part of my workout at the gym, good for endurance and cardio, and I'd never been happier about that fact as Laina's eyes twinkled in anticipation. "Do you want to bet?"

"What are we betting?"

She didn't hesitate for a second. "I give you two minutes to catch me. If you do, you get a blow job. If you don't, you have to eat me out."

My cock somehow got even harder. "Sounds like I win either way."

Laina's grin made her even more beautiful. "Me too. Ready? Go."

She barely gave me a chance to react before she took off, kicking the water behind her so it splashed in my face, and adrenaline raced through my veins as I took off in pursuit. While I might have had the edge in strength, Laina turned out to be very nimble, changing course when I least expected it. Once, I thought I had her cornered, but when I reached out to grab her, she dove down and squeezed through my legs, leaving me grasping at only water. The words 'slippery as a fish' had never felt more apt.

I had no idea how we would know when two minutes were up, but as long as she kept going, I'd keep trying to catch her, both wanting to win and wanting to lose at the same time. I honestly couldn't have said which I wanted more.

A moment later, I had her trapped again, and that time, she tried to fake me out by starting to go around me one way and then twisting back the other. I saw her eyes dart the other way, though, and when she made her move, she ran right into me.

"No!" she shrieked good-naturedly, squirming as my arms wrapped around her in the water, pulling her close to me so she couldn't get away again. Both of us laughed as the game came to an end, breathing heavily from the high-impact exertion, but as her body pressed against my still-hard erection, her laugh died away. Her tongue ran across her lips, wetting them in anticipation and making me even harder yet again. "I guess you win, then."

It certainly felt that way. "Do you need a minute to catch your breath?"

"Doesn't feel like you can wait a minute." Her hips tilted towards me, pressing against my cock more firmly and making me groan. "Come over here."

Slipping out of my relaxed hold, she led me to one end of the pool where a curved section of the poolside dipped down nearly to the water's edge. Following her instructions, I pulled myself up onto it, sitting facing her with my legs still dangling in the water but my cock almost entirely out of it. Laina remained in the water, at the perfect lap level.

"The realtor told me it was to make it easier for children to climb out, but I think it works better for this purpose," Laina explained with a laugh, gathering her wet hair behind her head before she took hold of my cock at the base. "Now, it's time for your prize."

Sitting in the warm sun, the water still dripping down my body as my new girlfriend's tongue dragged slowly up my shaft, her gorgeous blue eyes staring up at me the whole time, I had never felt luckier in my entire life.

She'd given me blow jobs before, but that time, it felt different. Before, it had only been about inspiring my writing, and pure lust. The lust remained, but other feelings had come into play. As the first sexual encounter of our brand-new relationship, it felt pretty fucking perfect.

Wanting to draw out my pleasure, Laina took her time, her tongue teasing and tasting me as it flicked around my head, tracing lines across every inch of me. My balls floated in the water as Laina played with them, her fingers gently stroking them as her tongue danced over my cock. Each time she reached the head, my breath caught, wondering if that would be the time she took me in. Would she take me all the way down her throat, as I knew she could, or would she suck on the end first, teasing me a little longer. When she moved back down without doing either, my anticipation only got stronger.

"Oh, fuck." Just when I thought I'd figured out her pattern, she surprised me, moving back to my head and taking me in half-way. As she pulled back, sucking me the whole way, her hand pulled gently at my balls, giving the sensation of me being stretched out in the most delicious way.

Smiling for just a second, Laina looked down as she took me in again, even farther that time, all the way, my head down her throat as I groaned again. How the hell had she learned how to do that? No one else had ever taken me that deep before.

The teasing had come to an end as Laina began to move in earnest, fucking me with her mouth right there in the open air, better than any scene I could have written. Her damp hair fell forward as she moved faster, so I reached down to gather it loosely behind her head while she bobbed up and down over my cock, and the sight of her, the feel of her mouth, the smell of the pool and the breeze and sun upon my skin soon overwhelmed me. I came as hard as I ever had, all the tension in my body releasing in an extraordinary wave of pleasure.

I must have blacked out for a second. When I opened my eyes again, Laina had let me go, wiping her mouth with the back of her hand as she offered me a sweet smile. "How's that for a memory?"

Still nearly weak with the aftereffects of my orgasm, I slid back down into the water's embrace. "It's a pretty damn good one," I told her, my voice raspy even though I'd literally done nothing but sit there. "But I think we can still make it even better."

Grabbing her again, I lifted her up into the seat that I'd just vacated.

"Put your knees on my shoulders. It's my turn now."

~Laina~

My legs shook as I hooked my knees over Dorian's shoulders, just as he'd asked me to. Already turned on from giving him the blow job and the pleasure he'd taken from it, the determined look on his face as we switched places had me fully throbbing with need. He'd already proven he knew what he was doing when it came to satisfying me, and for the first time, he'd be doing it as my boyfriend. It felt different to me, and I knew without him having to say it that it changed things for him too.

Leaning in close to me, his nose brushing against my clit, he inhaled deeply. "You know, I'm glad we never hooked up in high school."

"Oh?" I didn't expect those words, and forming an answer wasn't easy when he began to kiss me softly. Deeply. Intimately. "Wh... why's that?"

"I was a virgin until I was twenty-one," he admitted bluntly before dragging his tongue over my clit, making me shiver despite the warm sun shining down on my naked body. "I never even kissed a girl before college. I wouldn't have had a clue what to do with you."

"No one at that school did," I assured him. I had sex with a few of the guys there, not because I had any strong feelings for any of them, but because I was curious and bored, and there had been no shortage of willing partners. "Trust me, most men get much better with age, but I think you would have done your best even then. We could have had fun figuring it out together."

"Well, my best is a lot better now than it was then," he promised. "I think you must have gotten better over the years too, though. I can't imagine you being any more perfect than you are right now."

With that, his tongue plunged into me, putting an end to our conversation as my head fell back, my eyes closing as I focused entirely on the feel of him between my legs. His fingers rubbed my clit as he kissed my pussy, his tongue circling around my entrance and thrusting inside, as deep as he could go. A moment later, he changed it up, his mouth going to my clit as his fingers began to fuck me, slowly and steadily.

The best thing about my house's location atop the hill at the bend in the road was that my neighbours really weren't all that close. No one could see into my yard, and the sound didn't carry. Even if Dorian's mother were sitting out in his backyard, which she might very well have been at that moment, she wouldn't have heard any of the moans that came out of me as her son fucked me with his hand and his mouth.

"Fuck, just a little more, right there..." I gave him only the tiniest bit of direction and he figured it out, hitting all my spots perfectly until the tension inside me reached its tipping point. My legs trembled again, my thighs clenching around his head as I came, and Dorian raised his head in satisfaction, his lips still glistening.

"There. I think we both won."

To be honest, I'd forgotten all about our game, but I couldn't disagree. "I think we did. I'm not sure what to do now though."

With a deep, sexy chuckle, Dorian lifted me off the ledge and back into the water, holding me against his body firmly but gently at the same time. "How about we take it easy for a while? Curl up and watch a movie or something?"

Those were the kinds of things I loved most about being in a couple, and it seemed he felt the same. "That sounds perfect."

After we dried off and got dressed again, we headed back inside. I popped some popcorn while Dorian found something to watch on TV, and I grabbed some of my throw blankets to make us comfortable. Somewhat surprisingly, we made it almost the entire way through the movie before his hand, which had been resting on my hip most of the time, began to move higher.

Soon, we'd abandoned the movie entirely, having sex again right there on the couch. By the time we'd cleaned up from *that*, it was approaching supper time.

"You should go and eat with your mom," I suggested, even though I didn't really want him to go. The whole afternoon had been relaxed and easy and wonderful.

"I should," he agreed, sounding equally reluctant. "Or I could invite her to come and join us here, if that's okay with you?"

He didn't seem to want to be away from me for a moment, and though I made some half-hearted protests, in the end, I agreed to his plan. It didn't really matter anyway, because no more than ten minutes after he left to go and get her, Dorian returned empty-handed.

"She says she can eat on her own and that she's seen me a lot more in the last ten years than you have, so you can have priority for tonight. She told me there's no need for me to come back home tonight either." He shook his head in amusement as he relayed her response to me. "Her support is really sweet and a little disturbing at the same time."

Though I smiled at his assessment of the situation, I didn't say anything, and Dorian's cheeks immediately began to redden.

"I mean, that's only if you want me to stay. I know you haven't invited me to yet, I'm just telling you what she said..."

"Dorian." Pressing the tip of my index finger to his lips, I cut off his rambling. "It's fine. You can stay if you want to. I don't usually have men stay over unless we're in a relationship, but we said that we are, so you're welcome to."

"I would really like that," he admitted, still looking adorably flustered.

"Good. Let's have some supper, then, and we can have an early night."

We ordered some takeout and ate it in the backyard, watching the sun set over the ocean, and life had rarely seemed so perfect.

When the time came to bring him to my room, I watched his reaction carefully, curious to see what he would make of it. Like the living room, my bedroom had been inspired by the Italian villa I stayed in, and its large four-poster bed, antique sofas in front of the fireplace and yellow walls weren't to everyone's taste.

Dorian, however, seemed to appreciate it. "It's like something from a fairy tale," he exclaimed, his enthusiasm sounding completely genuine. "Do you ever film in here? It must look amazing on camera."

I loved that he brought my work up in a positive way, curious and respectful, and I answered him honestly. "No. This is my personal space. None of my co-stars have ever been in here. Jenny doesn't exist in here. Only Laina does."

Dorian's hand found my face, cupping my cheek gently as his fingers hooked under my chin, lifting it up until my eyes met his. "That's perfect, because Laina is the one I want to make love with tonight in that bed."

I wanted that too. It almost scared me how much I wanted it. It would be so, so easy to fall for him completely. I was afraid I already had, and it terrified me a little bit to put so much trust in another person. Could he really be as different from all the others as he said? Could he be the one I'd been waiting for?

Could he be 'the one'?

As he took me in his arms again, it really started to feel like he could.

Chapter Sixteen

~Dorian~

Having only been in my new house for just over a week, it didn't shock me when I woke up and didn't immediately recognize my surroundings. It did, however, take me a moment to realize that not only was I not in my old house, the room didn't belong to me at all. The canopied bed above me could only belong to one person.

Immediately, I turned my head to see Laina still asleep beside me, looking somehow even more beautiful in sleep than she did during the day. Maybe it had to do with how relaxed she seemed, how vulnerable and how trusting. Though I loved her feisty, independent nature, or the playful gleam in her eye depending on her mood, the softer side of the woman lying next to me made me want to wrap her up in my arms and protect her, just as she'd protected me so many times in the past.

I'd never felt luckier than I did at that moment, or happier, looking forward to what came next but also perfectly satisfied in the moment. That was the kind of stuff I wrote about in my books, the kind of feelings I'd never had before in my own life. The previous day had given me all kinds of new inspiration for my books, and I had a feeling that each and every day with Laina would be inspirational in its own way.

Maybe she felt me looking at her, or maybe we were just in tune enough that she woke up just after me, but either way, her eyes blinked open, slowly and sleepily, and when she saw me there, still looking over at her, a warm, contented smile spread across her face. "Good morning. Have you been up for long?"

"No, not at all. I'm sorry if I woke you."

"I'm a light sleeper, it's not your fault. Did you sleep well?"

We were both being polite and a little tentative, not sure how the other felt after all the intimacies of the previous day, sexual and emotional. Though I understood that, I didn't want tentative; I wanted her to know just how happy I felt to be there with her, so I leaned over to kiss her as my answer.

"I slept much better when you didn't kick me out immediately after we had sex."

She laughed as if it were a joke, but I hadn't been entirely joking. "Well, before, you were a hookup. Now, you're my boyfriend, and that earns you sleepover privileges."

I fucking loved to hear the word 'boyfriend' from her mouth, referring to me. "Yes, I am, and I need to know what Laina Macintyre needs in the morning. Breakfast in bed? Coffee? Another orgasm to start her day off right?"

My hand drifted down her body, still naked from the last time we made love the night before. I was naked too, mostly since I didn't have any clothes at her place. I'd have to put the previous day's clothes back on to go home, but I didn't care. My mom already knew I'd spent the night with Laina, and honestly, I'd shout it from the rooftops if I could. This incredible woman had somehow agreed to be mine.

Laina sighed as my hand brushed across her breasts, but all too quickly, the sigh turned to a groan. "I'm afraid I don't have time. I've got a meeting this morning, a few people are actually coming over here.

You don't need to rush out if you don't want to, but unfortunately, I do need to get up and get ready."

That disappointed me, but I understood. We both had careers that needed our attention. Not every day could be like the one before. "I really need to get my editor the chapters I promised too, so I should go anyway. Can I make you breakfast while you get ready?"

She lifted her head off the pillow to kiss me. "That sounds perfect, thank you."

My clothes back on, I headed to the kitchen while Laina jumped in the shower. With a little scrounging in her cupboards, I found what I needed to make some pancakes to go with the fruit and yogurt in her fridge.

Laina appeared just as the last of the pancakes came off the stove, holding her laptop in her hands, and her eyes glimmered with excitement. "I just had a new idea about my film. It came to me in the shower, but it's partly inspired by you. Can we brainstorm over breakfast?"

"Of course." My enthusiasm genuinely matched hers. I'd never dated anyone who also worked in a creative industry, someone who didn't mind examining the minutiae that went into an individual scene or debating in which order the words best belonged.

I could get used to it.

We got so caught up in our discussion that when Laina's doorbell rang, we both jumped in surprise. "That'll be Erica," she told me, getting to her feet. "My business partner. Do you want me to introduce you?"

"Sure, that would be great." I loved that she already wanted to include me in her life that way. Of course, I'd already flown my mom out to meet her, so I might have set the precedent.

As Laina went to answer the door, I typed in a few of the notes and comments we'd just discussed into Laina's document so she could pick up her work on it later. Just as I entered the last sentence, a loud whistle rang out from behind me.

"He's even better looking in person," the brunette at the door announced, tossing a wink at Laina before coming up to me and holding out her hand confidently. "Erica Chilton."

"Dorian Reid. It's nice to meet you." I got up as I shook her hand, taking quick stock of her as she did the same to me. She was very pretty, but she had an air of confidence around her that felt almost aggressive, nothing like Laina's cool, laid-back style. If she wanted to, she could have me in tears, I had no doubt, and I quickly made myself busy with clearing the dishes off the table. "I'll get out of your way so you can get to work."

"What were you working on here?" Erica asked, gesturing to the laptop I'd just been typing on.

"Oh, that's Laina's script. We were just brainstorming." The dishes in my hands went to the sink, where I knew Laina's housekeeper would take care of them. "Laina, I've got to take my mom back to the airport later this afternoon, but I'll text you when I'm back?"

"You better." She came over to plant a chaste, sweet kiss on my lips. "Have a good day, Dorian."

"You too. And you, Erica."

I gave her a friendly wave, and she returned it, trying not to smile. I had a feeling they'd be talking about me the second I left the room, and though part of me was curious, all things considered, I figured it would probably be better if I *didn't* hear what they had to say.

Still feeling on top of the world, I headed outside and back to my own house. The whole world felt brighter than it had in a very long time, and I was already counting the minutes until I could see her again.

~Laina~

Erica smiled slyly over at me after Dorian left. "Staying the night now, is he?"

"Yes, he is." Grabbing my laptop and cup of coffee off the table, I headed over to the living room on the other side of the house where we would be meeting with the rest of our team as soon as they arrived. Erica had shown up a little early, as usual, and I figured I would bite the bullet and introduce her to Dorian right away since I suspected she'd already guessed at the latest development. "We're dating now, which I'm sure you've already seen in the tabloids."

The photographer who found us on the beach the day before must have already sold his photos, though I hadn't gone looking for them yet. I'd been a little busy.

As I expected, Erica already had them loaded on her phone, and it only took her a matter of seconds to pull them up, handing the phone over to me as we both took a seat. "Pretty wholesome and sweet, actually. Not really selling the porn star vibe there, Laina."

Maybe not, but the pictures still brought a smile to my face. The memory of Dorian's hand holding mine and the tender way he looked at me sent a flush of warmth through me, even though the man himself had left the building.

"You'd prefer us being pictured going into a swingers club?" I guessed as I handed the phone back to her.

Though Erica laughed, she didn't deny it. "I'd prefer something I can sell. Him beating up one of your fans? Amazing. Photos holding hands on the beach? Boring."

It hadn't felt all that boring to me. "Well, maybe I'm just becoming boring. Maybe your days of trading off my personal life are over."

Erica's smile looked strangely enigmatic. "I have a feeling there's still a bit more we can wring out of it."

Before I could ask what she meant by that, the doorbell rang again and the rest of our team arrived, the four other women who headed up our different departments, ready to go over our entire operation for the month. Erica went first, giving them an update on the incredible week we'd had after the viral video with Dorian and the new short we'd released. We'd made more in a week than we often did in a month, and there were no signs of it slowing down.

"We need more new content," she summed up, looking pointedly at me.

"We've got the film we wrapped shooting on earlier this week," I reminded her. "It's almost done editing, we can certainly have it up by next week. Right, Michelle?"

Our content manager nodded in agreement, but Erica wasn't satisfied. "You're not in it, though. The new people that are coming to the site want to see you specifically."

"They have my whole backlist to get through. It's huge." Nobody could claim I hadn't done my fair share of work for our company. "The short was one thing, but I'd rather spend my time working on the script for the new film. With this extra income, we can increase our budget and make it even better. We've got this whole new audience, and I really believe this will be the way to make an impression on them."

"Right. Your script." Erica looked down at the papers in front of her, but not before I saw the smile she tried to hide. "Have you spoken to J.M. Everlee yet about putting her name on it?"

"What?" A chorus of surprised exclamations rang out around the room, the other members of our team all exchanging surprised looks while I shot Erica a disapproving one.

"That was supposed to be between us." First, she'd gone to Dorian's agent, and now, she'd mentioned the collaboration to the rest of our team without asking me. Had she always been so loose with my personal boundaries? Or maybe it had just never come up since I'd never really had very many before.

"Are you really working with J.M. Everlee?" Sarah asked, her eyes wide. She handled our accounts, and I knew she was a big romance reader. She'd probably read all of Dorian's books. "What's she like?"

"The marketing writes itself," Jordan crowed. Since she oversaw all of our advertising, her thoughts naturally went in that direction. "J.M. Everlee and Jenny Vixxen: A Perfect Marriage of Love and Passion. Or maybe Romance and Sex. Which do you think is better?"

They all began chatting amongst themselves until I cleared my throat loudly. "Alright, let's back it up a second. Yes, I've been getting some advice from J.M. Everlee. No, she has not agreed to put her name on the script and I don't know if she will. That information is confidential and does not leave this room. Understood?"

The others all nodded, accepting my decision even if they would have preferred a different one, but Erica pursed her lips. "If we can't get official agreement, I think we should leak it. You don't even need to confirm it's true. Just get people talking about it."

"No. Not unless h... she's comfortable with it."

Fuck, that was close. Hopefully, it just sounded like I slurred my words a bit rather than that I'd been about to say 'he'.

Erica still refused to back down. "If she really didn't want to be associated with you, she wouldn't be working with you in the first place, and it's easier to ask forgiveness than permission. This is the perfect time to bring it up, when you've already got the buzz going from the video. We could get the presale for the movie up to capitalize on it."

"I said no, and that's final."

The atmosphere in the room had grown rather tense, all the other team members exchanging concerned looks as Erica and I butted heads. I very rarely pulled rank, but in the end, the business belonged to me and my word ruled.

Finally seeming to remember that, Erica conceded ungraciously. "Fine. If you want to leave money on the table, we'll do it your way."

It took all my self-control not to roll my eyes. "We've got plenty of money at the moment. Peggy, how are things going for the shoot next week?"

We moved on, our production manager taking over before the rest of the team had their turns, talking over the rest of the business, but some of the tension remained. As soon as we'd finished, Erica excused herself and left, even though traditionally, they all stayed for coffee. The other women all stayed, and without Erica there, we were soon back to our normal, chatty selves. They tried again to get me to give them some info on what the mysterious J.M. Everlee was really like, but I refused to offer up any details, saying only that I'd been learning a lot from 'her'.

Once they'd gone, I had a meeting first with my personal accountant and then with my insurance broker, neither of which I got any enjoyment from, but they needed to be done. Finally, I had an interview that Jordan had set up for me with one of the gossipy entertainment websites. One of their reporters and a cameraman came to the house, and we filmed the interview outside by the pool, the backdrop working just as well for an interview as it did for one of my films.

Although officially, the interview was supposed to be about the state of the adult film market, the reporter mostly wanted to talk about the video and photos with Dorian. I confirmed that Dorian and I had known each other for a while, had lost touch but recently reconnected, and that he was every bit as protective and sweet as he seemed in the video.

When she asked if there were any plans for him to join me in any of my movies, I had to smile to myself, remembering the scene he'd written and how we'd acted it out in my kitchen, not to mention what we'd done in the pool the day before.

"He's not an actor, but he's very supportive of my work."

I couldn't wait to see him again that evening, and when she started to wrap up her questions, my stomach fluttered happily.

"So, I think that's it. Thanks, Jenny. I'll send your PR people the link as soon as it's live and we'll..." The reporter trailed off as her phone screen lit up, something on it catching her eye. "Sorry, just give me one second."

Annoyance flashed through me as she picked up the phone. I'd left my phone in the other room to give her my full attention; she could have paid me the same courtesy.

When she looked back up, her eyes were bright. "Are we still rolling?" she asked the cameraman, and once he nodded, she turned back to me. "One more question, Jenny. You said that Dorian isn't an actor. What *is* his profession?"

What did that have to do with anything? I kept my answer short and vague. "He's self-employed."

"Doing what?"

"That's not really relevant." It felt like she had a specific reason for asking, but I didn't plan to volunteer any information I didn't have to.

A second later, it became clear exactly what she'd been hinting at, and my stomach, so recently light and filled with excitement, dropped right down to my feet.

"So, what do you have to say about the rumours that he is, in fact, the popular romance author, J.M. Everlee?"

~Dorian~

The outcome wasn't always certain, but as I gave my mom a goodbye hug at the airport, I couldn't be happier that she'd agreed to come. "Thank you for making the trip. I know it was a bit of a whirlwind, but next time, I'll be able to give you a proper tour."

She squeezed me a little tighter, like I was still a little boy rather than a grown man half a foot taller than her. "I'm glad if I helped, and I hope it all goes well for you, Dory. If she'll make you happy, then I'm happy for you. She's a lucky woman."

It felt like I was the lucky one, but I thanked her for the sentiment anyway, waving goodbye once again as she headed into the terminal and I went back to my car, eager to get home and see Laina again. It would be supper time by the time I reached home, and I'd already decided I would cook for her at my place that evening and she could stay over there. Living right next door was pretty convenient. She didn't need to worry about bringing all of her stuff over when she could just go home in the morning to get ready.

Maybe before too long, we'd live even closer than next door, but I didn't want to get ahead of myself. Things were still very new, and I knew she would still have to learn to trust me completely after the negative experiences in her past. She might be a bit skittish, but she'd agreed to give me a chance, and I was determined to make the most of it.

Still twenty minutes away from home, while I was caught up in some afternoon rush hour traffic, my phone began to ping. At first, I thought it might be Laina, but the pings kept coming, faster and faster over the next ten minutes. Curiosity had me tight in its grip, but there wasn't much I could do about it while driving, not until I got a call from my publisher which I could answer through the car's system.

"Hi, Emily," I greeted my editor. "I'm in the car right now. Have you been trying to reach me?"

"Me and half the world, probably." Her voice didn't hold a hint of humour. "Dorian, your identity's been leaked."

If she said anything immediately after that, I didn't hear it. The whole world around me seemed to go fuzzy for a second as my pulse spiked, my heart thudding painfully within my chest as my face flushed hot.

She couldn't be serious, could she? Laina had just asked me if I could handle that happening. Maybe she put Emily up to this as some kind of test? It didn't make a lot of sense, but neither did the fact that it actually happened. After all the years I'd managed to keep it a secret, why had it come out now? *How* had it?

When the ringing in my ears faded, Erica was still talking. "We're putting together a response as quickly as we can, but we need to ask you some questions. I'm looping in the PR team, hang on."

I barely had a chance to process any of that before a new voice spoke up, one I didn't know. "Dorian, my name's Cristiano, I'm one of the PR managers. As far as we see it, there are two separate issues here:

the revelation about your identity, and your relationship with Jenny Vixxen. We can address them both together if you want to, but I would recommend..."

"Hang on. Stop. Back up for a second." Obviously, I was missing a lot of context, and my voice shook just as much as my hands which gripped onto the steering wheel tightly to try to give myself some kind of anchor. "What got leaked? By whom? What happened?"

Emily's voice came through my car speakers. "We don't know who leaked it, but a rumour started circulating online early this afternoon that you're J.M. Everlee. I caught wind of it maybe three hours ago, but our official policy is not to say anything. There have been other rumours about your true identity before, which were never correct, and we never said anything about those."

That much, I could understand. "Alright, so we should just ignore this one too, but it sounds like you don't want to. Why the sudden change of heart?"

"Because of Jenny's interview," Cristiano answered me. He must not know that Jenny and Laina were the same person, so I'd have to be sure to remember to refer to her as Jenny too. "I'm sure you know that there are separate stories going around about you and Jenny Vixxen dating after that video from a few days ago."

"Yes."

"Are they true?"

"Yes." I had no intention of denying it after promising Laina I'd be proud to be associated with her. Not to mention that I *was* proud of it. "What interview are you talking about?"

"Earlier this afternoon, she did an interview which hasn't been posted in its entirety yet, but clips of it are already being circulated. In it, she was asked about the rumours that you're J.M. Everlee."

My mouth went dry as I once again remembered Laina asking me how I would feel if my secret got out. She wouldn't have asked that because she intended to leak it? I didn't want to believe that, but my thoughts were all over the place. I couldn't believe this was really happening. "What did she say?"

"She deflected. Said that any questions about J.M. Everlee should be directed to the publishing house."

Feeling began to return to my fingertips as I relaxed my grip on the wheel, turning up the street onto the hill that led up to my house. "That doesn't sound all that bad. Why can't we leave it at that?"

"Because although that's what she *said*, it took her a few seconds to respond, and everyone's focusing on those few seconds. She obviously had no clue the question was coming, and she absolutely froze. You want to know what someone means when they say a person looks like a deer caught in the headlights? Just watch that video. Her reaction gave it completely away. From an actress, I'd expect better."

Shit. It sounded like she'd been completely blindsided, and although I still felt rather ill at the idea that my carefully-curated writing persona appeared to be dead, a wave of concern for Laina washed over me too. Assuming she had nothing to do with the leak, which I didn't really think she did now that I had more of the details, she must feel terrible.

She hadn't wanted to cause any trouble for me, and yet, the worst had happened anyway.

I reached my driveway but kept on going, parking in front of Laina's house instead. "What are our options?"

Cristiano answered me just as bluntly as I'd asked the question. "The way I see it, you've really only got two. One: you deny it. We say outright that it's not true. The risk of that is that if something else gets out which proves it *is* true, then you're caught lying. The second option: you come clean. The risk of that is the backlash from people who aren't happy that you're a man in the first place, and that you're dating a porn star in the second. You could lose some readers."

"Or you could gain some," Emily countered. "It would be a big story and people would be talking about you. People might read your books just because they're interested in all the drama."

That reminded me of what Laina had said after our encounter with her fans in the parking lot: all press was good press. Emily seemed to agree, but I felt less sure. "Are they going to be the right kind of readers, though?"

We'd spent a lot of time working on reaching my ideal readers, carefully curating my advertisements, doing market research to ensure my new books would appeal to those same people. All that work seemed to be flying out the window.

Emily obviously understood that, and she couldn't see the future any more than I could. "I don't know, Dorian. If you go public, things will change, that's for sure. I guess you just need to decide if it's worth it."

That wasn't an easy question to answer. I hated the idea of people talking about me, my face being plastered everywhere, or being stopped on the streets. I hated the idea of people judging my books based on my gender rather than my words. Those were the reasons I'd stuck with the pen name as long as I had.

But if I told them to deny it, not only would it be dishonest, but it might send the message to Laina that I didn't want to be associated with her. It might undo all the goodwill I'd tried to build up with her, and nothing in the world felt more important to me than that.

If I kept my anonymity but lost Laina, would that be worth it? I didn't have to think about that for even a second.

"Go ahead with the truth. Send me the draft statement before you release it. I've got to go for now."

Hanging up before they could say anything else, I got out of my car and headed up Laina's driveway, eager to see her and hear her side of the story. She'd probably tried to reach me too but I didn't even bother checking my phone. I'd much rather speak to her in person.

However, before I could even reach the doorbell, I saw the note taped to the door with my name on it.

In confusion, I snatched the piece of paper and opened it up, finding almost a full page of handwriting, which I had to guess couldn't have been easy for her with her dyslexia. Why wouldn't she have texted or emailed me instead?

As I tried to read it, my eyes refused to focus, my heart beating too fast and my hands shaking. Maybe that was how she felt when she tried to read too? I couldn't seem to take it in at all, but finally, a few phrases stood out to me.

... better if we're not seen together...

... I understand if you want to deny everything...

... I'm sorry...

At the bottom were the words that truly made my stomach drop.

I'll check in when I get back in a few weeks. I'm sorry it had to end this way, but I know you're too nice to take this step on your own. This is your career, a career you love, and I won't be responsible for ruining it.

I'll remember this time fondly always.

Laina

Chapter Seventeen

~**Laina**~

I knew the second I answered the question that I'd screwed up. The satisfied look on the reporter's face made it clear that she thought she'd got something good, and I felt almost sick as I ushered her and the cameraman out of my house as quickly as I could.

What the hell had I done?

When the woman asked me if Dorian was J.M. Everlee, several different things fell into place in my head. Erica had to be the source of the 'rumours'. It couldn't be anyone else. She must have figured it out when she saw Dorian at my laptop earlier, putting together all the puzzle pieces I'd inadvertently left lying around, and after the way she'd behaved during our earlier meeting, spouting that bullshit about it being easier to ask forgiveness than permission, she'd practically drawn me a map of her gameplan. I'd just been too naive to see it.

She wanted to exploit Dorian's wholesome popularity to make our upcoming film more palatable for mainstream audiences, and combined with the general goodwill people seemed to feel towards him after the viral video earlier, she'd wanted to strike while the iron was hot. She had a keen eye for opportunity, which was one of the reasons I'd hired her, but she'd never completely disregarded my express instructions before.

Worse than that, she'd endangered Dorian's reputation and his livelihood all for the sake of a little publicity. The very thing I'd feared most about getting into a relationship with him had just come true, partly through my own fault, but mostly through hers.

My hands shook with anger as I picked up my phone in the kitchen, and she answered on the second ring. "Before you say anything…"

Those four words were all the admission of guilt I needed. She knew exactly what had happened and why I was calling. She had probably texted the 'rumours' to the reporter herself.

"You're fired."

I paused to let the words sink in, and for a long moment, she didn't say anything either, probably trying to guess if I really meant it. "Listen, Laina, I know you're upset, but when you think about it…"

"I don't need to think about it to know that you went behind my back."

"It's going to be huge for us. I understand that you're upset right now, but we'll get through this."

"No, *I'll* get through this. There is no 'we'. I can't trust you anymore, so you're fired. Alex from HR will be in touch. Goodbye, Erica."

Years of partnership, dissolved in a matter of minutes. It left a bitter taste in my mouth as I called my HR director to ensure Erica's access to our systems were cut off immediately and to instruct her to sort out all the legalities of ending Erica's contract.

With that taken care of, I glanced up at the clock in my kitchen. Dorian had probably just left to take his mom to the airport based on the flight time he'd shared with me earlier. My stomach churned at the idea of having to tell him what happened, and I quickly placed another call, that time to my PR manager. As quickly as possible, I explained the situation before asking the question that was uppermost on my mind.

"If you were *his* PR manager, what would you tell him to do?" All I cared about was doing as much damage control as possible and making it easier for Dorian.

She answered me as honestly as she always did. "I'd tell him there were two possible ways to handle it: he can either deny the rumours or confirm them. If he denies it, there's a good chance people will still believe it anyway."

There really was no way to put the cat back in the bag, it seemed. "What happens if he confirms it? Will he lose readers?"

Again, she didn't mince words. "Without a doubt. There'll be people who are mad that he's a man, people who are mad because he hid his identity for so long, and people who are mad because he's dating you. Of those, the last one would be my biggest concern. From what I know of his books, his biggest audience is middle-aged women who'll be rather scandalized by the whole thing. I'm generalizing, obviously, but that's what I'd be worried about in his publicist's shoes."

"And what would your advice to him be?" When she hesitated, I pressed further. "Forget it's me he's dating. If he was your client and you had no connection to me, what would your advice be?"

"Well, that really depends on how he feels and what he wants. I'd ask him some questions to find that out first, but if we assume that he wants to try to maintain his current fan base, I'd suggest that he cut ties with you and find himself a quiet, 'normal' woman instead. Someone from a small town, probably with a dog, and have some new photos released with her as soon as possible. Sorry, Jenny."

She didn't need to apologize. I'd asked the question and though I didn't like the answer, I'd pretty much expected it.

Dorian's whole life was about to change unless he dropped me, but I knew him well enough already to know that he wouldn't do that. He'd be noble and insist he didn't care even while his whole world burned around him. He'd already proven his willingness to step out of his comfort zone and put me first, and now, I had to do the same for him, no matter how much I would prefer to stay and fight.

In the grand scheme of things, it had only been ten days since we reconnected, definitely not long enough for him to throw away years' worth of work for. Maybe we would have had something special. It certainly felt that way to me, but if it came down to me or his career, I would make the choice I knew he wouldn't make on his own. It would hurt us both, but in the long run, it would be the right thing to do.

The men who dumped me over the years had all been selfish, and I refused to be like them. I would break up with him not because it would help me, but for his own good.

After hanging up with my PR manager, I called my travel agent next. "Do you remember that Tuscan villa I've told you about before? The one in Italy that I designed my house after?"

Thankfully, she did, and after a bit of searching, she was able to confirm it was available. She could get me booked for the next day. "How long do you plan on staying?"

That was a good question. How long would it take Dorian to accept we were over and move on? "Let's say a month."

That would give me a chance to work on my screenplay, away from any distractions. Maybe I'd change the ending too. Things didn't always work out happily in the end, so it might be more realistic if the characters realized their worlds were just too different after all.

I could have video meetings with my team from Italy as easily as I could from Malibu. They'd have some work to do to pick up the slack created by Erica's absence, but I trusted the people I'd hired. They would pull through.

"I can get you on an overnight flight tonight," the travel agent told me. "How quickly can you get to the airport?"

"I'll leave in ten minutes."

I had enough time to grab my laptop, toothbrush and passport, along with a few toiletries and a small suitcase full of clothes. Anything else I needed, I could buy when I got there. Dorian was probably on his way back from the airport already, so I needed to get going before he got back, before he could look at me with those sweet brown eyes of his and convince me to stay.

The last thing I did was write a note for him, explaining why I'd gone and that our relationship was at an end. It had barely lasted a full day, but I already knew I'd remember it long after the others had faded from my memory.

The words swam before my eyes while I wrote, partly from my dyslexia and partly from the tears threatening to spill down my cheeks, but I pushed through and got it finished.

The taxi was already waiting for me outside as I taped the note to the door, and with one last, regretful look back at the piece of paper with his name on it, I walked away, trying not to imagine how he'd feel when he found it.

~Dorian~

In my kitchen, I sat with my laptop and Laina's letter, shoving peanut butter on bread into my mouth as a makeshift supper while I tried to figure out where she would have gone.

I'd tried a text first, simply telling her I wanted to talk, but an hour had passed and it remained unread. Either she'd gone somewhere with no signal or she was ignoring me; either way, I couldn't just wait for her to respond. There had to be something more productive I could do.

I'd read her letter so many times by then that I practically knew it by heart. She said she'd be gone for several weeks and that I shouldn't try to find her. She apologized, several times, for exposing my secret, and she firmly stated her wish that I should move on and do whatever was best for me and my career.

I didn't buy it for a second.

The girl who had come to my defense so selflessly in school had never hesitated to stand up for me, but when it came to putting her heart on the line, she was just as scared and unsure as that overweight, shy boy I had been. At the first hurdle, she pushed me away out of self-defense, making the choice to leave before I had the chance to leave her.

The problem with that was that I had no intention of leaving, and somehow, I had to convince her of it. I hadn't managed to do it yet. All the promises I'd made hadn't been enough to convince her that I was different from all those other guys who ran away at the first sign of trouble, but I was willing to try again. If she really couldn't put her past aside and believe in me, maybe we wouldn't work out after all, but I wanted to give it one more chance, to show her that even in what she'd given me as a worst-case scenario, I wasn't ashamed of her or her job.

To do that, I had to find her first.

Although she could have hopped on a plane anywhere in the world, or simply checked into a hotel down on Malibu Beach, I didn't think that was the case. Laina was particular about her living space. The care she'd put into her house proved that to me, and if she was going to go somewhere for an extended period of time, she would want something comfortable and familiar.

Would she have gone to our hometown? I considered it, but quickly discarded that thought. I'd never heard her say anything fond or nostalgic about it, plus she might guess that I'd look for her there. She wouldn't make it that easy for me.

Where else would feel like home, but be remote enough that I wouldn't stumble across her? Thinking back over all the conversations we'd had and the things she'd told me, I remembered her telling me how she'd decorated her house based on an Italian villa where she filmed a movie early in her career.

It felt like a long shot, but with nothing else to go on, I decided to start there.

First, I had to identify the villa. It took longer than I cared to admit, and I watched clips of Laina with far more men than I wanted to, but eventually, I managed to find the film she must have made on that trip. After grabbing screenshots of any scenes that showed the house itself, I edited out the naked bodies and put the pictures in a reverse image search. It took several tweaks and a lot of patience, but eventually, I found it: a villa just outside of Siena, still available as a rental property.

Glancing at the clock, I was surprised to see it was nearly one in the morning. My searching had taken me longer than I realized, but the good news was that it would be nearly ten o'clock the next morning in Italy. Rubbing my blurry eyes that had been staring at the computer screen for too long, I dialled the number on the villa's website.

A friendly-sounding woman answered the phone. "Buongiorno, Viaggio Toscano."

That must have been the name of the agency that handled the villa's bookings, and I quickly cleared my throat. "Yes, hi. Good morning. I'm interested in renting one of your properties."

I gave her the name of the property and she quickly pulled up the information. "When are you interested in visiting?"

"Immediately. Today, if possible."

I didn't have a back-up plan if she said it was available; I was simply going off adrenaline and a hunch, but I didn't need to worry about that as she checked her information. "Oh, I'm afraid it's not available. We have plenty of other properties, though. If you tell me what you're looking for, we can find you something just as good."

My gut told me I was on the right track, but I also suspected she wouldn't give out the name of the person staying there, so I'd have to be a bit creative. "Are you sure it's booked? I called last week and it was still available."

The clicking of her keyboard came through the phone from six thousand miles away. "Yes, I'm afraid so. It was just booked yesterday, actually."

Bingo. It could be a coincidence, but I didn't think so. As my best, and quite frankly only, lead, I'd have to take a shot. "That's a shame. Thanks for your help."

"Wait, sir..."

I hung up before she could try to sell me on a different place instead, and pulled up one of the airline websites instead. The first flight to Rome wasn't until eleven o'clock the next morning, which would put me in Italy the morning after that. It would have to do.

After a restless sleep, I got packed and got to the airport in plenty of time. In the airline lounge, the TV was tuned to the news, and I started in surprise when I saw my own face appear on the screen. The sound was down, but the closed captioning filled me in: they were talking about my books and the man behind them finally being unmasked. I'd purposefully been staying off my phone so I had no idea what the reaction was, and at that moment, I didn't care to know. I needed to talk to Laina first; everything else could wait. Keeping my head down, I went and bought a ball cap that I pulled down over my face to try to stay anonymous.

A confusing number of hours later, we landed in Rome where a car was already waiting for me to take me to the villa. The drive took a few more hours, during which I tried to get some rest since I hadn't slept on the plane, but every time I started to drift off, I'd imagine Laina slamming the door in my face, or even worse, a complete stranger opening the door instead, meaning my trip had been for nothing and I would have to start all over again.

At last, we turned onto a long drive, flanked on either side by tall, straight cypress trees that pointed up to the blue sky overhead, and at the end of it sat the villa from the website.

"You want me to wait?" the driver asked as he pulled up in front of the door.

"Yes, please." If I had it completely wrong, I'd need a ride back to the airport, slinking all the way back to Los Angeles to try to figure out my next move, but as I looked up at the centuries-old house next to the rolling vineyard, I felt unreasonably optimistic.

My heart told me she'd be there, and it pounded in anticipation as I walked up to the sturdy wooden door and knocked on it firmly, ready to make my case for the last time.

~Laina~

The Tuscan air felt different than I remembered. Thinner, somehow, and colder too. Maybe the time of year wasn't right, or maybe I'd just grown too accustomed to the fresh, warm ocean breeze in my backyard, but as I sat outside to have my coffee that morning in the small, internal courtyard of the villa, I had to pull my wrap tighter around myself to keep from shivering.

Or maybe my loneliness had just left me chilled.

Everything at the villa was just as beautiful as I remembered, and yet, when I woke up that morning to find myself there, my internal body clock still thrown off by the jet lag, I instinctively turned onto my side, hoping to see Dorian there. Gradually, the memories came back: the reason I had come there and the fact that I wouldn't be waking up beside him again. It had happened once, and that would have to be enough.

He sent one text, asking to talk, just after the news broke, but since then, there'd been nothing. No emails, no phone calls. Maybe he hadn't even read my note. Maybe he just went straight home and decided to pretend I had never existed. I couldn't blame him if he did, and yet, the thought hurt me anyway.

That was exactly why I'd travelled halfway around the world; if I'd stayed home, I wouldn't have been able to stop myself from going next door to see what was going on. By removing myself from the country, I removed that temptation for both of us.

As I sipped my espresso, my fingers flicked across the phone screen, reading through the news stories about Dorian. His publishing house had confirmed the day before that he was J.M. Everlee. They issued a statement that didn't sound a thing like him, saying he had kept his identity secret to avoid being stereotyped as a male author in a female-dominated genre. There were comments from people saying it had been fraudulent and comments from others saying they liked the books even more now that they'd seen what he looked like.

From Dorian himself, no one had heard a single word.

Author of sweet romance dating notorious porn star screamed one headline. Although I skimmed the article, I couldn't figure out what made me 'notorious'.

"He writes kind, deep men who see beneath the surface, but in real life, he goes for the blonde bimbos," one commenter had posted.

"He's definitely not with her for her brain," someone else added.

"I'm sorry I ever supported someone with such poor taste," commented 'soccermom37'. "His books are going straight in the trash."

I should have stopped reading but I couldn't look away. The comments got progressively ruder and more aggressive, speculating that he was using me, that I was using him, or that we were both as morally bankrupt as each other. Whenever anyone tried to interject with anything vaguely supportive - 'people can love whoever they want' or 'porn stars are people too' - they were immediately attacked.

Caught up in the drama on the bottom half of the internet, I almost missed the knock on the door. The housekeeper had already been there that morning to drop off some food and wouldn't be returning until later. I wasn't expecting anyone else and for a moment, I was tempted to ignore it, but maybe there was a delivery she'd forgotten to tell me about. With a sigh, I put my espresso down, shoved my phone back in my pocket, and headed to the door.

As I pulled it open and the man on the other side came into view, my heart seemed to skip a beat.

It couldn't be. I had to still be asleep and having a very vivid dream, because there was no way on earth that Dorian Reid could be standing outside my front door in the middle of the Tuscan countryside, six thousand miles from home.

"Thank God," he breathed out, exhaling in what sounded like relief. "I really didn't want to turn around and fly back home again."

"You... what? How? Why?" I couldn't decide on which question to ask him first, the words all coming out in a jumbled tangle of syllables. My heart had started beating again, faster than before. Maybe faster than it *ever* had before as my mind raced to put things together. At last, a coherent question came out of my mouth. "How did you get here?"

"The same way you did, I imagine. Big airplane, over the ocean?"

He seemed almost giddy while I still felt completely off-balance. "I mean: how did you know where to find me?"

I hadn't left any clues. Nothing in my note had mentioned where I planned to go. My travel agent was a personal friend, not someone related to my business, so Dorian would have had no way of knowing who to talk to even if he did get a hold of any of my employees. I honestly couldn't begin to imagine the path that had led him there, or why.

His gorgeous brown eyes pierced into mine as he answered me. "You told me about this place the first time I went to your house. You said how it inspired your own decorating, so I thought that if you were going somewhere away from home, you might have chosen somewhere that still felt like home."

I heard the words as he said them, but I could barely comprehend them. How did he remember me saying that? It hadn't been anything important, just a throwaway conversation as we were getting to know each other. How could he have guessed what I'd be thinking? And even when he did, how did he track down the exact location of the villa? It still seemed utterly impossible to me.

"What would you have done if I wasn't here?" I wondered out loud.

He shrugged. "Gone back home and tried again, I suppose. I would have kept trying until I found you or until you came back. If you want to break up with me, Laina, you're going to have to do it to my face. The fearless girl I knew in high school and the amazing woman I've come to know this month wouldn't hide behind a note. That's the scared, hurt side of you taking over. If you want to let that side win, that's fine. It's your choice, but you have to tell me so in person. Tell me you want me to go back home, that you meant everything you said in that letter and that we're definitely over, and I'll go. I won't bother you again. But if you want to be brave, as brave as you've made me feel, then you need to stop running away. You need to let me love you, because I could, Laina. I could love you so fucking much. You just have to give me that chance."

Passion and determination reinforced every word out of his mouth. Gone was the stammering, blushing man I found so adorably awkward. He held my gaze steadily, refusing to look away or back down.

Was that really because of me? Did I give him that confidence? Just the idea of it made me feel stronger too, as if we were lifting each other up.

I still didn't know what we were going to do about his pen name and his work and the stories about us, but at that moment, I truly didn't care about any of it. All that mattered was that the sweetest, sexiest man I'd ever known had tracked me down against all odds to tell me he wasn't giving up on us. Unlike all the other men in my past, unlike Brock and that stupid dinner he took me to the night Dorian moved in, if Dorian and I broke up, it would be my fault and mine alone.

He told me he wouldn't change his mind and he hadn't. So why did I assume I knew what would be best?

He asked me to give him a chance, and as the full reality of him being there finally sank in, my chest filled with happiness. What was I so afraid of? I was Laina fucking Macintyre, and if the world wanted to come for *my* man, they'd have to go through me first.

"Laina?" Dorian's confidence seemed to waver for the first time as I stood in silence, letting my epiphany wash over me.

I answered him the best way I knew how: wrapping my arms around his neck, I pulled his face down to mine and kissed him as hard as I could.

Chapter Eighteen

~Dorian~

A lot of feelings rose up inside me as Laina kissed me - joy, desire, satisfaction - but chief among them had to be relief.

Relief that I hadn't made a complete fool of myself chasing after a woman who didn't want me to a different continent. Relief that she wasn't ready to give up on us just yet.

Relief that our story wasn't at an end after all.

My arms wrapped tight around her as she held onto me, our bodies pressed firmly together, despite the fact that I really needed a shower. She didn't seem to care and so neither did I. All that mattered was that she was being open and vulnerable with me again. As long as she kept doing that, we could figure the rest out.

"So, uh... should I send the driver away now?" I murmured against her lips, gesturing over my shoulder to the car that still sat on the driveway behind him. "Are you going to invite me in?"

Laina looked over my shoulder at the car in surprise, as if she hadn't noticed it until right that minute. "Yes, of course you can come in. Do you have any luggage?"

"Barely." I gave her a sheepish smile before heading to the car and grabbing my small duffel bag from the back seat and telling the driver he was off the clock. When I returned to Laina, she was smiling at me like she couldn't quite believe I was real. "I had no idea how long I'd be staying so I only brought the basics."

"I didn't bring much more," she admitted. "None of this was planned in advance."

As she stepped back into the villa, I followed her in, my eyes immediately drawn to the large staircase that wound its way up to the second floor, the space soaring up into a painted ceiling that looked just like the sky. "Wow. This is…"

"A little much?" she guessed, still smiling.

"I was going to say it's very you, actually. Dramatic but beautiful."

"You do have a way with words." She leaned in to kiss me again, to my delight, a hint of coffee on breath, before pulling back. "You must be exhausted. What do you need?"

I could have said something cheesily romantic about how she was all I needed, but I didn't want to overdo it. "Coffee?"

"I can definitely do that."

With purpose, she led me to the kitchen, much more modern than the rest of the house, where an expensive coffee maker sat on the counter. With just a few presses of a button, she'd produced a hot cup of espresso that she handed to me proudly.

"That should wake you up. I left mine outside."

Taking a sip of the strong liquid, I followed her once more to a pretty little courtyard just off the kitchen where a cup identical to the one in my hand sat abandoned on a small wrought-iron table. She must have been sitting there when I knocked.

"Why did you run?" I asked her bluntly as soon as we'd taken a seat at the table, me doing my best to squeeze my larger frame into the narrow chair. "I told you I'd do my best to handle whatever came our way, but you didn't even give me a chance."

"I know." She reached over and took my hand, holding onto it as if I might disappear if we weren't touching. I understood it since I felt just the same. "I thought I knew what was best for you. I wanted to make it easier for you, but I should have spoken to you first. In a way, it's not much different from the guys who broke up with me because they didn't want me to feel bad when their friends made fun of me."

Indignation immediately shot through me, and I squeezed her hand a little tighter. "They actually said that to you?"

"That's the mild stuff." She smiled as she said but I could tell she wasn't exaggerating. "I wasn't trying to be selfish. Actually, I was trying to be just the opposite, but I should have just asked you what you wanted instead of assuming I knew better."

It made me so happy to hear that, and just to be having that conversation at all, openly and honestly. "Ask me now."

Her smile got a little wider as she got into character. "Okay. Hey, Dorian, it looks like your pen name isn't going to be a secret for much longer. I fired Erica, since she's the one who leaked it, but there's nothing I can do to stop it. How do you want to handle it?"

"Did you really fire her?" On the long flight, I'd come to the conclusion that the leak must have come from Laina's company, and as I remembered Erica asking me about what I was doing at the laptop, the pieces had started to come together. I was planning to mention my theory to Laina once we sorted everything else out, but it seemed she'd beaten me to the punch.

"Of course. She broke my trust and tried to take advantage of you. I won't put up with that."

That fierce attitude was exactly what I expected from her, and exactly what had been missing from the way she dealt with the challenge to our relationship.

"You didn't answer me," she reminded me, and I supposed I hadn't. She'd distracted me. "What do you think we should do about your identity getting out? Everyone knows who you are and everyone knows you're dating a porn star. Your reputation is ruined."

She was being deliberately provocative, so I played along. "J.M. Everlee's reputation might be ruined, but she doesn't exist. She never did. If people like my books, they'll like them just as well by Dorian Reid. If they don't, then that's their loss."

My publishers would probably faint to hear me talk that way, but I honestly believed it. I'd had a lot of time to think about that on the plane too. I'd had all the success I ever wanted, hidden behind my fake name. If I was less popular under my real name, so be it. It wouldn't matter what people thought of Dorian Reid, as long as he was happy with himself.

I hadn't understood that in high school, but Laina had. Now, I could remind her of it.

"And what about his girlfriend?" Laina asked, her tone somehow both teasing and tentative at the same time. "She doesn't really fit in with his romantic image."

"I think she fits just fine. I think we fit together pretty damn well." My voice got a bit deeper on the last words, my body and my heart reacting to the fact that she'd just referred to herself as my girlfriend. "So, you want to know how I want to handle things? I want to go on vacation with my new girlfriend. I want to take a ton of photos of us having a wonderful, romantic time together, and post them online to show people we don't give a fuck what anyone thinks. I've heard Italy is nice this time of year. What do you think?"

Laina's smile was filled with tenderness and happiness. "I think that sounds perfect. There's just one small problem."

"Oh? What's that?"

She reached up to run her hand through my hair. "You definitely look like you've just spent the night on a plane. If we're going to take photos, we'll need to clean you up first. How about a shower?"

Nothing she could have suggested would have made me happier. Draining the last of my coffee, I placed the cup firmly down on the table and pulled Laina roughly to her feet, making her giggle. "Lead the way."

~Laina~

Any lingering doubts I'd had were washed away in that conversation with Dorian. His eyes were fully open; he knew the challenges we'd face. He wasn't sugar-coating anything. He'd already seen the way that people would respond to him just for being with me, and he was willing to work through all of it because he wanted to be with me more than he cared about what any of those people had to say.

It was everything I'd always hoped for, everything I'd begun to believe no man could truly offer me, but apparently, I just hadn't met the right one yet.

And with my fears put to rest, my desire for him only grew stronger. Him following his hunch and getting on a plane to find me was the single sexiest thing any man had ever done for me. Some women would have found it too much, but those women weren't right for him, just as the other men in my past hadn't been right for me. We all needed to find the person who matched our own particular quirks, and at last, it seemed I'd met my match.

With that certainty growing in my heart, I really wanted him naked.

Dorian carried his duffel bag up the stairs and placed it beside the bed in the bedroom I'd claimed as my own. It featured another ceiling fresco, with naked men and women dancing above my head while I slept. It felt even more appropriate with him there.

Anticipation grew inside me as I led him into the large bathroom at the end of the hall. Like the kitchen, the bathroom had been completely renovated and decorated in a much more modern style than the rest of the house. The large walk-in shower had a deep shelf on one side, and I remembered it being put to good use when I was there filming years earlier. Hopefully, I'd soon be able to put it to personal use too.

Dorian chuckled as I began pulling off my clothes. "I thought I was the one who needed a shower."

"Oh, you definitely do. But you must be tired after coming all this way, so I'm happy to help."

"I appreciate that." His teasing tone was another sign of his growing confidence, a comfort in himself and around me that I found incredibly sexy. Quickly, he tossed his clothes aside, his cock already half-hard with the same anticipation that raced through my veins. I did my best not to stare as I got the water to a comfortable temperature.

"There, that should do it. Now, I'll just need to find you some shampoo since I assume you don't want to smell like fruit... oh!"

My rambling was cut off as Dorian picked me up, his strong arms lifting me as easily as he'd carried his duffel bag. He carried me straight into the shower and set me down on the ledge, just as I'd imagined. He'd obviously seen its potential too.

"I think this was designed for us," he murmured as he stepped between my legs which parted naturally to make space for him. "It's a perfect height."

My legs wrapped around his waist, trying to draw him closer. "I have a feeling you'd make it work even if it wasn't."

"I think you're right. When it comes to you, I'll always find a way to make it work." Gently, he pulled back, leaving me sitting there impatiently as he stepped beneath the showerhead, giving his hair, face and body a quick scrub. I would have taken him dirty, but I appreciated that he wanted to clean up for me.

My eyes followed his hands as they rubbed his limbs, making my fingers itch to do the same, and when he reached down to give his rapidly-hardening cock a few quick strokes, I nearly groaned in frustration. "I think that's clean enough. Get back over here."

Dorian shot me a satisfied grin, the water still dripping down over his face. "You're that eager?"

"What do you think?" I spread my legs wider to rub my clit, stroking myself just as he'd just done to himself, and his expression immediately turned more heated.

"I'll take care of that."

I figured as much, and as he came over to kiss me, his lips warm and wet, his fingers slipped between my legs, taking the place of mine that moved to his cock instead, stroking him slowly as he began to fuck me with his hand.

"Why does it feel so much better when you do that than when I do?" he groaned against my lips, making me laugh until his thumb brushed my clit again, choking off the sound.

"I'm not sure, but the feeling's mutual, I promise."

We carried on that way for a minute or two more, kissing each other while our hands kept busy, but eventually, Dorian couldn't take it anymore.

"Hold on," was all the warning he gave me, pulling me to the edge of the ledge and tilting my hips up before he pushed his entire length into me in one deep, perfect thrust.

"Fuck," I gasped, my hands grasping at his shoulders, holding on just as he'd told me to. "That's..."

"Perfect," he filled in. "You're..."

"Perfect."

No other word could quite do justice to the exquisite feel of him inside me, filling me and fucking me and loving me all at the same time.

That was what made it different. I'd been fucked many, many times before, both by men I cared for and those I only worked with, but never had any of them fought for me like Dorian had. Never had any of them looked at me with not only lust and appreciation, but true respect and affection too.

He hadn't said the word 'love' yet, and I wasn't in any hurry to hear it. I didn't need to. I could feel it in the way he held me, the way he put me first, the way he supported me. It had been missing from my previous relationships, but I recognized it immediately once I let myself be open to it.

His movements grew more frenzied, slamming into me as his fingers drifted back to my clit, his teeth grazing my neck just enough to make me shiver. The cool tiles of the ledge and the shower wall did little to quell the rising heat inside me, and when my legs began to tremble, I sighed out his name, softly, just a breath that evaporated into the air like the steam surrounding us.

His body shuddered with his own release as we clung onto each other, wet and sated, and stronger than ever before.

I'd always had the sex, but with him, I finally knew what romance really was. Together, we had the best of both worlds, and I couldn't wait to see what came next.

~Dorian~

We stayed in Italy for a week. After the long flight, neither of us were in a hurry to head home, and we had no reason we had to. Sitting by the pool, the sun shining over the vineyards that rolled off into the distance, Laina worked on her screenplay and I worked on my book.

"Which sounds sweeter?" Laina pondered out loud. "'I'll love you forever' or 'I'll love you eternally'?"

"They both sound pretty damn good to me," I teased, shooting her a grin over the top of my laptop so she knew I was joking. "Go with 'eternally.'"

She spoke quietly into a microphone and listened to it read back to her with her headphones, so when I wanted her attention, I sent her a message on the screen.

Laina pulled her headphones off. "Yes?"

"Should my male character swear during sex? He hasn't sworn throughout the whole book. He's pretty strait-laced."

"Absolutely," she stated without hesitation. "Swearing during sex is always hot, and the fact that it shows he's lost control? Even hotter."

I thanked her, expecting her to return to her work, but she smiled at me in that completely irresistible way of hers instead.

"Do you want to go test it out, just to be sure?"

Fuck, I really did.

Besides working and having sex, we also took some time to enjoy our surroundings. In Laina's rental car, we drove to a nearby town, wandering its ancient streets hand-in-hand, eating fresh pasta and drinking local wine. No one seemed to recognize us, so it seemed the celebrity gossip from home hadn't reached that corner of Tuscany yet. Laina asked our waiter to take a photo of the two of us, and she posted it to her social media accounts, just like she did with a selfie she took of the two of us in the pool, and one of us exploring the vineyards on the villa's estate.

On the last one, she included the caption: *Love is always sweet when it's new, but it's even sweeter when it's true.*

My cheeks flushed with pleasure when she showed it to me. "That's pretty sentimental for Jenny Vixxen," I pointed out, trying to hide the effect it had on me.

She shrugged. "If people can accept that J.M. Everlee is a man, maybe they can accept that Jenny Vixxen is an actual person too."

The crazy thing was: people *were* accepting it. Though each photo Laina posted got hateful comments on it, the positive ones far outweighed the negative ones, and a lot of them came from my readers. There were a lot of comments about how good we looked together, but also about how happy we looked.

More than that, my book sales had actually gone *up* since my publisher's statement, and preorders for my next book were through the roof, especially once Laina posted a shot of me sitting at my laptop and hinted that she was giving her input for the spicy scenes.

"You should put out a statement of your own," she suggested on our second-last morning there. "People have had a few days to adjust to the news now. You should let them hear your side of the story in your own words. On video would be even better."

That couldn't be much more outside of my comfort zone. Writing things down, sure, but speaking directly to a camera?

Laina immediately picked up on my discomfort. "It's just a thought, but I'd be happy to help. I can be your director and camerawoman. Together, we could make it really good."

Together, we made everything pretty good, so I decided to put my trust in her. "Alright. I'll give it a try."

She let me write a draft of what I wanted to say, and she suggested a few tweaks to it based on her much more extensive social media experience. Setting up a makeshift tripod for her phone, she put me in the villa's living room with just a hint of our antique surroundings behind me.

"Whenever you're ready," she said, giving me a thumbs up from behind the camera.

My heart pounding, I did my best to smile naturally at the round camera lens on the back of her phone. "Hi. My name's Dorian. You might also know me as J.M. Everlee. For the past eight years, I've been writing under that name and most people assumed I was a woman. As you can see, I'm not."

I gestured vaguely down at my body, and Laina gave me another thumbs up along with an exaggerated wink, making me smile despite my nerves.

"By using the pen name, I wasn't trying to fool anyone. I simply wanted to be judged on the merits of my books, not for anything about my personal life. To be honest, there hasn't been much there to judge. By nature, I'm a pretty private and quiet guy. However, as most of you already know, over the past couple of weeks, my life has been anything but quiet."

My eyes flitted over to Laina just to check that things were still sounding okay, and she gave me an encouraging nod, motioning to keep going.

"Jenny and I knew each other years ago. At the time, I was shy and awkward and she was beautiful and confident. Not too much has changed there, really. But this time around, I actually had the guts to get to know her a little better, and I found someone even more appealing than I previously thought."

Those had all been part of my prepared comments, and I was supposed to move on to addressing the comments about Laina's job, but as I reached that point, it didn't feel right. It felt like apologizing for something that didn't require an apology.

So, taking a deep breath, I went off-script. "Some of you probably want me to offer an explanation of why I'm dating an adult film actress, but you won't get one because it isn't needed. I'm not dating just an actress, I'm dating *her*, and I'd be dating her no matter what her job was. I'm in love with the woman she is, and that's got nothing to do with how she gets paid. As for my next book..."

I finished off by giving an update on the timelines for my next release, as planned, and when Laina hit the button to stop recording, I looked up at her nervously.

"Was that alright?"

She didn't answer me right away. She came to sit down on the sofa next to me instead, kissing me softly and tenderly. "Did you really mean that?"

"Of course. It doesn't matter to me what you do, I've told you that..."

"No, Dorian." She cut me off with a nervous, happy smile. "Is it true that you're in love with me?"

We still hadn't actually said the words, but I thought I'd made it pretty damn obvious. "Of course I am. Aren't you in love with me?"

A happy laugh bubbled out of her. "You'd better believe I am. Let's go make the most of the time we've got left here."

Leaving her phone behind, she led me to the bedroom where we made love again, and again after that, sharing a lazy afternoon in bed while the rest of the world carried on without us.

Chapter Nineteen

~Laina~

After we posted Dorian's video, I insisted that we turn off our phones and leave them off for the rest of our stay. When we got home to California, there would be plenty of time to see what the reaction had been. We'd had to reset the password for his social media accounts, it had been so long since he'd posted anything at all, and never anything about his books. It would be a change for him, but for as long as we could, I wanted to stay in our little bubble, content to hide from the world and make love in any rooms in the house we hadn't tried yet.

Dorian was game for just about anything. When he told me he'd never tried anal sex, I insisted that we give a go to see what he thought.

"It's... different," he said afterwards, his usual eloquence abandoning him in the wake of his orgasm.

"Different how?" I prompted. "Describe it to me."

"Well, your vagina fits me like a glove, snug and textured all the way in. Your ass is tighter to get in, tighter than your pussy, for sure, but once I'm in, it's much looser. I suppose it's like a water bottle."

"A water bottle?" I sputtered in surprise, the analogy striking me as so ridiculous that I had to laugh. "Did you just compare my ass to a water bottle?"

My laughter quickly caught on, Dorian's face turning adorably red as he pulled me close to him, both of us shaking as we fed off each other's amusement until my stomach hurt.

"I just... I meant... it has a narrow opening and is wider inside," he tried to explain, his chest still shaking as he tried to catch his breath. "It might not have been very poetic."

"Maybe all the sex is messing with your brain cells," I teased him. "For the sake of your career, maybe we should try some abstinence."

"I'd rather never write a word again," he growled, his laughter forgotten as he kissed me hard.

The flight home seemed to fly by compared to the one I'd taken a week earlier, alone and licking my self-inflicted wounds. Our anonymity quickly disappeared, though, as soon as we landed.

"Hey, aren't you..." from one person as we waited for our luggage was all it took, and soon, we had a small gaggle of people surrounding us, asking us questions and asking for selfies with us.

Dorian handled it all gamely, until someone walked by and tossed an insult over their shoulder at me. "You should be ashamed. Slut."

Instantly, the sweet man next to me tensed, but my hand on his arm was all it took to hold him back. The person had already walked off, probably feeling pretty smug in their hatefulness, and chasing after them wouldn't accomplish anything. "Some people are worth arguing with, and others really aren't," I reminded him, and taking a deep breath, he nodded.

"I hate that anyone thinks it's okay to talk to you like that."

"I know you do, and that means a lot, but you've got to pick your battles, Dorian, or you'll exhaust yourself. One random guy in an airport? Not the hill to die on."

As soon as we were in the taxi back to our neighbourhood, he pulled out his phone. "Guess it's time to see what's going on."

I could hear the way his nerves made his voice shake, so rather than checking on my own, I watched as he scrolled through the comments on the video, ready to give him my full attention as he processed whatever they might say.

The lines between his eyebrows grew deeper as he scrolled further, looking more and more confused until he glanced back up at me. "They're... good. Almost entirely good."

Honestly, it surprised me less than it did him. If I'd seen his video as an outside observer, I would have sided with him too. He'd been remarkably raw and real, and utterly appealing.

Alright, maybe I was a *little* biased on that last bit.

"I've got all kinds of messages too," he added, still scrolling in awe. "This one says she'd never read any of my books before but after my video, she just went and bought one. That's so sweet. This one says... oh."

His face turned beet red as his eyes skimmed over the rest of the message.

"What is it?" I asked, trying not to smile although I already had a pretty good guess what it involved. I got my fair share of explicit messages and unsolicited pictures, and although it had been going on for a while, I still remembered being shocked by some of the earliest ones I received.

"It's... uh... well, it's a pretty graphic description of what she'd do to me if I went to visit her."

"Should I track her down and beat her up?" I teased. "How does it feel to be a sex symbol?"

He tried not to laugh. "It's still not appropriate whether it's directed at me or you. There's more of them, too. And this one... oh."

He trailed off again, but that sounded like a different kind of 'oh'. Not shocked, but still surprised, in a different way.

"What is it?" I asked again.

"It's from Cody Morrison."

"From high school?"

That seemed unlikely, but Dorian nodded in confirmation, clearing his throat as he read the whole thing out loud.

"Hey. Saw you on the news. You probably don't remember me but we went to high school together."

I snorted in disbelief. "Probably don't remember him? That's code for he sure as fuck hopes you don't remember him."

Dorian grimaced in agreement. "Hang on, it gets worse: Looks like you're doing well for yourself, good for you, man. Your girlfriend's hot. She almost reminds me of a girl in our class, I don't know if you remember her. Her name was Laina."

The amusement instantly fled my body. Had he figured out my secret too? Were we both going to be exposed?

Thankfully, that didn't seem to be the case. His actual reason for writing, however, was even more bizarre. "I was just wondering if you knew what ever happened to her. I'm newly-divorced and I always kind of felt like she was the one that got away. You get that shit, right? You're into all that romance stuff. Anyway, if you know where to find her, let me know. Thanks, man." Dorian looked up from his phone screen in horrified disbelief. "Do you think that's for real?"

"I don't think anyone is wasting their hacking skills on pretending to be Cody Morrison," I pointed out, shaking my head at the ludicrousness. "Some people get better with age and some people apparently don't."

Pulling out my own phone, I checked my emails while Dorian continued to read through the comments. There were a few work-related things I'd need to deal with, and one from an email address I didn't recognize, but sent directly to my private work email, an address that not many people had.

Laina, it's Erica. It's been a week and I'm hoping you've had a chance to look at things a little more logically now. Things have played out exactly as I expected them to. Interest in both you and Dorian is through the roof. I haven't seen the latest sales figures on the website since you cut off my access, but I'm sure the numbers have been stellar. I've seen the photos you posted, so he'd obviously forgiven you. I'd really like to continue our partnership. I've put my heart and soul into this company and I have so many ideas for your new movie. I know we could still do big things together.

The words were all in one big paragraph, which made it harder for me to read, but after staring at it for a couple of minutes, I felt pretty sure I understood it all.

"What are you reading?" Dorian looked over curiously as I sat there staring at the words. Wordlessly, I handed the phone to him so he could read them himself. When he'd finished, he handed the phone back to me, exhaling deeply. "What are you going to do?"

In my mind, the situation wasn't all that different from my dinner with Brock, the night he broke up with me and I threw my drink at him. I'd burned all the bridges between us that night, and when I looked back at Erica, I couldn't see a way over the divide between us either.

"Just because things worked out alright in the end doesn't mean she was justified in doing it. She still betrayed my trust. She put your career at risk. She put profit and press above us as people, and that's not the kind of person I want to work with. There's more to life than money, and there's definitely more to life than porn."

"That's catchy. You should get that on a t-shirt." He shot me a smile before turning serious again. "Are you sure you don't want to try to work things out?"

"Are you defending her? She completely changed your life!"

"She did, but I don't want you to make decisions based on my feelings. You need to do what's right for you."

I shook my head at him firmly. "That's not how this works, Dorian. You want to protect me, right? It goes both ways. She went after you to boost herself up, and that's not okay."

"Noted," he assured me. "And also noted to never piss you off."

"Oh, you're going to piss me off," I promised with a laugh. "Everyone disagrees sometimes. But as long as you keep doing what you're doing, considering me when you're making decisions, then I'll never hold it against you for making an honest mistake. That's the difference."

He promised me he could see it, and when the taxi pulled up in front of my house, he got out too, heading with me to my front door to face the next step of our relationship: getting back to reality.

~Three months later~

~Dorian~

"That's it, Dorian." Emily smiled at me through the computer screen, looking just as pleased as I felt. "The edits are all in and the book is ready to go. The preorders are nearly double your last release, and our team will get in touch as soon as all the tour dates are finalized. Any questions?"

Mutely, I shook my head. As terrified as I felt about doing an in-person book signing tour, I was a little excited about it too. It would push me way outside of my comfort zone, but one thing I'd learned over my time with Laina was that pushing my limits could often turn out to be a very good thing indeed.

After promising to be in touch as soon as I had a firm timeline for my next book, I hung up, closed the laptop, and went in search of my girlfriend. Technically, I still owned the house next door, but I hadn't slept there for weeks. For all intents and purposes, Laina and I were living together, though we hadn't formally decided to. It just gradually happened since we didn't particularly want to spend any time apart that we didn't have to.

She was in her office, on her own business call, but she gestured for me to come in when she saw me in the doorway. Staying out of sight, I took a seat across the desk from her just in time to hear the person on the other end of the call say the words she'd been wanting to hear: "I'd love to work with you on this project."

Although she reacted calmly, I could see the adorable way Laina kicked her legs under her desk in excitement. "That's wonderful. I'll have my production manager send you the contract tomorrow and hopefully, we'll be able to start shooting in February."

They exchanged a few more pleasantries before hanging up, but once they had, Laine raised her arms over her head in triumph. "My first-choice director! I can't believe she said yes."

My chest swelled with pride and happiness for her. "That's amazing. But did you say February?"

That would directly conflict with my book tour, which had been arranged around a Valentine's Day release.

Laina lowered her arms and gave me an apologetic smile. "That was the earliest she was available. I'm sorry I'll miss your tour."

That hadn't been my concern at all. "I'm sorry I won't get to see you filming."

Although I had no problem with Laina making her adult movies, I didn't particularly want to watch her doing it. The scene I wrote where I inserted myself into one was the closest I'd gotten to taking part, but since her new film would have a lot of non-porn scenes, it would have been a great chance to see her in action.

"You'll get to see an early cut of the movie," she offered, but we both knew it wasn't the same thing.

Since we couldn't do anything about it, I pretended not to mind too much. "That sounds great."

Laina laughed as she got to her feet. "You're such a terrible liar. Come on, I have an idea."

Taking me by the hand, she led me over to the other side of the house where her team had been shooting a movie earlier that day. To my surprise, they'd left a couple of the cameras set up.

"Shouldn't they have put these away?" I asked curiously.

"They would have if I didn't ask them to leave them out." Laina adjusted the angle of one of the cameras as she spoke, pointing it directly at the couch that I would forever think of as the first place Laina and I ever had sex.

"Why did you want them out?"

Laina moved to the other camera, adjusting its focus too. "Because I've been thinking about that scene you wrote where you joined me on camera, and I think it's about time we made it come true. You just gave me the perfect excuse. Once you know how it feels to be in front of the camera, you'll be better able to imagine my days when you watch the finished movie."

I could almost follow that logic, but I still eyed the cameras warily. "What are we filming it for?"

"Just for us," Laina promised. "No one else will ever see it, but years from now, when I've lost my figure and you've lost your hair, we can look back and remember how hot we used to be together."

She never said exactly what I thought she would. "Why do I have to lose my hair? Maybe *you'll* lose your hair and *I'll* lose my figure."

She grinned at my teasing. "Either way, the movie will be a good reminder."

I'd never done anything like it before, but I loved that she was thinking about us getting old together. That would have almost been enough to convince me on its own, even if she didn't look absolutely amazing in her pretty business blazer, her hair and makeup matching the professional vibe. I wanted her day and night, and that day was no different.

"Are we doing a scene?" I wondered out loud. "Do we need a script, or..."

Laina walked up to me and pulled my head down to hers, her lips pressing against mine as she answered my question. "Just make love to me."

That, I could definitely do.

It didn't matter that I'd seen her naked a hundred times by then. It didn't matter that I knew what she looked and sounded and felt like. Every time felt different and new and exciting, and by the time she pulled my pants down, she found me as hard and ready as always.

"I'm going to bend over the coffee table, just like the first time," she whispered to me. "Ignore the cameras. Just focus on me."

Honestly, I'd almost forgotten them already until she brought them up. Kissing her as I pulled her clothes off, I groaned in satisfaction as her hands ran over my body. She knew exactly where to touch me to turn me on, just like I knew her, and when I'd removed her last piece of clothing, she turned around and bent over, exposing her beautiful pussy to me.

No man could resist such an invitation, but as much as I wanted to be inside her, I dropped down to my knees first. I wanted her taste on my lips when I fucked her. I wanted to be able to taste it in my memory every time I watched the video again afterwards.

Laina moaned happily as I ate her, concentrating my efforts in the way I knew would drive her crazy. Her wetness suggested she found performing with me just as much of a turn-on as I did, and when she came, pleasure flooded through me too.

Licking my lips, I got back to my feet and got into position behind her, sliding the head of my cock through the wetness between her legs and over her clit, once, twice, and three times, before I finally pushed into her, drawing another deep moan of satisfaction from her.

I loved the view I had: her blonde hair hanging down over her face, her sexy back, the curve of her waist and her beautiful, rounded ass, and especially the sight of my stiff cock disappearing inside her with each thrust, amplifying the feel of her body taking me in. I did my best to note each sensation, as she'd asked me to on that very first night, and to remember them so that when we watched the video back later, I could compare how it felt to be in the moment to how it felt to watch it. I never glanced at the cameras, though; my attention was entirely on her.

"God, I'm so glad you moved next door," Laina gasped as her arms began to tremble, her orgasm building fast.

"Not as fucking glad as I am," I grunted back, my body getting tighter and my thrusts more forceful until I felt her start to squeeze me. Knowing she'd gotten her pleasure, I could let myself go, and I came with the same all-encompassing satisfaction I got from every single encounter we had.

It was the best sex of my life.

At least until the next time.

Epilogue

~One year later~

~Laina~

The sparkly, silver dress reflected the camera flashes almost like a disco ball as the door to our limo was opened. A plush red carpet stretched out in front of me, reminiscent of the old-school Hollywood glamour I used to dream about. A touch old-fashioned, maybe, but I'd specifically requested it. I was never going to win an Oscar, so I wanted the premiere of my first mainstream movie to be as special as possible. My dream of being a Hollywood actress was finally coming true, after so many of my other dreams already had over the last year.

Ever since Dorian showed back up in my life, things had only gotten better.

A handsome young man working security for the evening offered his hand to me, helping me to make a graceful exit from the car in front of the gathered crowd and photographers. The warm California evening air enveloped me as I stood there, smiling at everyone on the other side of the barriers. My arms were bare, but I didn't feel cold at all. The attention and the heat of the lights sent a flush through my body, accentuated even more when Dorian climbed out of the car behind me, his strong hand slipping around my waist as he took his place at my side.

"Are you ready?"

I'd never been more ready, but as I glanced up at him, I couldn't help being a little distracted. "Do you have to make that tux look so good? I'm already imagining getting my hands down your pants as soon as the lights go down."

His chuckle sounded a bit tight, suggesting that I'd successfully planted the idea in his head. "Let's keep it PG in the audience. There'll be enough action on screen."

Together, we stepped forward to pose for photos and answer questions from the reporters in attendance. Dorian stayed half a step behind me, making sure the attention always went to me first, but right at hand if I needed him.

"Do you think the NC-17 rating will hurt or help the film?" a beautiful woman with a British accent asked me.

"It was always going to get that rating," I pointed out. Usually, filmmakers did their best to avoid the NC-17 rating that meant no one under the age of 18 could be admitted, but that had never been my intention. The film had actual sex scenes in it, nothing implied or suggested by editing, though they made up less than ten minutes of its hour-and-a-half running time. "We'll have to see whether it entices viewers or keeps them away, but it's exactly the film I wanted to make."

"Jenny!" a man shouted at me from further down the line. "How does your boyfriend feel about you having sex with your co-star on camera?"

I glanced back at Dorian to see if he wanted to answer that or if he wanted me to deflect, and he gave me a small nod, letting me know he was ready for it. "They're both actors. Jenny's *character* has sex with Curt's *character*. That's what the audience is seeing. Trust me, I can tell the difference."

That earned a few laughs, and I quickly moved us on before the conversation got sidetracked.

After half an hour of talking to the press and taking photos, I headed over to the fans to sign a few autographs. Dorian signed some too, for women who'd shown up with copies of his latest book, before we finally made our way inside. Silence seemed to swallow us up as the doors closed behind us, blocking out the buzz of the crowd outside.

Most people had already gone into the screening, with just a few people still milling around the elegant theatre lobby, drinking wine and enjoying the complimentary food. Dorian and I were swept straight into the auditorium, where the director had just started to say a few words. Two seats had been left empty for us on the aisle of the third row, and we quickly settled ourselves into them.

"When I got approached to do this film, I had never directed an adult film before. What drew me to it was the story, the characters, and the idea that even the most unlikely characters deserve romance. I hope that after seeing it, you'll agree."

As she took her seat, the lights began to dim and a round of applause swept the theatre while Dorian took my hand in his, holding it tightly for support.

We'd seen the finished film before, on our TV at home, but seeing it on the big screen with a theatre full of people felt entirely different. Normally, my movies were watched in the privacy of people's homes, something intimate and personal, and while I loved that, there was something special about being out in the open too.

There had been a lot of lines to remember, but Dorian suggested I hire an assistant for the filming whose only job was to help me with my lines before each scene. Nobody had any idea during the shooting that I struggled with reading.

Dorian had also helped me with the script quite a lot, not taking over but encouraging me in his kind, supportive way, and the film was better for it. He refused to let me give him any credit, even though he dedicated his last book to me.

He was always so giving, so selfless, that I wanted to do something special for him too. As the movie came to an end and everyone around us applauded, my nerves kicked into high gear, knowing what came next even though Dorian didn't have a clue.

No one moved during the credits, eager to give everyone who worked on the film their due, and once they ended, my face suddenly appeared on the screen again. Dorian looked over at me curiously for just a second before turning his attention back to the screen.

"Thank you so much for coming tonight and for supporting this movie," the recorded version of me said. "There are so many people who helped to make this a reality, but there's one person in particular who made it happen in more ways than I can count, someone who didn't want his name in the credits."

"Laina." Dorian murmured my name in warning, and despite the dark surrounding us, I could guess just how red his cheeks were turning in anticipation.

"Dorian Reid is the best man I've ever met, and the most romantic man too. He's kept every promise he ever made, and he hasn't pushed me into moving forward with our relationship even though I know he bought a ring months ago and has it hidden in his sock drawer."

Affectionate laughter circled around the audience as Dorian glanced over at me again, that time in utter surprise. I'd never told him I knew, and I knew he was waiting for the right time. He wanted it to be perfect, but I had always been more practical than that, and I truly hoped that I'd found a good compromise for both of us.

"So, I've asked his mom to help me out and show him just how much he means to me."

That was the cue we'd been waiting for, and as the lights came up, Dorian's mom walked out in front of the screen while Dorian's jaw dropped.

"She told me she couldn't come," he reminded me, sounding adorably confused.

"She lied," I whispered. "I asked her to."

In her hand, she held a ring box, and she lifted it up as she spoke directly to me. "I think this belongs to you."

Dorian looked more confused by the second. "That's not the ring I bought."

"No, it's not." Leaving him with those words, I got up and walked to the front of the theatre, taking the box from her. "Thank you, Ruth."

We might never fully agree on my job, but we'd spent enough time together for her to know that I did truly love Dorian, and because of that, she accepted his choice without hesitation. "Thank you for making my son happy."

With the box in my hand, I turned back to the crowd, my eyes on only one man as I opened it up to reveal a wide gold band.

"Dorian, I used to be able to predict how my relationships would end, but you've rewritten everything I thought I knew. So, I thought I'd change the script too and take matters into my own hands. Will you marry me?"

The whole room seemed to be holding its breath, hundreds of people tense and silent as they all turned to the gorgeous man I'd fallen in love with.

His face was no longer red. He seemed to have forgotten anyone else was there as he stared straight back at me, his expression bewildered and joyous all at the same time. "Of course I will."

The whole room erupted into applause as he got to his feet and jogged towards me, picking me up in his strong arms and lifting me off my feet as he captured my lips in a passionate kiss worthy of any Hollywood ending.

"I love you," he whispered against my lips, and somehow, I heard him above the roar of the crowd.

"I love you too."

Whether the movie made me a star or not, my dreams had already come true.

Keep in Touch

Thank you for reading X-Rated! I hope you enjoyed Laina and Dorian's story. If you did, please take a moment to leave a review.

For more about my other books and keeping up to date with new releases, find all the links here: